good deed rain

Different Planet ©2017
Allen Frost, Good Deed Rain
Bellingham, Washington
ISBN 978-1-64008-158-1

Writing: Allen Frost
Covers "Different Planet" & "Day's Fantasy"
    & Illustrations: Laura Vasyutynska
Apple: TFK!
Production Assistance: Fred Sodt
    Maggie Feeney & Klaatu Mothra

Quotations from:

The Book of Joe, by Vincent Price, Doubleday & Company, NY, 1961

I Caught Flies for Howard Hughes, by Ron Kistler, Playboy Press, Chicago, IL, 1976

Travels with Charley, by John Steinbeck, The Viking Press, NY, 1961

Different Planet

DIFFERENT PLANET:

Robots, rockets, outer space, clones—the four adventures in this collection take you to a different planet.

My experience with Science Fiction begins with *Sci-Fi Theater* every Saturday afternoon. Our black & white TV showed amazing movies about monsters, other worlds, time-travel. In elementary school, I ran into Ray Bradbury's books. Recently I gave my son a copy of *The Martian Chronicles*. Then, out of the blue I found Philip K. Dick. That was life changing. I searched all over Seattle for his paperbacks. Here's a story about that: I was in a Capitol Hill bookstore, in a maze surrounded by crowded aisles stacked to the ceiling. I asked the guy behind the counter where the Sci-Fi books were. He gave me an icy cold stare and said, "You mean the Speculative Fiction?" Somewhere far out at sea a giant octopus is pulling a ship apart, there are robots in our midst, people are living on Mars. Words can take you anywhere.

Allen Frost, Bellingham
Summer, 2017

"But why should we hear about body bags, and deaths, and how many, what day it's gonna happen, and how many this or what do you suppose? Oh, I mean, it's, it's not relevant. So, why should I waste my beautiful mind on something like that?"

—Barbara Bush on *ABC/Good Morning America*,
   March 18, 2003

"Returning to the moon is an important step for our space program…the moon is home to abundant resources. Its soil contains raw materials that might be harvested and processed… With the experience and knowledge gained on the moon, we will then be ready to take the next steps of space exploration: human missions to Mars and to worlds beyond."

—The 43rd President of the United States of America,
   NASA headquarters, January 14, 2004

THE NEXT PRESIDENT

Part One:
THE PROFESSIONAL LAUGHER

A slap stung his face and woke him up into the dark room.

She was leaning over him, close, with her hand returning in its hitting arc.

"Ow!" he yelped and caught her hand before it struck again. "What'd you do that for?!"

"How can you do it?" she seethed.

"What?! You were dreaming! Calm down, dear."

She pulled her arm out of his grasp. She was sitting up now.

"What's the matter?"

"It doesn't matter if it's a dream or happening for real!" she snapped. "You're a beast!"

He rubbed his numb cheek. "I don't know what you're talking about, Carolyn."

"How can you laugh at that monster's jokes?"

"Sylvan Moore?" He was beginning to understand. "Oh, we've gone through this so many times before, Carolyn. He's my employer. That's what I do, I laugh for him."

She folded her arms over her bare skin. "Well, he's sick! And I'm not the only one who thinks so, Rupert. There's plenty of people who can't stand him. Nobody likes that show. Nobody has any respect for that man, or for what he does. Don't you see how he's using you? If he didn't have what you do, the show would be over, they couldn't hide it anymore."

"Carolyn…"

"Don't touch me, Rupert!"

He pulled his hand back. "Listen Carolyn, I understand. But I can't help what he's like. I have to laugh at him, that's what I get paid for. All this…" he swept an arm at the shadowy large luxury apartment bedroom, "It's because of him."

"Well, I can't be a part of it anymore." She threw off the sheet and stood out of the warm bed. "I'm leaving Rupert. Try laughing at that!" With that, she snapped up her satin robe and slaked across the carpet to dress and fly away.

"Ohhh…" he groaned. He fell back on the bed. He was too tired for a fight, besides it was better to let her storm and get it out. He decided he would talk about it tomorrow. He needed his rest. His sides hurt from all that laughing and he had to get up early and start all over again.

The rickshaw ride was a breath of fresh air. Rupert could clear his head and curse his bad luck losing Carolyn in the middle of the night. He felt like asking the driver's opinion, but he didn't. He figured that guy had it rough enough already, pulling this contraption all over town in whatever turn of weather, day after day. Still, that was his lot in life, so it goes.

Rupert straightened his clip-on tie. He stared up at the building tops where the clouds seemed to steam to life. Before he went to the studio, there was something else on the agenda: a visit to his past.

Because of rioting, they had to take the long way through the park. That suited Rupert fine, he needed the fresh air. And the road had enough bounce and sway in it to soon take Rupert's thoughts off Carolyn going away. He felt an edge of nervousness as they neared the Dino Lamza Museum. "I should have prepared a speech," he thought, "But what's the point? I'm just talking about myself." A smile found his way. It was a beautiful day after all.

The sprinklers were going on the wide lawn before the museum, causing the sight of it to shimmer and float on a veil of water.

The rickshaw stopped beside a blooming lilac tree. The perfume gushed. Past the purple flowers, Rupert could see the big opened entrance doors. They were surrounded by a thick violet frame of climbing wisteria. An old man wearing a bright yellow suit was waiting there impatiently.

"Say, could I pay you to wait here for me, driver? This won't be long, I just have to make a speech then I'll be right out." Rupert pulled out his money clip and offered a twenty. "This for waiting?"

The driver shrugged, "Sure."

"Thanks," Rupert beamed. "You can come in if you want. I'm sort of a hero to these folks."

"That's okay," the driver said, "I'll wait here."

"Alright…Well, I'll see you in a bit." Rupert stepped out of the rickshaw and waved at the old man by the museum entrance. As Rupert approached, he watched the yellow arm rise to shade out the sun.

Rupert bellowed out across the lawn, "Hello! It's

me, I'm back!" He took a look at his cufflinks and waved. He had only been to the Dino Lamza Museum once before, when it opened. Even though he was only a grade-schooler back then, the reception had been brittle. They had watched his every move, trying to see through his disguise. He hoped this time would be better.

The man at the door raised a cane. Rupert took that as a good sign. Approaching the museum was overwhelming. Of course it was more than just a memorial to the life of Dino Lamza, it was also his tomb. The embalmed body of the superstar rested under bulletproof glass with a sort of supernatural grace.

Rupert could see all the buttons and medals on the old man's yellow suit. This must be a bigwig, he thought, maybe the director. Had he known this old man leaning on his cane? "Good morning!" Rupert greeted him.

"Yes it is," the director answered severely. He held his silver ear pointed at Rupert Wells.

"It's good to be back here." Rupert stuck his hand out and was surprised to be offered the tip of the outstretched cane instead of another hand. "Oh…" he fumbled, then accepted and shook the cane. It trembled like a birch branch and found the cement again.

"Everyone's waiting for you."

Rupert apologized, "I know. My alarm clock didn't wake me up. I've had a heck of a morning already."

"Follow me…" The old man opened the door and scraped in. "This wasn't my idea anyway," he grumbled in a rough whisper meant to be heard. "Someone else wanted to see you again. Not me."

Rupert resisted saying something in reply. So this is the way it's going to be again, he fumed. Once he was in the museum though, he was awed. He remembered every one of the relics in the displays.

The director led him past the manikin dressed in one of Dino Lamza's finely tailored suits. The blue sharkskin caught the light with matching sparkling gold cufflinks and tie clip. Rupert sighed.

They made it to the auditorium where the sound of crooning and orchestra swelled behind the door. A big gold star on the door proclaimed it The Dino Lamza Theater. The music rushed out when the old man opened the door.

Rupert walked calmly and slowly with the director down the aisle. He waved at the gray and blue shapes of people sitting in the dark. Slides were flicking over the screen up front. Dino Lamza in his glory days…

Rupert stepped onto the stage and stood in the black and white shutter of the slides that ended with a brassy fanfare and a huge smiling face folding around him. As a spotlight faded onto him, Rupert basked in their applause. "Thank you…Thank you…It's an honor to return to you. I want to thank all of you for your warm welcome here to the Dino Lamza Memorial Museum." The houselights were now on so he could plainly see the audience regarding him.

"Although you knew me well," he smiled. "You may not know me now. My new reincarnation name is Rupert Wells." He cleared his throat. This was a tough audience. He smiled. He restarted, "Thanks for the turnout folks. Let me just suffice it to say that Dino Lamza would have been very impressed and appreciative of the turnout here today." The mention of Dino had got them clapping. He held up his hands, "That's great, you're great." He grinned at the old remembering faces. Actually, he couldn't remember a single one of them, but it had been all the years of this life since he had known them. "Thanks for the welcome. It's good to know I'm remembered so fondly. I'd love to share whatever stories I can about my past life. I know you're all fans of Dino Lamza and eager to hear news. That's what I'm here for."

"Mr. Wells, will answer some questions now," the museum director's voice came from a speaker, "Then we can finally get to the breakfast buffet."

"Oh! Sure, I'd be happy to answer your questions." Rupert held a hand over his eyes to shade out the bright houselights. "Does anyone—yes—yes, you in the back there."

"Yeah!" the silhouette said. "Why didn't Dino Lamza go to heaven? Why'd he come back as you?"

There was a ripple of mumbling voices.

"Well..." Rupert stalled, "I'm certainly not the one to—to judge these matters. Perhaps upon his— *my* death—Dino Lamza's death—there was still some unfinished earthly business. Some mountain left to climb. You know," he brightened, "I've continued to press along in show business. I'm doing quite well working for Sylvan Moore." The audience reacted as if jolted, an outcry that rolled at him. He let it pass, he was used to it from his girlfriend and everyone it seemed. "Or maybe Dino Lamza did something wrong and got set back a little?"

The audience glared at him.

"But that couldn't be possible, could it?" Rupert joked flatly. "And in a way, isn't this kind of heaven to be alive again, to be doing what I am meant to do, to be recognized by all of you?" He put on the smile and swept an arm to include them all. Someone out there clapped for that.

"Thank you," Rupert bowed.

"Oh cut it out!" A woman in the front row stood up. She glared at Rupert. "Why don't you sing us something?!" Her bold command brought a flutter of applause around her as she sat down again.

Rupert felt like laughing out loud at all this. He could feel it wanting out, but he took a deep breath and calmed himself. They were waiting for him. "I don't do that anymore…As I said, I'm in a different line of entertainment now. What I do now is I make people laugh." He shoved his hands in his pockets casually. "Maybe that's what Dino Lamza was missing in the end."

Suddenly Rupert had to hold out his arms to balance himself. The stage underfoot was moving, he was being pulled off by gears and unseen pulleys. The old music was blaring. So he waved goodbye to them as he disappeared behind a red velvet curtain.

Backstage, there was no sign of the director. Rupert was there in the gloom, wondering what to do, when a door opened a ray of light on him and an elderly woman called him.

"Dino—I mean, Rupert? Oh, there you are."

"Yes, I'm over here."

She leaned herself against the door and waved him forward. "Come out of there," she smiled warmly. "It was kind of you to show up this morning. I apologize for the crowd. They're anxious to get to the buffet, I'm afraid. Why, even if the real Dino Lamza—I mean— even if he was back—if *you* were back in your original form, they'd still—"

"Don't worry about it Lydia."

She froze. "You remember my name?"

Rupert smiled shakily. "Oh, there are people I knew who I could never forget."

Her eyes were melting blue behind those thick owlish spectacles. "I can't believe you remember…" she faltered.

"It's okay, Lydia." He drew her close and let the door shut. He remembered the feeling of her too. Through her frailing structure, what the years had done to her, he still felt her youth. "How are you, Lydia?"

She looked up at him, crying, not a word to give him.

Rupert squeezed her and tried to laugh, but he was choked up too. She had her head leaned on his shoulder and he touched her white hair. "It's okay, Lydia," he repeated. "I'm still around."

A voice crackled from another doorway. "Are you going to the breakfast buffet, Lydia?" The director glared and Rupert let his arms drop from her. "I'm saving a seat for you, Lydia," the old man rifled.

Her answer was a, "Yes," like drowning water. "I

have to go," she told Rupert. "Will you please give me a call?"

"Lydia!" the old man in yellow snapped.

"I'm in the book. I'm still Lydia Waincoat."

"Sure," Rupert nodded, "I'll call you sometime."

"Don't forget me."

"I won't," Rupert promised.

The director hooked an arm into her and caned out of the hallway.

It was a strange beehive she left him with. It wasn't often that this life of his ghosted back with such force to another past world. When it happened, Rupert felt out of body and out of time, a victim of his own mirage that came and went.

Lost in that phantom state, he could have remained for another while, but the hall door sprung open again and the director pegged back into sight.

"I'm not convinced," he croaked at Rupert. "Never was. This wasn't my idea," he pointed his cane behind him. "It was Lydia's. She's very…" he paused to look for her word, "Sentimental." He swung his cane back around to Rupert. "You're free to go, mister. The door's that way."

Rupert was all smiles; he always seemed to manage. "No breakfast?" he grinned.

"Members only," the old man rasped and tilted.

"Well, I'll be on my way. Thank you." Rupert gave a bow and opened the door.

The flowers stewed in the air, the warm throw of the sun, dappling shadows. After being inside, this was like being born onto a new planet. Rupert hurried across the lawn away from his past.

The driver sat beside his rickshaw, playing a game of dominos against himself or some invisible opponent. When he saw Rupert clipping across the grass, he scooped the clacking black tiles into a sewn purse and stuffed it away. He climbed up onto the seat and swiveled the pedals back and forth until he felt the cab sway with passenger weight.

"Thanks for waiting," Rupert told the driver. "Tough crowd…" he jerked a thumb at the museum.

The rickshaw had already begun to move.

"Can you take me to the Airwaves Building?" Rupert asked the back, straining with the pull of him and the cab.

"Okay," the driver puffed.

Rupert felt inclined to relax a bit now, to breathe in the thick flowered air and stare as the wind played and the green leaves pinwheeled by. They began to dip down off the museum hill, parks clotting into the traffic, while towers of the city downtown grew.

Rupert straightened his clip-on tie. He stared up at the building tops where the clouds seemed to steam.

"You got a job at the studio?" the driver startled Rupert.

"Yeah," Rupert grinned for him, "I work on *The Sylvan Moore Show.*"

The driver clammed up. Then, as the light turned green he hopped onto the pedal and jerked them forward.

Rupert sighed. He got that reaction a lot. Every once in a while someone would be interested, but not very often it seemed.

They rattled past a caravan parked in the square. There was a puppet show going on, some little jester smacking an alligator with a stick. Rupert smiled. The crowd that gathered around loved it. He thought Sylvan Moore might enjoy bringing them on the show sometime.

"Here we are," the driver said as he pulled the rickshaw into a space left vacant by a wooden cart.

"Thanks comrade." Rupert stuffed a paper bill into the man's calloused hand. "Maybe I'll see you again some lifetime," he added with a friendly wave, because who knew with reincarnation where one's soul would land. Rupert smiled and climbed onto the cobbled street.

The driver pulled away, slowly adding his voice to the crowded air. "Rickshaw for hire! Rickshaw!"

The Airwaves Building reached fifty stories tall into the sky above them all. Antenna towers went on beyond that. Rupert was only a drift of sand moving before its shore, pouring about, then inside.

A silver robot stood on the other side of the revolving door. It stretched out an arm until Rupert showed his I.D tag. Those eyes scanned him and let him pass.

The door's wind pulled him, propelled him on to the lobby. This was the first level where, he smiled, if he wasn't who he was, he would have to fight his way on and up and up like a video game, with time against him.

After every day here for years, he knew the way. But this wasn't every other day. He needed to talk to

Carolyn and see if he could try to patch things up. So he followed the diamond-shaped floor tiles that took him to Studio 1-C.

A small portly guard who wore a gray uniform with silver buttons running up him from shoes to hat, stood post by the grand door. He watched Rupert approach and then snapped a hand up to salute him. "Good morning, Mr. Wells."

"Hello, Hugo. How are you?"

"Just fine, sir."

Rupert stared at the gold lettering on the door: *Chimp Champions.* The On Air sign above the doorway was glowing red. "Alright if I sneak in, Hugo? I really have to see Carolyn. I'm afraid we had a quarrel."

"I'm sorry to hear that, Mr. Wells, but you know once the show is underway, I'm obligated to—"

"Hugo. Take it easy. I'll be quiet as a shadow. She's pretty steamed at me." He plucked the rose out of Hugo's lapel. "This might help though. As a matter of fact," he reached in his pocket and took out his billfold, pulling off some money, "See if you can deliver some flowers for me. Have them ready for her after the show. Just tell her I was thinking of her. And oh—" he touched Hugo's braided shoulder pad, "Maybe I'll see if I can get you a gig like this upstairs, on *The Sylvan Moore Show.*" He smiled and touched the door handle.

"That's quite alright, Mr. Wells," Hugo replied. "I'm happy at this door. I really wish that you wouldn't go in now though. They're—"

"Hugo. I promise it will be okay." And with that assurance, Rupert opened the door enough to slip through into darkness on the other side.

Down stairs and past chairs filled with audience, the stage area was lit by blinding white light. Rupert leaned against a pillar to quietly watch. His heart struck a chord as he saw Carolyn. She wore a long blue dress that made her glow, while she pointed at the row of busy chimpanzees. They wore suits and ties. A couple of them wore glasses, one had a monocle. Rupert muttered, "Wow…" They were typing away furiously.

Carolyn drew the spotlight onto her and attracted the camera. "Fifteen more seconds," she announced silkily. She looked so beautiful among the chimpanzees.

Oh, Rupert sighed inside, how he wished he had the power, or superpower, to leap down there and sweep her away over skyscrapers in a single bound.

"Ten, nine, eight," she started to count backwards and voices in the audience numbered back with her, "seven, six, five, four…"

Rupert held to the pillar like a vine.

"Three, two, one!" She threw her arms up as an invisible orchestra responded with a flurry of sound. Carolyn spun round and round to the dance of it, pulling pages out of their stopped typewriters, gathering together an ever growing thicket of paper.

Rupert watched her effect on the crowd. He sneaked glances to see if they felt it too. And they did. The shimmer bounced off them, watching mesmerized. Whatever happened next was waiting for her to move. Even from this distance, Rupert held his breathe, enchanted. Every day she had them watch something marvelous. The apes may have been capable of more than the ordinary, but so much of the appeal of this show had to be because of her charm. They were luckier than him; they were lucky to have her nearby. He knew that and hoped he hadn't lost her.

Her voice purred from the stage, reading the typewritten title page, "Hamlet 2!" The spellbound audience clapped again and she waved the show to an end. She probably was doing something grander than he, Rupert sighed. Maybe he was wrong. How could a Laugher like him (even if he was the best) compete with those chimps? It had been such a joy to see her, but now as the lights came back on, and the audience stirred, and the music was lost in the shuffle, his hopes felt as far away as Mars. He turned for the door.

"Hey Rupert!"

"Oh hello, Vera," he tried to smile. Vera Haskins, Carolyn's rabbit robot had stopped him with her cold metal paw.

"Boy are you in the doghouse!" Vera chirped.

"Yeah, I know."

"You should have heard her this morning! I never—"

"I know, Vera. Listen, that's why I came by to see her. I was hoping—"

The silver rabbit laughed at him, her glasses shining, "Nice try, Rupert."

"Is that Rupert Wells?" Another rabbit appeared.

"I thought you were history."

"Very funny. I need to see her."

"You're serious?" The new rabbit spoke into a microphone, "This is Esther. We need some backup."

"Come on Esther, Vera. I just want to talk to her. Look, I brought her a flower." He held out the rose and put it in the rabbit's metal claw. "Could you give her that, please? Tell her I miss her, okay?"

The rabbit named Esther pushed up close and batted blue phototropic scanning eyes, "Oh Rupert… You shouldn't have…" with cartoon sarcasm.

Rupert held up his palms. It was too much. This day had been trying to unravel him. He had to leave before it did. Ignoring the gathering rabbits, he pushed the studio door open again and hurried past Hugo. Time to move on.

The elevator wasn't far. If the brassy golden doors didn't open right away, all he had to do was wait beside them and soon he could be on his way.

"Hello Mr. Wells," said a voice near the floor as the elevator doors opened.

"Hey Ditty, how's the elevator business?" Rupert got inside the elevator beside the little man.

"Oh, you know…"

"That's a joke, Ditty. An old one. You're supposed to say it has its ups and downs."

"Right, right," Ditty recalled. "I forgot for a minute."

Rupert laughed, "You're okay, Ditty. Don't worry about it."

"I won't, sir. Fifteenth floor?"

"You got it."

The doors slid closed and Ditty spun a dial to 15.

Rupert admired his gold cufflinks. He turned his hands so his sleeves rotated and glittered. He thought of asking Ditty about the puppet show outside, when the elevator made a terrible rasp and the entire contraption stopped.

"Not again…" Ditty sighed.

"What? What happened?"

"Oh, the elevator's stripped gears again." The overhead light blinked and buzzed.

"What do we do?"

But Ditty was already doing it. He pried the doors open. They were stuck between floors 5 and 6. "I'll have to call this in," Ditty said and he walked calmly through the door crack, dropping out of sight down to floor 5.

"See you around, Ditty!" Then Rupert groaned and mumbled, "I hope the elevator chain doesn't snap and cut me in half while I try to get out." He pulled himself up onto the sixth floor level, rolled over the carpet and stood up in the hallway. A bland music pawed out the speakers in the walls. "I'll take the stairs up to 15," he decided.

"Mr. Wells!" a yellow haired secretary called out to him. "We've been trying to get in touch with you all morning!"

"I know. My telephone and alarm clock are conspiring against me. My museum hates me and this moving carpet doesn't work either. Oh, and my girlfriend left me too."

"Yes, that's awful, Mr. Wells." She seized his arm by the sleeve.

"That elevator's broken by the way."

"Mr. Wells, Mr. Moore needs to see you immediately."

"Oh no. Not more bad news?" Rupert hurried to match the speed of her pace down the hall.

"I don't know, Mr. Wells." Her voice steamed, "I just happen to know he got summoned."

Rupert groaned, "The boss is in trouble, huh?"

"I don't know about that. He's in Makeup right now. You can find out." She opened the door and stepped aside for him. "Good luck."

"Thanks." He glanced at his gold cufflinks and went into the room.

"Rupert!" Sylvan Moore roared.

Rupert caught the eyes of his boss reflected in the mirrored wall and gave a startled reaction.

Half of Sylvan Moore's face was painted with makeup, the other half was untouched, stressed and pale. The mask hollered, "Where have you been? What's the point of having a Laugher if I can't get you when I need you?!"

So Rupert started to laugh. It took him over completely and shook him like a seizure. His face was breaking with the hysterics until he gasped for air. Leaning on the wall, he tried to catch his breath. When its storm passed, he still remembered it, with laughing backfires for a little longer.

Sylvan Moore was grinning, "That was great, Rupert. Thanks, I needed that."

Rupert swayed away from the wall. "I—no problem, boss—that was—" he laughed again. "That's hilarious!" He straightened his tie and looked at his cuflinks, then back to Sylvan Moore. "What's up, boss?"

"Ohhh," Sylvan Moore sighed and became grim again. "Listen, there's no way to put this lightly. The president is dead."

Rupert was quiet, while his mind whirred.

"And we need to locate his incarnation quick, before the news breaks. You can imagine the pandemonium…"

Rupert slumped down into the chair next to Sylvan Moore.

"I know what we're up against, Rupert," Sylvan Moore spoke solemnly. "It won't be easy, but we have to act."

"What happened to him?"

"I don't know. Someone found him dead. It just happened today." Sylvan Moore allowed more make-up to layer him. The robot painted his peaked skin until Sylvan held up a hand for it to stop. "We'll go on the air as usual though. Feed them something, stall them with cartoons. Meanwhile, I want you to go out looking."

"Yeah, but…It's a big world. He could be anywhere. Where do we start? It's impossible."

"That's not what I want to hear, Rupert." Sylvan Moore pointed his finger, "He's out there and you will find him!"

"Yes, of course."

"Get out to the stage. That's where we'll start. I'll

meet you there. Business as usual."

Sylvan Moore closed his eyes and allowed the brush to paint color over him.

Rupert said, "See you there," and left the room. He almost turned for the elevator but he stopped himself. He didn't want to go through that again. He opened the door to the stairwell and heard a loud train of footsteps coming down. He stood there waiting in the doorway until he saw Ditty round the handrail corner from the seventh floor above. Ditty was leading a group of people down.

"Sixth floor!" the little man piped as he stopped beside Rupert Wells. He mopped his forehead with a white handkerchief.

"Elevator still broke, Ditty?"

"Yes sir."

"Well I'm going up, Ditty."

"Alright Mr. Wells." Ditty stood aside for a frail couple carrying a birdcage. "Next stop, fifth floor." Ditty gave Rupert a choppy salute and led the crowd loudly down the next flight of stairs.

"See you, Ditty!" Rupert climbed away from the tromping sound. Nine floors…step after step…it didn't take long before he began to feel the effects. Stopping by the door handle he decided he needed to rest a second. Far below he could hear the strange burble and clatter of Ditty leading another group through the building. Poor little fellow, Rupert thought, he's going to wear out before long if they don't get that elevator fixed.

Floor 15 was one gigantic set designed for the

Sylvan Moore broadcast. A huge metal camera was wheeled past. People went by with boom microphones and light stands. A stage was being set up on the other side of the vast room. It was a background panorama of blue sky and white cumulus above an orange lit prairie. Stagehands hurried over every detail.

Rupert sighed. Another broadcast from the ranch. He wished they would try somewhere new, like Peru, or Europe again, or anywhere else. The president rarely left his ranch though…Especially not anymore…

"Mr. Wells!" Virginia Atkins, one of the show's producers hurried up to him. "Did you see Mr. Moore?"

"I just got back from seeing him."

She whispered, "Did he tell you about the president?"

"Yes…It's hard to believe. What happened exactly?"

"He didn't tell you?"

"No, not really."

"Oh, well…Then I probably don't know. We better get you prepared now. Over there please."

"Sylvan said we're going to act like nothing has happened."

She nodded, "Business as usual. We already have a story prepared. You just do your part, Mr. Wells."

They wove between the machinery of the program and in a moment, they were walking on sand, and sagebrush rubbed against their legs. The phony sunlight glowed from banks of orange and yellow panels. Rupert blinked. Virginia Atkins held her electronic clipboard over her eyes. "You'll get used to the brightness. Here, you stand by this fence, Rupert."

What at first seemed like a strange dream was now fooling him for reality. The fence had been worn and chipped by the weather—some thorns caught on him—he could smell cattle—and in the background of all the hammering and finishing touches, he could hear birds and wind.

A crew was still working on a scale model windmill in the background.

"Let me get you some makeup, Mr. Wells," she decided. She touched his forehead.

"Okay." He settled against the lean in the sand. He looked at the gold reflectors on his cufflinks. It wasn't long before he felt his face being brushed. He closed his eyes and listened. When he heard, "Okay Mr. Wells, you're all ready," he opened his eyes.

"Thanks."

Everyone else had left him too. Except for one man working on the branches of a sorrel tree.

"Hey Ed!" Rupert called him.

Ed Hume, the show's gardener, gave him a curt wave. "Hello Mr. Wells."

"Think you could put a hammock on that tree for me, Ed? I could use a nap."

"I don't think so, Mr. Wells. This tree is made of paper-maché."

"I was just joking with you, Ed."

"Oh." Ed Hume continued to pin leaves and shape the tree like a dressmaker.

Then a new voice boomed behind Rupert, the loud arrival of Sylvan Moore with his entourage. "What a beautiful day in Texas!"

Rupert turned and almost yelped in surprise; Sylvan Moore wore a big white cowboy hat tipped on his head.

"Rupert!" He slapped him on the shoulder. "You ready for this, buddy? Is everyone ready for this?!" He called to the crew.

Rupert nodded and agreed with everyone else in a chorus.

"Well alright then! Let's get this show going!" Sylvan Moore sidled up against the fence and allowed the cameras to trundle in nearer.

In the commotion and shifting of equipment, Rupert said, "What are you going to say about the president?"

Sylvan Moore laughed, "Oh we've got some great footage of him fishing and maybe you could work up a laugh for us."

Rupert nodded slowly, "But when do we tell them about—"

"Relax, Rupert! All in good time. Once we find his incarnation. Okay?" he smiled winningly.

"Okay."

"Can we get a sound check, Mr. Moore?" A microphone swayed above.

"Hello Americans!" he bellowed his trademark greeting, "This is Sylvan Moore."

"That's great, Mr. Moore." The sound technician faced Rupert, "And you, Mr. Wells?"

"Ha ha ha ha."

"Perfect. Whenever you're ready."

"Ten seconds!" announced a voice from the dark offstage. The vast room had become silent. Rupert stared down at his cufflinks nervously. Sylvan Moore grinned fixedly at the lens of the nearest camera.

"Five seconds. Four, three, two, one."

A fanfare from the orchestra machine flared up and melted into Sylvan Moore's, "Hello Americans!" He rested an elbow against the fence and assumed his folksy manner. "We're here at the president's ranch once again. A beautiful place," he turned his cowboy hat gaze to the side and back. "No wonder he spends so much time here." The soundman cued the sound of a hawk's shrill cry. "It's just what the president needs. Well folks, earlier today we caught up with the president fishing on his well-stocked pond. Take a look at this footage and get ready to laugh at his joke." While the film of the president fishing last month was run, Sylvan Moore waved at Rupert to begin.

Rupert let it start low in his belly, the feeling that soon conjured into a full awakened charge of laughter. He held onto the fence, rocked with it while the film rolled across the air. At last the pictures ended with the president reeling in and holding up a fat trout and Rupert gasped to a halt.

"Hope you feel wonderful, America!" Sylvan Moore signed off. An overhead bank of lights shut down, and fake Texas was in dusk. "Nice job, Rupert."

Rupert held his side. It felt like he had been jabbed with a sword. He'd have to lay off the laughs for a while. "Thanks boss."

"We're sending you, Rupert. There's an airship leaving from the roof. It will take you to the real ranch. See if you can pick up on the president's trail." Sylvan Moore slapped him on the shoulder, then he was off into the crowd disassembling the stage.

Rupert watched the windmill topple over. It made a loud crash on the cement floor. Someone was sweeping the sand away. The fence folded up into bundles. He stood back and watched the fake Texas ranch fall apart. Well, he thought, here I go. He left, the stage crew dismantling him like the scenery.

The elevator was still out of order, so he took to the stairway again.

He climbed six floors alone with his echoes. No sound of Ditty above or below.

Rupert rested after a few more floors. He had a long way to go. Maybe Ditty had given in to exhaustion. Then a robot appeared clonking through the doorway behind him.

The big gorilla robot held out hands to him and Rupert said, "Thanks!" and climbed on its back.

The gorilla took him up and up to the final floor where a ladder went to the roof level. "Thanks again, pal!" Rupert smiled. "I'll take it from here."

Rupert pushed on sunlight, opening the trapdoor. Coming out onto the bright green turf and yellow flowers of the roof, he felt like he was climbing out of a grave. He let the trapdoor fall closed into the grass.

There was a breeze on the roof, setting all the dandelions tipping and turning. Some of the blue sky was moving with white and gray cloud flocks, but no sign of an airship yet. In his time of wondering mind,

Rupert thought of Carolyn. He felt like a heel.

From his jacket pocket he took an envelope and quickly dictated a message. "Carolyn. Okay, I'm sorry. I wish last night never happened—I mean, the part about you leaving me. I'm going to Texas now. I can see the airship. I miss you. Rupert."

He couldn't see the airship yet. He listened to the letter over. It wasn't great, but at least she would know he was thinking of her. He hoped she was thinking of him, missing him. Maybe it would take a few lonely days and nights.

He sealed the envelope. With a Sylvan Moore Show pen, he addressed the envelope and pressed the stamp to activate it. A pair of cellophane wings whirred open and the letter fluttered out of his hands. It made a compass circle then flew off east in the direction of Carolyn's riverside apartment complex.

He watched it go, and though it had disappeared quickly into the hazy blur burning above the city, he continued to stare in her direction.

About ten seconds later, he could discern the approach of an airship dotted in the watercolor sky. It drifted closer. Above the whale-slooping shape of it, great sails were unfurled to catch the jet stream. The thing rolled like an ancient clipper ship. He imagined himself strolling the iron catwalks a thousand feet above the ground, while the four bladed propellers clashed them along above the red sandy desert.

Without slowing, the airship sped past the Airwaves Building, going west. Rupert watched it leave, waiting for the rudders to turn it around again to get him.

"Mr. Wells?" a mechanical device greeted him.

When he turned, Rupert suddenly realized what airship Sylvan Moore had found for him. There was a lawn chair anchored in the grass; above it a bunch of white weather balloons. "Oh no…"

"Are you not Mr. Wells?"

"No, that's me, it's just I'm not going to Texas on that thing." Did the robot think he was stupid? Probably. Most of them did. "Forget about Texas…"

"Mr. Wells." The robot lifted its flimsy arm. "Your employer has requested your immediate departure. You're in the safest possible hands. I've flown over fifty passengers and never had anything go awry. Plus, I also served in the war." It clapped its hands together in prayer, "Thank God I'm out of there!"

"That—*chair!*—can't get me to Texas. Even if it could, it would take me months."

"No, I disagree, Mr. Wells. You'll be pleasantly surprised. If you hurry on board, we can try to catch a ride in the wake of the Grand Duchess."

"I don't know," Rupert paused. How could he be lured into this? I should just take the train and forget about it. He was going to say that when the robot interrupted him.

"Okay Mr. Wells, no more Mr. Nice Guy." It seized him and dragged him across the dandelion garden, got him pinned in the chair before Rupert could struggle, locked him in with a seatbelt, held onto the chair controls, and cut the anchor line.

The shoot into the air cut Rupert's breath off. His

cufflinks were ripped off his sleeves, the roof was gone in a jump. He clenched the arm rests as he watched gravity tear out from under him. A scream formed in him, about to go, when the robot spoke.

"Thank you for choosing to fly with Air Chair, Flight 262. I'm your captain Lou Murphy. Looks like some good flying conditions today. We'll make good time, so sit back, relax and enjoy your flight."

Rupert was still getting used to seeing planet Earth from a bird's perspective. Every dip in the wind and swerve it threw, the lawn chair jumped him like a puppet.

"At this time I'd like to ask our passengers to refrain from smoking."

"Get me down!" Rupert screamed.

"Take it easy, Mr. Wells," the robot answered him. "Don't be a nightmare. We'll catch up with the zep, then you'll really see some traveling."

The fear was too much though—the jet-stream shook him like a tornado, until a rush of darkness covered him over and out.

Part Two:
ON MARS

When Rupert opened his eyes, it occurred to him that he was looking down at a vast green forest. Yes… He remembered what happened…Wasn't he flying to Texas on a balloon?

He must be hundreds of feet in the air now, staring at the earth below. Something tickled his face, and when he tried to move, it became evident that he was lying down. He turned his face on the grass and he saw yellow. Dandelions…Where was he? Back on the roof? Did he even leave?

He struggled to move. He was sore everywhere, as if pummeled by an eggbeater. So he lay there for a little while, to allow his eyes to wander slowly over the green and yellow.

The backs of stooping gardeners worked in a row off to the left. He didn't see the cherry trees that marked the corners of the Airwaves Building roof, so he decided he had gone somewhere else. It was warm as afternoon wherever he was.

"You're Mr. Wells, aren't you? Rupert Wells? Let me give you a hand." A cardboard robot extended its arm to him.

Rupert laughed. Normally the cardboard ones stuck to light chores like dusting or feeding carp. It looked like the arm would tear right off if Rupert grabbed it. "Thanks," Rupert smiled and took the grip lightly. When he was suddenly and easily pulled into the air, Rupert laughed and burst out, "You must be from Texas!" It was an old joke.

"Mars," the Robot corrected.

"What??"

"That's correct sir."

"We're on Mars?"

"Yes sir."

"Ohhhh, I wasn't prepared for this," Rupert groaned. "I didn't expect to leave Earth."

"Well sir, you're here now."

Rupert took a deep breath of the Martian air. It was sweet with flowers. People said it was better here than on Earth...It was like Earth used to be. Also, the different gravity made him feel lighter and stronger. "I need to get to the president's ranch," he quickly told the robot. "Can I get transportation?"

"Why sure! Follow me." The robot swayed and tilted as he walked like an old-time cowboy movie star. The patch of dandelion greens and flowers ended in a tall red stone wall, where the robot pushed open a wooden gate and there they were. "This is midtown," the cardboard told him. "Welcome."

Rupert stepped out beside him onto the dusty orange pavement. It was a Martian postcard scene.

"Try the bait shop for a horse," the robot offered, bending a finger at the gray building with all the hand-painted signs worn all over it; an antique on another planet. "And good luck."

"Thanks." Rupert failed to answer with a smile though. He hoped he wasn't losing his humor. What was he doing way out here in space? Why couldn't the president live in the old Texas? But Rupert knew what had happened to the old Texas…He just hoped that wouldn't happen here.

Some piano music came out of the saloon across the street. A robot cow pulled a flat overcrowded cart, piled with rattling spindly hard Martian trees. Rupert stepped around it and aimed for the bait shop.

He managed to smile when he imagined himself buying a bucket of bait to take out hunting brainees in the outback. He knew that's what a lot of the settlers here did. Well, he shook his smile away, this was certainly a long, long way from *The Sylvan Moore Show*.

He stepped up onto the plastic wooden porch and stood there for a moment staring blankly at all the painted signs and neon. It seemed they were in a different language.

"Howdy pardner!" someone greeted him.

Rupert noticed the coin operated child's rocking horse ride talking to him. It was the sort you would find outside of supermarkets on Earth. "Oh, hello."

"You're from Earth, right? The horse nodded its plastic head. Its whole body moved up and down on a pole that attached it to its rectangular metal base.

Rupert returned the nod.

"You're not hunting brainees in that suit, are you?" A soft chuckle came out of the speaker.

"No. I was told I could get some transportation here."

"That's true!"

Rupert paused, "I guess I'll go in then and see what

they've got." He reached out for the screen door but the horse interrupted him urgently.

"Woah there, pardner! Look no further!"

"What? You mean…You?"

"Yep."

"You're serious??"

"Sure! Where you headed to? I'll take you there."

Rupert paused, "Ummmm…How?"

"Just put some coins in the old slot and awaaaaaaay we go!" the horse announced with a buck.

After a sigh, Rupert agreed, "Okay…But I'll need to get change for that meter."

"I'll be waiting for you. Oh—you might want to pick up a cowboy hat too while you're in there. The sun gets awful fierce on the plain."

"Okay…Thanks."

The horse was right about the sun. Rupert was thankful for the sombrero he wore. It cast a blue shadow down over his shoulders, over his suit onto the loping, rocking plastic neck of the talkative, slow moving kiddie horse. As its longwinded story about lost prospectors was drawling out of steam, its pace had been slowing to a crawl. Predictably, it begged for more money again.

"You better put another couple quarters in me, pardner…I'm gettinnnnng riiiiight tiiiiiiiiired."

Rupert still had a heavy pocketful of silver, but he wondered how long it would last, and would it be enough to get them to the ranch? "How much further is his ranch anyway?" He dropped some money in for the answer.

The horse gave a buck of new life and Rupert grabbed the thin leather rein.

"We're near about there. Getting closer all the time."

Rupert groaned. "I hope we're not lost. It all looks the same to me." Rust colored rocky plain sloped without ever seeming to get entirely up. The horse, rising and falling on its pole, directed its tank-like base around larger stones, while its wheels underneath left a double track path like a railroad.

The horse laughed at him, "All Mars looks like you're lost! That's the way it is up here. But I'll tell you, I wouldn't have it any other way. I was—Hey now!" he hushed and leaned. "Look a' there!"

Ahead of them was the sight of three glowing blue objects on the rusted sand.

"Brainees!" the horse excitedly seethed. "You got a gun?"

"No, of course not."

The Martian creatures had sensed them though, moving around the edges.

Rupert had seen pictures of brainees, but wondered, as he saw them this first time, what kind of thing they were? They almost seemed like birds, the way they ruffled themselves as if to fly.

"Too bad you don't have a gun," the horse clucked.

"Shhhh!" Rupert pulled the rein.

The brainees began to quiver into single file, motioning away.

"Let's get closer," Rupert told the horse and he dug his heels into the plastic. The retreating brainees put on some speed, but he could see them better now. Now he saw them as sort of moving flowers… Maybe two feet tall…Blue petals waved around a central whorl that pulsed with a darker pumping color. That's how they got their name, he guessed: brainees. It looked like a big fissured lobe, the cerebellum of a fiendish science fiction monster.

The horse couldn't go much faster than their current rate and when the brainees dipped into a shallow full of shadows, they easily disappeared from view.

"We lost them…" the horse panted, "Should have had a gun on you…" He was running out of coin again. "You betttttterrrr…put sommmmmme mmmorrrrrre…"

"Yeah, I know!"

The horse was almost stopped.

"Where'd they go though?" Rupert stood up in the saddle and shaded his eyes, pushing back the rim of his sombrero.

"Where…theyyyyyyyy…alwaaaaayssss…..go."

"Where's that?"

"They….go….unnnnnnnderrrrrrr." But with a loud click the horse froze into a statue.

Rupert groaned and dug in his pocket. He wondered how much money he'd already spent on this slow moving slot machine. I bet the bait shop had mechanical camels out back, he raged at himself, I could have been at the ranch by now.

The horse came right back to life with its money,

finishing its sentence, "—ground."

"Underground?"

"Sure, pardner! There's where they live. I know a rancher peeled open the soil with a backhoe and found fifty of them sleeping under there."

Rupert said, "What exactly do they do? Are they a pest or something?"

"Sure! They're Martians! Oh, it's too bad you didn't have a gun! You could have made 600 bounty, maybe more."

"I just want to get to the ranch," said Rupert quickly. "I don't want to kill brainees. It sounds like the TV special we ran on the buffaloes last month. Back in American history, they killed them all off. So what are people doing here? Taking themselves to other worlds and continuing their bad habits? It's shameful."

"Awww," the horse growled, "You're just not from here. You don't know what it's like."

You're right about that, thought Rupert.

"You'll get used to it though, if you stay here long enough. Heck…I wouldn't live anywhere else. I took another Earthman like you for a ride last month—his first time here too—and he—"

"Isn't there anything you can do besides talk?" Rupert cut the horse off abruptly.

"Isn't there anything you can do besides *laugh?*" the horse snapped back. "Yeah, I know all about you and your show and your president! We can't stand it! He's lucky someone hasn't taken a shot at him."

Rupert held up his hands, "Alright! Alright. Woah, okay so you know who I am." He didn't know a robot horse could be so angry. It steamed at him like a hot teakettle. Besides, he wanted to say, since I got here I haven't laughed once.

After a little break in conversation, filled in by the slow movement of the cracking Martian stones, the horse continued, "Listen, I'm sorry mister. I didn't mean to snap at you like that. That's not my job. That wasn't right of me and I sincerely apologize."

"That's okay," Rupert tried to smile, but he thought, let's see if I put any more quarters in you when you run out of steam. I can cover more ground walking.

"Well, I feel like a right heel for that behavior nonetheless, and I'd like nothing more than to—Hey!" the horse seized up again, "That's a brainee hole!"

They were stopped at a place where the broken clay fell in.

"You ought to at least take a look," the horse told him.

"Okay—I'll take a look, but then, you know, I'd like to get to the ranch at some point today."

The horse snorted, "Just take a look-see. You might be able to grab one out. I knew a—"

"Here I go," Rupert said bluntly and stepped off the slick plastic saddle. His knees were a little sore, still he bent down to peer in.

What a gloom. No sign of the blue glowing brainees. He was about to draw himself back when he heard a faint sound and tremor. The ground moved ever so gently, some dirt fell in front of his face. "I think something's in there!" Rupert hissed.

Like a dummy, he got up and turned around to see

the mechanical horse galloping off, raising hoofs of red dust, ditching him in this desolate part of Mars. He had to admit, the thing could really move when it wanted to.

Rupert took off his sombrero and clocked it against his knee, calling out an Earth curse at that fleeing blur.

Here he was, who knew where…

The sun shined miserably. The sky looked metallic and as he turned slowly to take in the lost landscape, he saw smoke signals.

That's a place to go, Rupert decided. He started in that direction.

It looked like the clouds were coming from less than a mile ahead.

It wasn't so far after all. As he got closer, the sight came into focus. Rupert kept trying to figure it out and then he could.

There was a mechanical steam-car parked next to a boiler shape that was creating the clouds every half minute. Rupert could also see the stick-like figure of a tall man standing there.

Rupert paused to wave his sombrero at the cloud operator.

The person waved back and leaned over the boiler-thing. It made a racket, like violins falling down stairs.

In the next moment, a new cloud puffed out and arose.

This one, Rupert realized with surprise, was shaped like an elephant.

He walked the rest of the distance smiling, watching the elephant walk overhead Mars.

"Hello there!"

"Hello!" Rupert called back. "What do you have there?"

"Hah!" the man laughed. "Come on over, friend."

Now that he was near, Rupert could count flywheels and cogs and dials bolted all over the copper machine. "That looked like an elephant you just made."

"So it did." The man beamed and tipped his black peaked hat. A long black robe covered him. There were blue stars stitched onto the cloth.

Rupert got it when he read the hand-painted sign on the steam-car parked near him.

The Cloud Wizard.

"My name's Denton Clyde," the wizard said and, "This is what I do. I go around Mars and make clouds. Clouds like that one that went thatta way, that elephant you saw."

"That was a good one."

"Sure it was! I have plenty more in store. I can make them in all shapes and sizes. Mars has never seen clouds like mine. I think it's about time for another one. Watch this…" and he turned the machine cranks and pulled levers to release a noisy new rush of vapor into the air. The roiling swirl took form high over them, pushing and twining into the surreal outline of what looked like the Cheshire Cat. Denton Clyde laughed at that, "Or I can do regular Earth cumulus too. Anyway, it all depends on how you look at it."

"I like them," Rupert said. "I see that's something I've been missing since I got to Mars. There are no clouds. It's pretty empty here isn't it?"

"Well, that's what I'm here for!" Denton beamed. "I've got a whole set of clouds I special ordered from Montana—those will be going up in an hour. Wait til you see them!"

"I'd like to stick around, but I'm trying to get to the president's ranch. Do you know where it is?"

The cloud wizard took a deep breath of silence. He seemed different suddenly, as if he'd put on a new mask. "What brings you there?"

"I have some business to attend to there. I've wasted the whole afternoon riding a horse to nowhere. I need to get to that ranch before dark."

"Well…Everyone on Mars knows where that ranch is…"

"Would you take me there?" Rupert pleaded.

"No. No, I don't go near there. Neither do my clouds. You're fresh from Earth, maybe you haven't noticed it, but the president isn't exactly well liked here. However…" he pointed a robed arm west, "There's a horse stand in that direction. A good horse will take you to that ranch before nightfall."

"That way?" A small hill of rocks climbed up to block the horizon. "Thanks wizard. I'll be watching for your clouds." Even on Mars, Rupert got the cold shoulder. The wizard turned his back on him and was cranking a silver wheel on his cloud machine. "Goodbye," Rupert mumbled.

The legs of his suit pants were colored from the orange of Martian traveling. He entertained the possibility that Sylvan Moore had sent him here to be marooned. It was possible; a power play on Earth. But he had to hope for the best—like Robinson Crusoe, he had to turn his mind to survival. The dry country-side didn't seem to offer much to eat. He wondered what exactly the settlers did with the brainees. Did they eat them? He shuddered at the thought. Why were they after them?

At least Denton Clyde hadn't lied…Rupert came down the hill on the other side to see the spindly sight of a camp, a corral of tin planks pushed up with horse heads looking over. I'll ask for the fastest one, Rupert hurried, enough of this puttering about.

The horses watched him approach, a few of their heads bobbed like puppets to neigh at him. A man in a cowboy hat came out of his tent and cupped his hands to yell at Rupert, "What's the big idea?!" Then his hands went down to the pistols he wore on his belt.

Rupert halted. A Martian Western was unfolding. "I need a horse!" he yelled.

Keeping one hand on a gun, the man waved him forward with his left hand. "I've got horses—if you've got money."

With all the calm of a tree branch in the wind, Rupert reached slowly into his pocket to show he still had dollars.

"I'll take that," the cowboy grabbed all Rupert had displayed. "I'll give you a horse. This way." Leaving a hand on a gun just in case the deal turned, the man walked along the gray tin wall. Horses nuzzled over the edge watching. He stopped at one leaning towards him and he reached for its halter.

In one pull, the cowboy lifted the horse up over the fence and planted it beside Rupert. It was a chestnut brown horse head attached to a stick. The horse opened its mouth and whinnied. It looked like a discount Christmas tree.

"That's—" Rupert lost the next word's direction.

"She's a good mare. She'll take you where you're headed." The cowboy leaned her over to Rupert.

Rupert sighed. This was Mars, he had to realize. "Thanks…Pardner…" he managed to say, as he took the horse by the handle. He paused with it held in front of him, holding it like a top-heavy popsicle.

"You know how to ride, don't you?" the cowboy grinned a yellowed smile. "Just put her between your legs and go." Then he burst into abrupt laughter.

Rupert carried the horse away. He tucked it under his arm and made for the sand behind another countless boulder. No reason for anyone to see him perform for laughs when he was up here on Mars. He was penniless, lost, and on top of it all he had a stick-horse companion.

"Where do you need to go?" the horse asked him in a husky voice.

The shock that it talked caused Rupert to drop the stick in alarm.

"Ow!" the horse yelped with eyes closed.

Rupert sputtered an apology and gingerly picked up the stick, keeping it at arm's length though.

The horse gave him a hard stare. "What's the matter mister? You're not going to drop me again, are you?"

"Sorry about that…I just wasn't…Umm—prepared. I'll be careful now. So…How do we get started?"

The horse showed its teeth with a laugh. "How do you think? Just put your leg over…That's right…"

Rupert held the reins. The horse pulled and Rupert started walking with the stick horse between his legs. "Wait a second!" Rupert stopped walking.

"What's the matter now?"

"I'm doing all the work here!"

"No you're not."

"Yes!" Rupert insisted, "I am! I'm doing the walking!"

"No."

"Yes! Look at me! I step, one leg, then the other, and again."

The horse tugged on the reins. "Why don't you stop playing games, I don't see what you're trying to prove."

Rupert almost screamed, but he didn't. He started to walk. He crunched his feet into the Martian surface and went about twenty yards biting silence. The horse's head had assumed the lope and attitude of one attached to an actual horse.

"See!" Rupert yelled. "I'm doing the walking! I'm carrying *you!*"

The horse shook its rein, snorting, "No you're not."

"That's it!" Rupert roared. "I've had it with you." He stabbed the horse stick into the sand so it stood there, horse head sprouting like an aghast flower.

"Thanks for your help, but I'll go on alone."

"What are you doing?!"

Rupert didn't care. He let it yowl on and on as he departed across the crumble. Fuming thoughts blocked it out, so enough time went by and he was on his own, on the plain.

He was on another planet's desert, the sun's day was dimming, and where was he anyway?

A noise went off in his coat pocket. He had forgotten that contraption. There was a cell telephone in there. He stopped and tore it out and answered it anxiously, "Hello?"

"Rupert!" the voice scratched at him from 35 million miles away, "How you doing up there?"

"Sylvan?"

"None other." Static jumped in to block some words, "—that done."

"I'm not at the ranch yet!" Rupert yelled at his hand.

"—and—"

"I need directions, Sylvan! I'm out here walking in circles."

"—told Carolyn." The telephone paused.

"What?!"

"I told Carolyn."

"What did you tell her?!"

"I said you'd be okay."

"I'm not!!" Rupert bellowed.

"Everything will work out, Rupert. Just talk to

them there, someone will know something. You'll find him."

"Can I talk to Carolyn? Can you transfer me? Please."

Sylvan Moore laughed. Who knows how far that laugh traveled on past other stars and meteors and unnamed things in space? "Sure. Hang on."

Rupert did. He listened to the seashell sound in his hand, the faint crackle and stir of water and sand, and then he heard a ring on the other end. He made a wish.

The answering machine picked it up with the slow ballad she chose to talk over, "This is Carolyn. Do you miss me? Leave me a message."

So he did. "Oh—Carolyn…It's me, Rupert. Can you believe I'm on Mars! I—" He tried for the right words. "I'm so far away from you and I've never been here before. I'm—I—I hope you're—" then the connection broke and he was left staring at the sky.

It happened so fast, this Martian night, not like on Earth where the sun settles slow to dim and melts into gone: this was sudden, and Rupert was left cold, very cold.

Desperation seized him. He wasn't used to roughing it like this. He knew he needed heat and he scrambled looking. Around him were those silhouette wisps of Martian weeds so he pulled all he could into bunches and piled them on the ground. If he could only get through the night, however long it lasted. He wasn't sure if it was more or less than what he was used to, where he came from. A glance at the sky for a second, looking for his home.

After freezing minutes of running around gathering enough weeds to make a thatch stack of brambles—if only there were trees, he seethed, or something bigger to burn—he halted and in movie-motion, reached slowly to pluck the sombrero off his head. This heavy lid on him must burn as well if not better than anything in the Martian wilderness. He set it down, a crown on top of the bird's nest, and took the matchbook out of his suit coat pocket.

He struck the red end against his shoe and the match broke uselessly. That should have worked, but it didn't, so he struck the next match along the roughened edge of the matchbook and orange blinked like a coyote eye. Tremblingly, he brought the fire close to the bent sombrero visor.

The flash blinded him for ten seconds. His vision was white then purple then gradually he could see in the dark again. No sign of the flammable sombrero, only the shriveled burnt out tangle of weeds he had gathered.

What cold dream was he sliding into?

Stars were thrown all over above. Mars was cold. Freezing. Rupert held his arms around himself tightly as he shuffled through the crunching stalks of papery weeds. Sometimes he came across old brainee tunnels, dead feeling, like broken cemetery tombs. This ground was haunted and waiting for him to fall. He knew it would only be a matter of time before he dropped, he knew he didn't have long. What a fate…

As he recovered from a near fall in the dirt,

staggering and scattering a splash of small rocks, he caught sight of a faint light off to his left. His tattered thoughts moaned aloud, "It's probably brainees closing in, coming to get me and drag me underground," but he plodded towards it anyway. It might be mercy, there was always a chance. The closer he got to it, or it got to him, or they got to each other, the light began to separate into a string of blue colored pearls in the night, like fireflies attracted to him.

Rupert had the strength to panic, he wanted to run the other way, but he tripped and was sliding down a black hill of sand towards them.

When he could stand, he heard music coming from the lights. Also, he seemed to see shadows flickering back and forth, making the lights blink a little. He couldn't climb up that cold collapsing landslide behind him, so he used the last of his power to steam ahead, to call out before he sunk.

He lay that way for a minute or so, still in the same dream he realized, then he began to move again. He discovered it was easier to shuffle along on his hands and knees. So he forced himself across another hundred yards. "Someone help me…" he chattered. He didn't know what it was, or who, but someone did.

"Ahh!" Rupert shouted.

The twins stared at him with the same surprise in their eyes. Two girls dressed alike in long flowing robes, veils, silver bells that shook when they jumped away from the carpet he lay on.

He tried to catch calm. He tried again. "I'm sorry—I—Where am I?" Around him circled a gently flapping tent world of patterned cloth walls. Candles flickered on tall gold stands. It was warm. He sat up. The girls watched him like two cats caught in headlights.

"It's alright," Rupert said. "I'm glad I'm here… Where am I?"

"You're Rupert Wells, right?"

He shook like a flower. "Yy—ess."

"We see you on TV." She turned to her sister, "I told you it was him!"

Her sister was silent, her eyelids dropped.

"What are you doing on Mars?" asked the girl.

Rupert rubbed the side of his face. "I'm just trying to get to the president's ranch." His fingertips were stubbled with the sand that had been on him. "Thanks for finding me, if that was you."

"Oh my God!" The girl gasped. "We're going to the ranch too! Are you going there to see daddy?"

That was when Rupert figured out who he was with. "You're the president's daughters?"

"Yeah!"

"Mm-hmm," the other, quieter one, nodded.

"Ohhhh…" Rupert dropped back like a dead weight and sunk into sleep.

Each step the big mechanical animal took rocked Rupert in his chair. It was morning, Rupert was part of their caravan, riding steam camels across the sand.

Rupert held to the cradling armrests. The surface of Mars was still largely a dead world. He thought somehow they should be planting trees all over it, if there was water for that, of course. It would take more than a few Earth shipped clouds, Rupert mused. They could use Lake Erie right there, he scanned the horizon…some misty Appalachia growing on those ridges…redwoods for miles and miles…He daydreamed the dry landscape getting rivers, becoming prairie with buffalo. He was on a roll, imagining Mars brought to new life, when the twins yelled down at him.

They were leaning over the balcony at the top of the camel. "Rupert! Are you sick?" They laughed. They were greenhouse flowers. What did they know beyond the soft and cradled? They couldn't venture without vast care and entourage.

He waved to them. "No!" His metal chair was bolted on the wide side of the camel. For fear of falling off, he kept a hand gripped to the armrest. "I'm just—How much further to the ranch?"

Up there in the bright sun they laughed down at him like two spoiled silhouettes.

He held on with both hands. He was from a big city on another planet, he wasn't used to any of this. He was glad when the twins disappeared and he could return his mind to wondering, comparing this world to the one he came from.

Rupert grew close to meditation, listening to the rhythm of the electric hydraulics and the feet plodding. Behind them a fine cloud of dust kicked up and obscured the rest of Mars. It made the terrain look like an ancient television program.

There came a thud on the tin ribcage above Rupert. He looked up. The twins had tied a shoe to a long string and it was swinging and echoing on the hull.

"There's the ranch!" the girls yelled.

All Rupert could see was a hill growing up high off the plain. But they were right, the desert ahead had changed, it glowed bright red through the dust. As it got clearer he could see what made the color…Flowers…Scatters of them grew.

"Poppies?" Rupert wondered out loud. Were the rumors true?

The girls were getting excited, chattering above him like squirrels. They were glad to be getting home and of course, Rupert, after all he'd been through since landing on Mars, was just as relieved to see the brilliant red hillside getting closer and closer.

The camel leading the caravan suddenly clanked to a snapping halt and Rupert had to hold on tight as the rest of the camels bunched up and locked gears.

A black iron fence had popped up out of the sand before them. They must have triggered it. It formed a protective circle, ten feet high all around the flower fields surrounding the mansion.

Something else was rising out of the baked soil too. On the other side of the wall, a pointed striped sentry box arose then stopped when it was completely out of the ground. Some rusted dust clung to its black and white paint. The silver door creaked open and a very old sentry shuffled out. Dressed in black, from his right leg dragged a chain attached to something that took a little longer to come out—a big iron ball, like a cannonball. The coppery skinned fellow heaved that weight across to the ironwork. It took him a while.

Rupert was dumb with the recognition. Abraham Lincoln! Or??...Could it really be him? It must be—or...was he cloned, or fit into a robot who looked like him? The zoo Lincoln reached his arms up to cling to the other side of the fence. It was an effort. He almost seemed to be holding himself from falling down. A thin cloud of blackish steam spilled off the stovepipe hat like a smokestack and a weary voice addressed them.

"Fellow citizens..." Lincoln held his big flat hands up to them, "Finding this condition of things, all such collisions tend to excite misapprehensions."

Someone in the bow of the camel in front of Rupert called back, "Open the gate, Abe!"

The giant continued anyway, "In cases of these kinds I have, so far as possible, heard and redressed complaints which have been presented by friendly powers."

With a yell, the driver of the forward camel swung down from his controls on a long hissing rope. He landed in front of the locked gate. "I said open the gate!" He drew a steam-gun from his coat and pointed it at Lincoln's chest.

That was too much for Rupert. He came alive, fell out of his seat and bounded over the sand. "Hold on! Hold on!" He couldn't bear to see Abraham Lincoln hurt again.

Still pointing the weapon straight ahead, the driver turned around. "Who are you?" But then the man's sunburned face wrinkled up, "Hey, I know you!" His gun lowered. "You're that guy from the TV. The joker! Hah!"

"Yes…That's me."

"Say something funny!" the driver said.

"Well—I'd like to—of course I'd like to, but I think maybe instead, I could talk to Mr. Lincoln here and see if he'd let us through."

"Oh no," the driver answered, raising his gun again. "He won't let us through. We always shoot him. That works fine." He drew aim at the old president again.

"No! Wait!" Rupert practically shrieked.

"What for?"

"Just…Just let me try? Okay?"

"Look at him." The driver pointed the barrel. "You can see all the times we've had to shoot him before. That's what we have to do."

It was true, the Lincoln figure's clothing had been patched repeatedly and there were bullet sized scars dented into spots on his skin.

"Wait!" Rupert shouted again at the gun. "We don't need to shoot him. Let's try to be rational. I can talk to him, can't I?"

The driver cursed into his hand and shouldered his gun disappointedly. "Alright, Laugher. I'll give you two minutes."

"Thank you sir…" Rupert took a deep breath of relief and faced Abraham Lincoln alone. "Mr. Lincoln," he began. The great eyes stared at him and Rupert seemed to lose his language. Rupert was swimming in them. In the middle of a desert, he was drowning in those sorrow pooled eyes.

"I deem it my duty—"

"No," Rupert interrupted him. "Listen to me please, Mr. Lincoln. I'm here to tell you," but then he laughed skittishly, "You're one of my heroes you know…See, I want you to be safe, I don't want anyone to hurt you. I can't explain. Maybe you could just open the gate kindly for us. Look, the president's daughters are returning."

Before the Lincoln eyes could open from a slow mechanical blink, Rupert gushed, "You know, since you're here, I'd like to tell you you're probably the greatest president. We all look up to you still. I—Oh my gosh, Mr. President—Can I break up the moment here to tell you how much you mean to us Americans?" Rupert felt like one of those dunces who followed him on Earth, hounding him for an autograph. He clapped a hand over his eyes, "I hope you understand…"

Lincoln shifted his heavy weight. The chains across to the big cannonball rattled his decision. He clasped his hands in a praying manner. It was an effort to lean from that coupled metal weight when it happened.

Rupert couldn't believe his eyes as Abraham Lincoln smiled, he had never seen a picture of that before. The president spoke, "It gives me pleasure to report a decided improvement. Physically speaking, we cannot separate. We cannot remove our respective sections from each other, nor build an impassible wall between them."

Rupert beamed and replied, "I knew you'd understand! You know, you should be on our television program! I'm sure you'd be most welcome."

Just then a gunshot cracked past Rupert and with a loud impact Abraham Lincoln fell backwards to crash on his back.

"What the—?!" Rupert yelped as he whirled around so fast his feet caught and he tripped himself. He let out a yell as he hit the hard ground. Mars was like landing on a bag of cement.

The twins were laughing uproariously, pointing at Rupert's shoes, the laces they had tied together when he wasn't looking.

Rupert had to undo their knots while the whole caravan laughed.

"Load up, Earthling!" the camel driver leader yelled. A blast of black locomotive smoke came out of the lead mechanical beast's stack. A shrill whistle hit the air.

The twins raced back to their ladder.

Rupert hurried and snapped the laces free from each other. Lincoln lay dead as could be in the dust, tied, sunken to that big metal ball.

The camels were creaking, starting to move, the tall legs leaning like trees.

"Okay!" Rupert choked. He ran and caught the rope rungs hanging down. Gears and pulley pulled him back up to his chair. He buckled himself while they passed through the opened gates, plodding by the dead president. The top hat was clunked off his head like a broken chimney.

Most surprising of all, on the other side of the fence, in not more than fifty yards distance, the desert had patches of bright red flowers growing on long green stalks. They were poppies alright, Rupert confirmed, growing on Mars. The camels started walking uphill. The president's ranch was on the other side of the incline. Rupert held on tight as everything tipped.

One by one, the camels topped the ridge and stopped. Their engines groaned from the exertion. Rupert almost fell out of his chair in surprise as the other side of the hill was revealed.

There was no more desert: the landscape had changed to a glowing bright red. It looked like a crimson lake cut down inside the bowl of the hills. Tomato soup. In the center were the spires and slanting roofs of the president's ranch castle. It was quite a sight.

Rupert jumped again as each camel in unison let go a whistled shriek of arrival.

Far below, a horn sounded from the mansion.

"This is it..." Rupert murmured. As the camels began to descend, sand scudded down in slides ahead of them. How many people besides this inner circle of the caravan had ever seen this sight? It was the real ranch...not on Texas, but on Mars.

A path cut a narrow way through the crop. Soon the camels left the sandy hill behind and their steel ankles brushed leaves and petals as they threaded themselves in. This near, Rupert could see the knife cuts in the big flower pods. The ooze that came out would be prepared and sent to the nearest planets. Martian opium and heroin was talked about in hushes back home. Rupert had heard all this mentioned before, and now he was seeing it with his own eyes. The air was like a vapor. And Rupert felt like nodding, he was so tired from the journey here.

"Hey Rupert!" one of the twins up above him screeched, "Aren't the flowers beautiful?" Two laughs fluttered up there.

But he wasn't thinking about them, or the enormous crop, he was thinking about Abraham Lincoln. He had a plan. If Rupert got a chance, somehow he was going to get back to that spot where the president landed on the dust and craters. He would bring cutters or a saw so he could cut that ball and chain. He would take that president off this planet someway, in disguise or whatever, and call up Sylvan Moore. "I've got him," Rupert would say, "I've got the president. Let him lead us again." That would be amazing. That's what they needed. All the televisions would freeze and Sylvan Moore would announce to the worlds that the next president had been discovered on Mars. It was more than reincarnation, it was the actual manifestation of the one we were all waiting on, and missing, for so long.

Another thing hit his head and Rupert woke up. A silver coin dropped past him.

"Damn!" one of the girls cussed. "I missed him."

"Wake up Rupert!" her sister screeched.

They laughed again and a shower of coins rattled over and around him.

"Okay, thanks!" Rupert replied. That was strange,

what dream had he been dreaming? How long had he been asleep? Not long, he decided. The caravan waded through the tree sized poppies. It was dusty. He rubbed his hands over his face. The leaves brushing against the hulls made a lulling sound like ocean waves. He just wanted to get the Martian business over with as soon as possible. Then what? Then he thought of Carolyn. What made him remember her? She was so far away.

The camels started to whistle again. The flowers fell back and they were through, to a sea green lawn. The presidential palace was a hundred yards from them.

The camels stopped. Ladders fell down off their sides like brocades so all the passengers could disembark.

The twins scrambled past Rupert's chair. They were so happy to be back they shot across the lawn. They quickly grew distant as Rupert let himself down the swinging ropes off his chair. Below, people were unloading all the things they brought, precious cargos of rare spices and lumber, mahogany, gold and silver sparkled in piles. Rupert set foot on the grass and walked towards the marble columns and shining windows.

It was breathtaking alright. He hadn't seen anything like it on Earth. A fortune had gone into making this possible. He felt like he was walking from one dream into another. Anything was possible next.

What exactly was he supposed to do? Was the president's death still a secret here too? The twins didn't seem to know. There would have to be someone to talk with.

Rupert froze as he realized the immense size of this lush green lawn. On Mars! It was a field! This was the one oasis he had seen on a dry planet.

Where were they getting their water?

"Well, well, well, look who the wind blew here!" snapped a voice that made Rupert jump and whirl.

He stared at the source of the mechanical laughter braying at him. It was that horse he rode at the start of this journey.

"We meet again, pardner."

Rupert had to stand on the desire to kick the metal beast as hard as he could.

"Aw, don't feel that way! Let's let bygones be by-gones! Look, I'll give you a ride up to the front door." The horse jerked his head and his reins swished loose. "Free of charge," he added.

"No thanks," was all Rupert could come up with.

"I hate to see you so bent out of shape," the me-chanical horse drawled. "It just isn't neighborly."

The horse shuffled along not far from Rupert who ignored it, walking towards the ranch palace at a faster clip.

"Say…Wait…You wouldn't happen to have some spare change, would you?" the horse begged. "It was a long way here, I'm pretty tired." The horse followed along in the Earth man's silent wake for a little bit more. "Heck, you should be a little grateful. You saw a whole other side of Mars than most visitors." The horse looked over its shoulder at the camels, "Looks like you traveled in style too."

Rupert glared down at the green lawn rushing by his feet. He felt like a helicopter above a jungle. This was the first time he'd seen this much green on Mars; it didn't seem possible here, it was what they used to call a mirage in the movies. Somewhere along the way, the horse was left behind as Rupert hurried to the door.

He couldn't believe his eyes again. The door was open and he could see gold light shining from inside. The twins had left the door open. It had been carved from a single round slice of tree trunk, reinforced with silver poppy shaped bands. A jewel handle was set in the middle.

"Hello?" Rupert paused in the entry. Before him awaited a golden walled room lined with mirrors and framed paintings, mostly of cowboys and broncos. Three halls led away in different directions.

He could hear the screech of the twins echoing down one of the hallways. That studio set they had on Sylvan Moore's show was nothing like this. How could they ever have known, or even begun to duplicate this? This was truly a palace.

"Good afternoon. What is your business here? If you're a peddler, I'll have the Martian tigers unleashed." It was the painting talking. Butler paintings had been all the rage quite a few seasons ago. Since then, Rupert had seen them in yard sales; he was a little surprised to see this one—an Eric Blore—still serving on the wall. Oh well.

"Hello," Rupert began. "I'm here to find the president."

"Hmmm, not an uncommon request." The painted butler rolled its eyes, thick in oils, and let a long moment pass.

Rupert tried again, "Could you tell me, does the president have any close friends here? Someone he could confide in?"

The portrait struck a thinking expression. "Of course there's Patches…"

"Patches? Who's Patches?" Rupert knew a clown with that name.

"Patches is our ranch boss, a genuine Martian wrangler. He's—well, he's as much a part of the family as Spot." The painted eyes peered over Rupert's shoulder, "As a matter of fact, he's crept up on you."

"What—huh?!" Rupert spun.

Someone Rupert hadn't seen creaked leather next to a potted saguaro cactus. The lanky weathered man moved towards him. "You come here from Earth," he rattled in dry judgement of Rupert in his suit.

Rupert shuffled uneasily.

"Well, I might as well admit it now," Patches said. "I did it."

"You did it?"

"It wasn't an easy thing for me to do," Patches told him, "but it had to be done. So I did it. Come along, I'll show you where I buried him."

As if roped and taut, Rupert followed.

Patches put on his black cowboy hat and pushed open a panel door. Harsh Martian light streamed inside at them. "This way."

The man halted under the skeletal canopy of an imported Texas jack pine, to roll himself a smoke.

"You know, I had a hand in raising the boy. I feel responsible for the way he turned out, much as I would any heifer or mare…He always wanted to be a cowboy…" His slitted eyes regarded the distant, small rare herd of Earth cattle. "I taught him how to ride. It was me showed him the way of life out here on the range."

Patches struck a match and puffed. He let out smoke, shook his head. "You know as well as me how he turned out, and what he ended up doing when he became president… Sickness…I've seen his same madness take over half a herd before. Person's no different than a sick animal, even if he's the president… Even if he was like my own son."

He smoked another blue cloud up into the spiny needles. "Somebody had to put him down. The system sure wasn't going to work…So…That's why it happened. See, on the range we have our own law… Still, he kind of broke my heart." He pointed, "Come along. It's not far."

True, just another minute walking along the rocky path, in the space between two pecan trees, there it was: a mound of red soil, planted with dwarf yellow roses. Glassy native sandvines were already choking the flowers.

"This is it," Patches said and toed the ground.

"How…How did you do it?" Rupert stammered at him.

"The quickest end to the whole thing." The old rancher tapped a revolver Rupert suddenly noticed holstered beneath the hide coat. "I just asked him to come over, which he did so willingly. He's always known to trust me. I touched the barrel between his eyes and it was all over, that fast. So…" Patches flicked the roach off into the dust and he unrolled his sleeve to reveal an arm bronze as a Remington sculpture. "That's the story, my confession. If you have need to cuff me, here's my arm."

"No," Rupert replied. "I'm not a cop. I wasn't sent here for you. I'm here to find the president's reincarnation. I work for *The Sylvan Moore Show*. You probably don't watch a lot of TV, but it's pretty popular back on Earth. Sylvan Moore sent me here so we could be the first to rediscover the president." Rupert darted a look from the grave to Patches' eyes.

"Hah!" Patches laughed all the lines on his weathered face. "What do you want to do that for? You ought to let him be. He's got to start all over again from scratch." He eyed the herd again, "Of course… What you say is possible…Maybe he did come back as one of them? I had a calf born last week at about the right time…" He stirred his coffee with a dry branch and chuckled. "Sort of looks like him too…"

"That's very funny, Patches," said Rupert, thinking about it for a bit, "But he did love this place the most, didn't he?"

"Sure. Who wouldn't?"

"Since you were the last to see him alive, maybe you know where he planned to pop up next?" In the quiet that followed he let the thought drop. This felt hopeless to him. It would have been wiser to send a trained team with Tibetan crystal balls, karmic mantrameters, ghost-map cryptologists.

"You mean, did I see anything in his eyes?" Patches finally grinned. "In those last moments? Or afterwards, caught in his dead stare?"

Rupert couldn't bear to look at him.

"Well, I did," Patches said.

Rupert stopped breathing, the crickets shrilled.

"I did see something, clear as day. He had the moon in his eyes."

It looked like Rupert's luck on Mars was finally getting better. While Patches was out at the blast-pad preparing a rocket, Rupert was in the presidential library looking for something to read. There were a lot of Westerns on the shelves and World War picture books.

At last he found a book entitled *Martian Riddles*, pulled it out and opened it.

"Pah!" he announced, very funny. The pages were all blank.

He pushed it back on the shelf and took another book at random. *The Soul of Modern Man*. Also no words. Four more books were the same way. He turned around—was the entire library nothing but empty pages?

"Hello stranger."

A woman stood next to the door. Like a paper lantern, she wore a white and yellow trimmed hoop skirt. Her face was heavily mottled with makeup. She turned the cane handle of a parasol.

She was no stranger to him. Rupert recognized her

immediately; he had interviewed her three times before, laughing at her jokes until he was in pain. She was the president's wife, now the president's widow.

"Imagine!" she gasped. "I had no idea you were coming to our little plantation, Rupert."

"Yes, well…I just got here."

She glided over to him and spun the opened umbrella to her side.

"You're looking well," he said tremulously. "I saw your daughters, both of them, they're—"

"My goodness but you're nervous, Rupert!" she exclaimed. She put a hand on his shoulder, brushed the red dust and cooed, "You've probably had quite an experience getting here."

"Yes, yes I have actually. Your husband—"

"My husband!" she blurted icily, "That lampoon! Why he's probably out there riding his tricycle or some such nonsense." Then she batted her eyelashes and fluttered, "It's been so long, I'd like to think you came all this way just to see me."

"Naturally. I, I got here as fast as I could."

"Oh Rupert," she sighed. All the perfume she was wearing stung his senses. "Hold me," she purred. "Like you did in San Francisco."

It was his good fortune again that at that moment Patches knocked on the library door and boomed, "Ten minutes to blastoff."

"Oh, I'm sorry," Rupert told her, "I have to go."

"Go?!"

"You heard Patches," Rupert shrugged. "Well, it was nice seeing you again." He put on a Hollywood smile and tried to leave.

But she hooked him with the parasol. "Rupert!" Roaring eyes at him, she cried, "You can't leave me like this Rupert. Not again…" Then she cooled, "But if you must…At least let me give you a gift…To remember me by…" She dug into her Little Bo Peep pocket.

For a second Rupert expected a derringer, but she retrieved a small metal American flag. "This is for you, Rupert." She pinned it to his suit. "Wear it here, over your heart and think of me now and then."

"Okay. Okay, I will. Take care of yourself."

"Oh…I will."

"Bye then," Rupert bowed and left the room.

He shut the library door and as he passed down the hall, he took off her pin and tossed it in a potted fern. That was another stroke of luck for Rupert. Twenty minutes later the little flag bomb blew up, disintegrating half the ranch and leaving a hundred foot crater reminder.

Patches led Rupert to a lush green square of lawn covered with dandelions, where a silver rocket towered in the middle. There were no markings or numbers on the ship—it was a bootlegger, the fastest dagger available. Fifty feet up its polished metal skin, a door was open, a rope ladder dangling.

"There's your ride," Patches said.

"Wow."

"Far as I'm concerned though, that's the last one out of here."

Rupert looked at him quizzically.

"I never liked this operation, it's not in my nature. No, this was his idea all the way," Patches nodded back towards the ranch. "As a matter of fact, there's going to be some changes around here when you leave." He swept at the air in a circle. "The hell with all this opium." The glare he gave it was fierce as burning prairie. "I've been wanting to tell someone what I know about him and his operation, but who would believe it? But as soon as this rocket leaves, the whole world is going to see the change. I'm going to give Mars back its water. What do you think of that?"

Rupert nodded, "Mars could use the water," he agreed. He coughed dryly. "Where are you going to find that much water?"

"You're standing on it." He shook his head dismally, guiltily. "Once he became president, it was like he was waiting all that time to start wars on Earth and Mars. He had an entire ocean full piped in underneath this ranch. And look what that did to the rest of the planet. Let's just say I'm going to reverse the damage."

"Listen, Patches, what are the brainees exactly? I've been wondering."

He cupped his crowed hands around another smoke.

"One minute to blastoff," cawed a speaker above the lawn.

"You better hurry or you'll miss that rocket," Patches said.

The spaceship had begun to rumble.

"Anyway, thanks for helping me out." Rupert

repeated the famous lines of an old movie, a scene they reenacted on *The Sylvan Moore Show* every Casablanca Day. "It might be a good time for you to disappear from—" but the second rocket motor had fired and Rupert knew there wasn't time. He saluted the old cowboy and ran the distance across the dandelions. He grabbed the stringy skeleton ladder.

"Forty seconds…"

He fished his way up trying to fly to that door. He slipped a couple times as more seconds clocked by.

"Twenty seconds…"

The rocket whined like a leashed animal.

Rupert clawed through the doorway and pulled the door closed behind him. He bolted it with a plank sized bar.

"Ten seconds…"

He turned from the door and gasped at the sight: two chairs in the middle of the round floor—the battered figure of Abraham Lincoln already in one, the other chair waiting for him.

"Seven seconds…"

Rupert bounded over and seated himself. He shot a look at Lincoln and gripped the sides of his chair. There was no time to think anymore.

"3…2…1…"

Part Three:
FINDING ZERO

"Zero," Rupert was still repeating, as he blinked into awareness. How much time had gone by? Where were they? But he could see out the window straight ahead and he could tell. It was familiar. Now they were on the moon. He stretched, rubbed his eyes, and yawned, "That was a quick trip wouldn't you say, Mr. President?"

Abraham Lincoln was silent. He gestured at the bandage that had been wrapped around his neck. He made a gun with his hand, pulled the trigger and showed how the bullet had passed through his neck.

Rupert winced. "You can't talk anymore?"

Abraham Lincoln nodded then mimed the motions of taking an invisible pocket watch from inside his black coat. He whirled a forefinger over the face of it, pointed to his wound and shrugged.

"Maybe in time…" Rupert translated. It was charades.

They both agreed.

"Well," Rupert continued. "That's okay. There's been miles of inventions since you were in America. When we get back, we'll have you cured in no time." He sat up and looked out the glass. "We're almost there too." He frowned, "I don't know why we had to stop on the moon."

Lincoln took out a piece of old parchment paper and wrote, "The next president."

"Oh," Rupert sighed. "Is he here?"

The ancient president looked distant.

Rupert moved to the door and opened the latches, pushed it open to the black sky and lunar ground.

It looked like a bone.

"What a dead place," Rupert said. "No wonder nobody lives here."

The rocket growled meshing gears, lowering a ramp to the curb.

"Mr. Lincoln," Rupert addressed him, "You ready to go?"

The grand old man joined him and the two of them clomped down the decline.

A few scraggly dandelions withered here and there around the rocket landing. It was hard work for flowers, they pined with the barest yellow electricity.

Rupert in his blue suit, well colored by Martian red soil, took a stricken look about him, but creaky Lincoln seemed right at home in the stark black and white world.

"Any suggestions?" Rupert asked him. "Intuitions?" His breath showed clouds in the cold air. "I hope another long walk isn't about to begin..."

Lincoln shrugged.

With a sigh that added cumulus to the musty starry air, Rupert led the way in the obvious direction, following the path littered with old signs from the aborted colony days, the foot stamps of those pioneers and their wheeled carts and animals. Rupert read the fading ghost town words on the signs, *Luxury Real Estate...Enjoy Moon Mist...Have Your Crater Filled For Less...Buy A Melchior Moon Buggy No Money Down!...*

Earn Money From Your Dome… others were too faded by the harsh light of planets and stars to read anymore, or the words were worn away, cracked and peppered by lunar storms.

Rupert was lost in that faraway when his phone rang in his pocket. He stopped walking and Lincoln halted too; Lincoln, silent as a garden post. "Hello?" Rupert said and waited. He stared off into the stars.

The voice crackled at him, "Rupert, tell me you found him. Tell me you're not running around in circles up there. You know I like good news." Sylvan Moore cut him off before Rupert could reply, "And speaking of news, you've seen *The Bert & Janet Show* haven't you? No—No—How *could* you have, you've been out *getting lost in space!* Don't ask me how they found out, but Bert and Janet broke the news about our dead president."

"Oh."

"Oh?! Oh, he says. Do you have any idea—?"

Rupert said, "I know where he is."

"What?! Where?!"

"On the—"

"No!" Sylvan Moore shouted. "Don't say it! There's probably a super-computer tracking this conversation. Just get back to Earth quick with the…the *merchandise.*"

"We're on the way."

"Okay. That's good to know. Hey Rupert, while you're there, how about giving me a laugh. I've been under this unbelievable stress since Bert and Janet burnt us. Come on, Rup."

With effort, Rupert managed only to cough. "I don't know Sylvan. I don't think I can."

"Okay Rupert, okay. I'll just watch a repeat. Once you get back here, if this stunt works, you can have a vacation, relax and work on your laugh again. I'll see you soon then." Sylvan Moore cut the conversation.

"So…" Rupert asked Abe Lincoln, "Any idea where he might be?"

With the wide eyes of a Labrador, the sixteenth president had seen something familiar off the path and down in the ravine. Rupert could see a coal black pool of stagnant water. Lincoln wagged a finger and nodded that stovepipe hat of his.

"Okay, if you say so." Honest Abe, Rupert remembered pleasantly. Who knows? I bet someone like him, revived from the dead, can see more than we can.

Abraham Lincoln purposefully and mechanically walked over the cardboard and plastic signs—*Vote for Chives…Lost Zingwer…*scraps of paper and junk thrown out down the hill.

Rupert wished he could laugh at the awkward stork-like figure in front of him, but he couldn't. He caught some baling wire on his shoe and kicked it off. Those settlers may be long gone from trying to homestead the moon, but they left behind plenty of dumped relics.

The desert here was different than Mars. It wasn't sand. It was mostly dime-sized stones white as bones. Rupert hadn't seen any plants after they left the rocket launch pad. If the president had returned to life here, he really was starting all over again.

Lincoln had gone fifty yards ahead of him before Rupert realized and he hurried into walking again. Small rocks slid down the hill in the path they were making. Too bad they hadn't brought skis, Rupert thought, then he imagined Abraham Lincoln on skis. He still couldn't laugh though.

By digging his heels into the scree, Rupert followed Lincoln into the ravine, towards the pond, and whatever they were looking for in there. Rupert thought of the ratings boost *The Bert & Janet Show* must have got. There better be a basket floating on that bracken pool, he heard Sylvan Moore's voice crabbing in his head. And there better be a beautiful newborn baby in it too!

Lincoln had already made the shore and was standing at it, scanning the ironed water.

As Rupert neared, he saw something break the surface and trail sharkishly towards Lincoln who stooped beside the pool.

"Oh no...." Rupert responded with the slowed timing of a dreamer.

The thing in the moon water stopped next to Lincoln and by then, Rupert was there too; he and Lincoln both watched as the dim shape pushed slowly out of the rank fluid. That's when Rupert took a horrified flop backwards. The face!

The startled creature pulled itself back into the wet in a hurry.

Abraham Lincoln had to calm everything down— a hand on Rupert—a hand dipped into the cold water to pat starfish-gently. If he could have talked, these gestures would have been another Gettysburg. It was okay though, even without words, he addressed them.

When the water parted again, Rupert recognized what it was…Four seasons ago, Sylvan Moore did a show at Sea World. They had dolphins to talk with, a green swimming turtle to ride, manta rays had flapped around them while Rupert laughed on cue…Then they showed the eerie creeps of the deep, the things lacking humor and colors.

"A wolf eel," Rupert hissed. "That's what you've come back as."

"Ohhhhhh…" the wolf eel opened a slathered maw to groan. "Lincoln…" the thing's slurry eyes rolled over, "And the TV clown? You too? Ohh, this is awful. Would one of you tell me this is just a dream and wake me up." The reincarnated president slithered pitifully into a coil in the shallow.

Lincoln couldn't talk, and Rupert couldn't say what he was thinking.

A painful silence stood there for a while.

At last Rupert drew out his telephone and said, "I guess I better tell Sylvan Moore about this."

"No!" the eel president yelped, hiking his face out of the soup. "No television! Not when I look like this!" He raised himself on his fins to beg. "We need a magician or something. Or—Or—Make a robot and put me inside of it! We can do that, right?!"

Rupert stared at the blubbering face, a caricature of that well known world leader. Such a pathetic sight might have wormed at his heart, but the realization that rushed at Rupert was the pure golden wonder:

This was how the president had to be. It was just like Patches said.

Rupert pressed the button for operator assistance and swiveled towards the thin blue curve of Earth.

"Hi, this is Overly Friendly. To whom would you like to place a call, Mr. Wells?"

"Sylvan Moore."

"Oh! What a fine choice. Allow me to assist you immediately. By the way sir, how are things on the moon?"

But Rupert shut his eyes and concentrated on what he could tell Sylvan Moore.

There were some clicks on the phone line followed by a sound like water going down a drain, then ringing.

This is it, thought Rupert. Each ring cut him through closer.

He opened his eyes to stare at his home planet for inspiration. Clouds whirled over ocean.

"Sylvan Moore here."

"Hello again. It's Rupert. I've got the president if you want him."

"Of course I do!"

"Well…" Rupert braked.

"What? What is it Rupert?"

"Well, yes, he's…"

"He's what? Is he ugly? He's not a lochinkop or something?"

"He's an eel."

Sylvan Moore's reply was stuck 250,000 miles away.

Rupert started over, "I said he's an eel. A wolf eel actually, like the one from Sea World you put in Garby Zabor's dressing room that time…" That was back when Rupert could laugh.

"Tell him to make me a robot!" the president spouted, "One that can hold water!"

Rupert shook the phone. "You there Sylvan? What should I do?"

Sylvan replied in a defeated tone, "Alright, Rup… Very funny…I guess I deserved that…Just get him here and we'll figure out what to do."

"Okay," Rupert said softly.

"When I see that rocket land, I want to see the next president." And that was that.

Rupert returned his attention from his planet to the gloom groveling on the moon.

"What did he say?" the eel asked.

Rupert started to say, but a blue light caught like summer in the corner of his eye, blinking his attention to it. The light was getting closer. "Is that a brainee?"

Lincoln, who had seen them for years on Mars, turned slow as a spindle, while the eel immediately thrashed into deeper water.

"What do you know?" Rupert marveled. "Here on the moon too."

The light moved rapidly closer, becoming the shape Rupert had last seen on Mars. It came partly down the slope of the path he and Abe Lincoln had made, then stopped near a cleft. It hovered about a foot in the air.

"Rupert Wells," a voice resonated between Rupert's ears. "We've been following your progress with great interest. We understand the importance of your task and we have decided to help you again."

"You have? You followed me from Mars to help me?"

"We're not only on Mars, Mr. Wells. And we're not just helping you."

"What do you mean exactly?"

The brainee glowed its pilot light. "The success of this adventure has always rested with you, Mr. Wells. Now this is where you make the final decision. There aren't enough flowers here. Your rocket only has power to carry one of you back to Earth. You must choose."

With the abrupt click of a lightbulb string being pulled, the brainee blue was gone, leaving them to blink at a moon as desolate as before.

"What was that last part? I missed that last part." The eel had splashed back to the shallows near Lincoln's feet. "What did he say? Only one of us can go home?"

"Yeah," Rupert said.

The eel drew himself out of the slop to address them. "Listen folks, I won't forget you all. I'll send a rescue rocket back for you first thing. You can count on me."

He was answered with silence.

"You came all this way to get me! You found me!" The eel's voice rasped importantly, "I'm still the president!"

Rupert examined the briny face, harshly cut by moon glows and shadows, the black round soulless eyes, blunt jaw and carving teeth. It was hard to look at him, much less acknowledge this creature was the president of the United States of America.

"I made my decision a long time ago," Rupert told him.

"That's right, you know what to do. You can be trusted," the eel president squirmed. "You follow orders. You've always followed orders. Laugh when you're told to, then you get paid. I won't forget you. After you send me back, I'll pay you more than you've ever seen." The blunt fangs grinned at Rupert.

Rupert pictured the eel's triumphant return to Earth. The parade to the White House, the carefully screened audience pushed up to see the motorcade… The black limousine with a bulletproof fish tank… That should be a comedy scene, but Rupert saw it as a grim possibility. That would be reality if he didn't tell Lincoln, "Come on Mr. President, your rocket is waiting."

At first the wolf eel could only drop his jaw in stupefied astonishment, until Rupert and Lincoln began walking away.

With a shriek, the eel threw himself out of the water. He snapped at the other president and tore some black cloth off his leg, but Lincoln was unfazed and on his way.

That eel can bellow all he wants, Rupert thought, he can stay here forever on this cratered dead land. There's a reason he is here: he brought himself. Decision made, Rupert and Lincoln hiked up out of the ravine leaving that eel.

Of course Rupert realized that the brainee terms

meant that he himself would also be stranded on the moon—that was how things turned out—try laughing at that if you can. But he was able to smile at what he had done. This time he didn't really notice the forgotten junk strewn or leaning along the path…He was imagining Abraham Lincoln stepping out of the rocket, onto a field in green America.

They reached the rocket and stopped on the brittle soil underneath its silver fins. What the brainee said was true—there were barely enough dandelions growing there.

"So…" Rupert spoke, "It looks like I'm staying on the moon." This was a good time to revive the *Casablanca* speech again and he might have, but suddenly his telephone sobbed out the voice of Overly Friendly.

"I can't take it!" Overly Friendly cried. "This is the saddest ending. Rupert Wells, noted television laugher, stranded on the moon…I can't go on!" The phone cracked open and curled smoke in Rupert's coat.

"AH! My pocket's on fire!" Rupert batted his hand on it, but Lincoln calmly poured some of that dark ravine pond water out of his sleeve to extinguish the phone.

"Thanks, Mr. Lincoln."

"Liftoff in one minute," the rocket speaker blatted.

Rupert set a hand on the ramp. "Here we go again. You better get up there, Mr. Lincoln. They're waiting for you on Earth."

Lincoln started up the ramp, but stopped his lope when Rupert called out.

"Oh, Mr. Lincoln, when you get a chance to talk again," he grinned with force, "You might want to work on your new speech. America's been through some changes since you were there last. At core though, it's still the same." He shrugged, "You'll see. You better go now."

The mute president hoofed up into the rocket, tipping his stovepipe hat before he crawled in the door. It banged shut.

Rupert backed away.

The dandelions began to tremor.

Rupert stepped back over a tinfoil pan, and in a blink the rocket was gone.

When Rupert stared at the blue and gray planet floating overhead, he liked to imagine great things were starting to happen.

Not long afterwards, a meteor shape fell out of space and crashed on a long abandoned lunar Waffle House restaurant. Inside the shattered crater, dandelion greens sprouted and quickly grew yellow flowers. An instant landing pad was formed. Ten seconds later a brightly painted rocket appeared. Words were splashed along the hull: *The Bert & Janet Show*. In the next moment, the iron door popped open and a dune buggy soared out onto sand.

Bert drove wildly, while Janet stared into the camera.

"This is another news breaking report," she taunted. Her lime green hair whipped around. "Bert and I are following a homing device." She grabbed the crash bar on the ceiling to hold on as the buggy jolted. "But ladies and gentlemen, this is no ordinary homing device we're tracking. This one is on the moon! This one will locate the next president of the United States of America!"

Bert hit a low organ sound with his elbow pressed to the dashboard keyboard.

"Bert, are we there yet?" Janet whined.

Bert nodded silently. That was part of their act. Bert never spoke, he was the quiet straight man for Janet's chatter.

She burst, "Yes, there on the right, I can see where the path leads down the ravine. That's where the president awaits." She clutched Bert's arm to heroically confide, "We're making history on the moon again!"

Bert grabbed the handbrake and raked the buggy to a stop. Gravel pushed from their overinflated tires.

"Follow me," Janet told the camera, as she hopped out and ran. Her violet tights glowed against the stark black and white background of cliffs and spires. Automatic floodlights in the soles of her boots lit her prancing way. Bert leaped behind her, playing a wrist piano, as the camera hovered around them flittingly. They leaped over the camera and surfed down the rockslide to the bottom of the ravine.

Breathlessly, Janet gasped, "Ladies and gentlemen…in thirty seconds, before an audience of eager millions, we hope to reveal the president's new reincarnation! But first we need to hear from our sponsor, Taggit's Beetle Chips."

The camera shut off and Janet turned to Bert. "That's the place?" she grimaced.

"Yeah…" Bert sneered. "Get a load of that swamp."

"Maybe laughing boy was telling the truth about the president being an eel."

Bert snorted, "It's probably an improvement anyway."

"Hah!" Janet guffawed, then faced the revived camera seriously. "Taggit's Beetle Chips! One hundred and forty flavors to delight you," she said. "Now Bert, what do you say we reintroduce ourselves to the leader of the free world?"

While Bert played an ominous run on the keys, they crept towards the brackish pool. With the camera riding next to her, Janet confessed, "I just hope he's not an alligator."

Bert banged a dissonant chord and Janet cried, "Look! There! Something's swimming this way!" She turned her green hair at the camera to whisper confidentially, "This is it…"

The eel burst from the water and Janet screamed. The fanged creature bounced off Bert's arm, ripping off the mini-piano and swallowing it whole. The eel slapped viciously onto the shore, hissing at them.

"Stop! Stop! We come in peace!" Janet blurted. Bert held his wrist and mimed shutting himself inside an invisible box. The camera flew about like a startled insect. "We're Americans! Is that you Mr. President?"

The camera zoomed in on the stony looking charcoal portrait face of the eel. The jaw groped open. "What?" he said. "Why are you here?"

Janet forced a tear to run down her cheek, made sure the camera caught that, and said, "We're here to take you home, Mr. President."

"Ohhh…" the eel sobbed. He dabbed at his round wet eyes with the tip of his curled tail as his gnashed teeth came together in a wicked looking grin.

"Are you…" Janet wept, "Are you getting this on film?" With trembling hands she took an American flag from her utility belt and extended its gold metal pole, then with great solemnity she pushed it into the white dust next to the eel.

"We're here to take you home, Mr. President," she repeated chokingly. Instinctively she knew that would be the phrase marketed shamelessly into millions of items, onto clothes, coffee cups, stickers and soon a #1 Billboard song. *The Bert & Janet Show* had of course done it again.

Great things may have been happening on Earth, but Rupert Wells could only see a slow collapse for himself. He would go until he couldn't go anymore, then a few cold seasons would turn him into dust.

He plodded along, heading for a pyramid shape, as good a place as any to give up. "Here's to the King of the Moon," he toasted the sky, a wide open frontier full of stars, worlds and suns so far away.

He fingered the burnt cloth remains of his coat pocket. It was too bad the phone had blown, he would have liked to call Carolyn; she had been in the back of his mind all along, like a garden in the backyard.

He stopped and kicked a rock futilely. "Aww," he said, "What would I say anyway?"

He watched the stone bounce down the hill and stop before it got halfway to another dead settlement that looked like so many of the dustbowl shadows, with junk in the yard, everything dried to a deathly pallor. Maybe because he had nothing else to do and all the rest of his life to do it, Rupert followed the stone down the hill. He wanted that rock to make it to that yard where it could spend eternity with the broken plows, tractors, rusted crippled winches and slumped playground toys. Rupert gave it a last good kick to send it there.

It clanged against a red wire roll of fencing.

He had been alone for such a while, he thought he was hearing his own thoughts waterfalling his way. Or was it real? There was tinny music, chatter and laughter coming from one of the domes.

The front door was open. Rupert walked right up to it fearlessly. Why not?

It sounded like a party alright; Rupert brought a grin up from cold storage. He touched the door and opened it the rest of the way to see what was going on inside.

He didn't expect to see the room full of furniture, gathered around a blasting jukebox. Bottles of wood polish cluttered the table.

"Wellllll!!" a tipsy ballooned chair came down from the ceiling. "Looookeeee heeeere!"

"It's you!" Rupert gasped.

"Yeah it's me. And look who's you?" Lou Murphy

slopped across the floor and stopped next to him. The music still blared. "How's things going?"

"What are you doing here on the moon?"

"Why, I'm visiting my family. Sure, I got relatives here. That's," the chair rocked, "That's my Aunt Mabel. And my uncle. Their kids are—oh I don't know where they went. And let's see—oh, there's a bunch of us here."

Rupert grabbed the chair, "Listen. Can you get me back to Earth?"

"Sure, sure I can get you back there. What's the hurry? Don't you like it here?" The chair wiggled to the samba beat. "It's a party mister, so relax."

All the chairs, footstools, sofas and tables jammed around him. A lamp bent hotly to his ear and asked him his name.

Rupert grabbed at one of the quivering balloon strings and pulled. "Hey!" he caught the chair's attention, "Couldn't we go now? I really need to get back."

"Sheeeesh!" The chair shrugged and jabbed a coffee table relative, "Can you believe this guy? I take him to Mars, now he thinks I'm his chauffeur! Listen pal," he leaned towards Rupert, "I don't wanna. I like being on the moon! But since I'm in a good mood, I'll tell you what I'll do. I'll let my kid nephew take you back to America. That way maybe he can earn a merit badge too. Hey, Philip!" he called out.

Several other voices took up the call jovially, "Philip!" "Philip!"

"I don't want—" Rupert tried to explain, "It's just that—"

"Relax, relax! It'll be good for Philip. Between you and me, the kid needs some confidence."

Rupert clutched his forehead in despair.

"Philip! There you are!"

Rupert watched as a plush overstuffed purple chair minced through the rambunctious crowd.

"Philip, get over here! Hey Philip!" his uncle boomed warmly and threw a leg out in greeting. "Philip, I got a job for you. Mr. Earthling here," he tipped at Rupert, "needs you to take him to his precious planet right away. What do you say?"

"Gee, I don't know," Philip hesitated.

Rupert stared nervously at the young chair. The upholstery looked like it had never been sat on before.

"Philip," Lou announced, "this is the sort of job you've been waiting for! What good is it always reading about space travel, but never taking that big leap? Didn't you get straight A grades on your last school report?"

"I guess so," Philip shuffled.

"This here's a smart kid," Lou boasted. "All you need is some balloons." Philip's proud uncle listed and whistled for everyone's attention.

Rupert stood flattened to the wall for the next few minutes as the pack of furniture shifted and scraped and knocked off of one another. They finally found a stack of weather balloons in another room and spent the next few minutes tying them securely around and around Philip's porky shape.

It took a while, with more falling over and a chaise lounge passing out, before they managed to get Philip to the doorway where outer space awaited.

Philip whined, "But what if we wind up in Alpha Centauri, or—"

His uncle gave him an aluminum reassuring squeeze, "You'll do just fine, Philip! It's time for you to leave the nest, kid."

The next thing Rupert knew, he had been whisked over and dumped on Philip's amply sewn lap. More ropes were secured around him and with a raucous roar, Philip and Rupert were hoisted out the door.

The cold was a shock as the balloons sprang through the doorway and tugged them up.

The partying furniture cheered at first, but all groaned when Philip came back down with a hurt "Oof!" pancaking on the hard white sand.

The chair dragged along sending a cloud of dust behind. "Up!" Philip despaired while he hopped and prayed, "Come on balloons! Up! Take us up!"

Rupert clutched the freezing armrests in silence. If he was a little stronger, it would seem absurd.

Ahead of them, one of those thousand nameless ravines loomed like a broken floor. Either they would crash to their doom or recover, over and out.

Philip's typewriter heart was pounding like crazy at the end of the page.

THE SCHUBERT STORY

Pictures of Joe went out on the wire services. Joe and I were posed in loving poses and the picture was in every paper. Long columns appeared, telling the whole story, and we became a one-day wonder that everyone thoroughly enjoyed.

—Vincent Price, from *The Book of Joe*

I told her that I had seen enough screwy things already to be convinced that this was a nowhere job and that it was only temporary and I would continue to look for work more suitable to my qualifications.

—From *I Caught Flies for Howard Hughes*, by Ron Kistler

His name was Varney Decker, but he wasn't the only one. There were at least five others, maybe more by now. Three months had passed and a lot of things had happened.

It didn't seem like such a bad idea to begin with. He worked fulltime in an insurance agency, and his wife Miranda worked part time. They had two children, a pet ape, and one car which had just been converted to steam power. Add to that all the other expenses, mortgage on their house, utilities, bills, etc. etc. and the Deckers were just making it by. Varney was an honest man, but hopeful as any other American that there was an easier way out. He kept hoping it would happen. Once a week he played the lottery at the corner store and that's where his adventure began.

While he stood outside, set his briefcase down between his shoes to scratch the ticket and groan at the jumbled numbers, a man wearing an expensive suit stepped beside him.

"No luck?"

"No…" Varney shook his head amiably. "I keep trying though."

The elegant man took a card from the silk lining of his coat and held it out to Varney. "Allow me to present you with an opportunity to make quite a sum of legitimate money."

"What?" Varney took the card and looked at it. "Superior Genetics?"

The man nodded. He explained.

After listening to the spiel for a few minutes, Varney tucked the card into his pocket and agreed to an appointment the next morning, at 9 AM.

That was three months ago.

There were two rabbits watching them. Fort Lauderdale was wheezing, pulling Varney along with all her might, her front paws pedaling the air as she leaned towards them.

"Come on!" Varney told the dog. "What's the big deal?" It was like this every time she saw a rabbit and the woods were full of them. He tugged her back onto the path. Her stiff legs dragged in the gravel. It was like pulling a wooden chair.

Once the rose bush hid the rabbits from view, Fort Lauderdale settled into a moan and they were able to continue with the walk.

This was the morning shift. This was his job, walking a dog named Fort Lauderdale.

Fort Lauderdale! What kind of a name was that for a dog? He didn't ask. It meant $40 a day, $200 a week, $800 a month. That paid rent. So who was he to ask why a dog was named Fort Lauderdale?

Varney could see a cloud chasing another one very slowly between two alders. He watched that slow drama above while the dog peed beneath an overhang of flowering blackberry vines.

Fort Lauderdale gave a kick at the soft mossy earth and led the way again. Varney let himself be drawn along, holding the leash like a water skier over the rough green weeds on the path. He kept replaying the thing that had happened. He couldn't avoid the past;

it seemed to be running right along with the present. While he was here now, he was also in the parking lot of Superior Genetics three months ago.

Standing at the door in the gray blue light of morning, he thought this could be a terrible mistake. Then he remembered if time got away from him, he had the possibility to go back. Accommodating Time Travel Inc. had billboards all over town, and radio commercials that drove him up the wall. He couldn't listen to a baseball game without that jingle breaking in. But because of them, Varney knew the principles of time travel. Before any major decision you might regret taking, he knew you had to leave a marker, a beacon that your future self could signal in on, to draw you back to that spot in time before your life diverged.

So that morning he dropped a 2010 penny into the garden beside the curb of Superior Genetics and he gave it a nudge, covered it with a layer of beauty bark. If things got crazy later on, Accommodating Time Travel Inc. would take him back to that penny waiting in the dirt. Varney stared hard at his reflection cloned in the glass door, then he went inside.

Fort Lauderdale brought him back to the present with a growl.

There was a guy who lived in the woods. Varney first noticed his camp last year. Everyone had. It wasn't well hidden behind the fallen tree, where the path took a crooked turn towards Joe's Garden. The cops had come and run him off, so now he was hiding deeper in the trees. Alders, thick mounds of blackberry, everything snarled and whorled with vines and leaves.

There could be another world hidden off the path. Sometimes a twig would snap, or a bird would startle a branch, and Varney and Fort Lauderdale would freeze and stare.

"Come along," Varney said.

After Fort Lauderdale's walk, Varney had to take the key from the hollowed part of the tree and unlock the Van Harlow's garage door. Fort Lauderdale had a plastic kennel about the size of a small refrigerator. It seemed weird to jail a fancy breed like her in a cell like that, but Varney just had to get her in there, close the door and retreat. She would howl and bay while Varney sprung the latch, closed the garage door behind himself and walked across the driveway to replace the key in the oak. Nobody likes to be locked up.

It was almost noon. A jet was pulling two white threads across a blue sky. Varney could do what he wanted now. It all happened so fast.

The day after he sold Superior Genetics the rights to clone him, Varney got to work a little late and saw himself already there, sitting in his chair with the typewriter going. His clone also had a tall cup of coffee next to him. Varney never bought coffee at work. It was too expensive: $4 for that cup!

"What's going on?" Varney mumbled. Although his clone was wearing a suit and a grin, it was like looking in a mirror.

"There you are!"

"The bus was late…" Varney said.

"Uh huhh."

"What are you doing here?"

His clone laughed. He was cheerful, Varney noted. It was probably the coffee.

"Remember the contract?" The clone reached in his suit jacket and took out the parchment, unfolding it neatly as an origami flag. Then he took out a pair of eyeglasses. They looked good on him.

"You need glasses?"

"Oh yeah. Say, I bet that means you do too. You should get that checked."

"Go to a doctor?"

"Correct. An eye doctor. Here it is…Listen: I will allow my clone(s) to freely interact." He looked like Cary Grant in *Bringing Up Baby* as he solemnly took off his glasses and refolded them for his pocket. "I like that sentence. The Thomas Jefferson of clones wrote that masterpiece." He resealed the edges of the contract.

"So, you decided to come to my job?"

His clone laughed again.

Varney frowned at that. Then he noticed his boss appearing. You could hear the green corduroys chirping.

"What took you so long, Varney? Your bus get a flat tire again?"

Varney's clone laughed. "Good one."

His boss clapped a hand on the clone's shoulder. "I like this one!"

"The feeling is mutual," said the clone.

"Oh brother…" Varney muttered. That's when he

should have known he was in trouble, that his life was transforming and leading him to a boarding house basement apartment on September Hill.

"I can't have two of you though," their boss told them. "Here's what I suggest. I flip a coin. You're heads, and you're tails." With that, their boss got a coin, tossed it, caught it, took a look and gave the job to the Varney in the tailored suit. "Okay, this Varney wins."

It didn't end there though. That evening Varney lost his family to his clone. While Varney slouched on the couch, his clone arrived home at 5:30. With a bound, his impersonator scooped up the children and leaned over to kiss Miranda. It was quite a scene, like a piñata party, as they laughed and carried on around Varney's clone.

By eight o'clock, Varney was checking into the Aloha Hotel. He paid in cash and gave his name as Walter Pidgeon. He stayed there for a week, until he found the room at September Hill.

He followed the steep path, past cars parked with tires digging into the curb. It was early July and the weather was gray. There had been clouds and raining for weeks. The summer felt more like November. Or was it only him?

He could see the window of his new home, low as a glass cat asleep in the lavender.

Varney made tea in the communal kitchen down in the basement. An open door led up the wooden stairs to outside. He could hear a lawnmower a block away. It sputtered and buzzed while he read the Employment section of the newspaper. He never expected to be doing this again. Something was circled with a penciled loop. *Stockboy Wanted. Pay $7.50/hour.* Varney took another sip of tea.

Herbert Leopold showed up and took a loaf of bread from the cupboard. "Lunchtime," he said.

Varney hummed.

Herbert carried a slice of bread over to the table and sat down opposite Varney. He took a bite, chewed it, finished and asked, "You looking for a job?"

Varney nodded.

Herbert stared at the bitten shape of his bread, then said, "Didn't you say you used to work in an office?"

"For ten years."

"So you can type?"

"Type?" Varney looked at Herbert with curiosity. Bad as Varney felt about things, Herbert looked even grimmer, like a medieval woodcut. "Of course I can type."

That was all Herbert wanted to know. He stood up and took the rest of his bread with him.

It got quiet in the kitchen again. Even the lawnmower stopped. Varney's eyes drifted out of the words. He flipped the newspaper over, he had seen enough. Walking Fort Lauderdale twice a day wasn't going to make him rich, but it was better than the slow agony of hunting for a job in a newspaper map.

Finishing his tea, he thought about taking himself

for a walk.

He wondered if Miranda would come back to him…if the kids would want him…hell, even the ape. But no, he knew it wouldn't make any sense. He hadn't seen them in weeks. That's how they wanted it. They had chosen the version of him they wanted. The loneliness was the worst part. He had been used to the sounds of them, never being alone, which at the time he sometimes wished for. Now he had to do something, anything, to fill his day, to distract his sadness, heartbreak and blame.

He stood up and walked. He put the ceramic tea cup in the sink and splashed some water in, gave it a swish and set it in the drying rack. "Can I type?" he repeated. That Herbert was an odd one alright.

He left the basement kitchen, went up the stairs and out into the day that was turning sunny after all.

Every color on September Hill was glowing with the break in the clouds. On the edge of the park that grew over the top three quarters of the hill was Varney's boarding house. There were also other houses, a main street called Underhill, cars parked along its edges, and a blue painted waterfall stairway that Varney took every day to get to town. He descended through a weedy lot filled with wildflowers, went between houses, the one with the harp in the window and the Harp Lessons sign, a canopy of madrone trees, curtains over windows, an old red circus poster pasted to the wall of a garage, finally to the wooden morning glory covered arch at the landing on Gerard Street.

He passed the pet store and the bowling alley where he sometimes went. Believe it or not, 20th Century Bowling was a calm place for him. The lanes in there shined a glowing beauty like the beams in a temple.

In a little while, he stopped at a screen door and opened it. He went inside and climbed worn stairs. Up on the slanting second floor in that wooden hallway, there was a dentist office on the left, a detective's door to the right, and straight ahead the green door was open to Old Books. The last time he was here, he bought a video of *Invasion of the Body Snatchers*. The familiar handwritten calligraphy sign written on yellow paper welcomed him.

The woman who ran the place, sat at the big wooden desk. He really should have known her name by now, but he was in another world these days. "Hi," he said.

She held three books in her hands. "Hello."

Navigating Old Books was a sort of voyage; it made sense if you let yourself wander, knowing that sooner or later you would find something interesting. There were shelves and also towers built of stacked books and you could wind around three rooms.

Standing in front of her desk, Varney cut right to the chase. "I'm looking for books on dogs." She had big glasses and she gave him a goldfish stare, then she set a book down and pointed to her left. "Far corner…That room."

"Okay. Thanks."

"Mmhmm."

The floor creaked him into the next room, past a framed portrait of Groucho Marx, to the corner. The dogs were there, from the ceiling to the floor. It was hard to believe that Fort Lauderdale would drive him to this, but there was something about her. And now he had time during the day to do whatever he wanted, he was curious about her. He spent a while going over the titles, craning his neck back and forth until he found an interesting one. *The Book of Joe*, by Vincent Price. On the cover, the actor's orange and gray dog was sitting on the cobblestones, looking over its shoulder soulfully. Varney was pleased with that, but he had a question for the lady whose name he forgot. He carried the book to her desk.

She was writing something long-winded on a yellow tablet of paper.

He didn't want to interrupt her, but he did. "Hi."

"You found a book?"

"Oh yeah, a Vincent Price tell-all shocker. I was wondering though, do you have any books on Schuberts?"

"Schubert's what?"

"The dog breed. The dog I walk twice a day is a Schubert."

"Schubert? No..." she shook her head. "Schubert the composer...uhh, sherbet the ice cream...That's all I know about that."

He nodded. "Yeah, I've never seen anything like it before either. I thought I'd read up on the breed

though. You never know, I might find something useful."

"Sure."

"I'll get this book though."

"I thought maybe you were collecting books on famous dogs," she said as she examined the book. "Actually, I wondered about this one myself. Do me a favor and tell me what you think of it."

"Okay." He paid for the book.

She put the receipt into it like a bookmark.

Just before he left, he turned around and said, "If I like it, I'll pass it on to you." He didn't know why he said it, or what it meant, but after he left the book-store he felt like the Hound of the Baskervilles.

He took his time in town. He carried *The Book of Joe* to The Last Exit where he bought a pot of twig tea. He found a seat on the bench in the light of the big window. After the first page of the book, he didn't mind the movie going on around him. By the time Varney put the receipt in between pages 18 and 19 and finished the little left in his cup he was glad he bought the book. It made him think of Fort Lauder-dale; it made him feel like they were starring together in their own book. With words and chapters being written about him, Varney left the café and rejoined the sunlit sidewalk.

He couldn't believe the pigeons just walking along at the feet of everyone like wind-up toys. One of them whirred and popped next to him for the rest of the block on Gerard. When Varney got to the blue stairway, he looked up the steps like a salmon before a tall waterfall.

Fort Lauderdale hopped down the last step in front of her large house and stopped to smell the hydrangea. This was her territory. She took all these smells very seriously, testing Varney's patience, fixating on something crushed into dandelions. Varney tugged the leash and led her the other way.

The park started right behind the Van Harlow's three story house, and Fort Lauderdale sniffed the boundaries of the fenced yard to where the forest started. They picked up the trail and Varney followed a wagging tail.

Funny there were no books on Schuberts, Varney thought. Old Books seemed to have every other breed of dog covered…and that led him to think of the woman at the desk with her big hazel eyes. He replayed his parting words, sounding to him like some maniac Humphrey Bogart, "If I like it, I'll pass it on to you." Oh, he crumpled his hand on the leash and halted Fort Lauderdale's head in a fern. It didn't feel right to him. What was he doing? He thought of his wife and family. It wasn't like they had abandoned him really—they hadn't left him for someone else—they were just with a better version of him. Miranda, the kids, and even the ape loved his clone.

Then he thought of the message taped to his apartment door. His memory projected it like a vast billboard.

Varney your ex called. She has a box of yours at the house. Come get it.

The house meant the new house his clone had moved the family into. Out of the two-bedroom, 1937 claptrap they'd been living in for almost ten years. Varney didn't blame them for abandoning it. He had spent untold hours on that house, patching holes, dragging himself through crawlspaces, cursing the furnace, setting rat traps, laying new floor and on and on. It was like a wooden cartoon ship he could barely keep afloat. Who knew what his perfect clone had provided for his family? But Varney was sure it was something wondrous.

No, it wasn't like Miranda was seeing someone else. She was still with him, wasn't she? The situation was so confusing. And here he was reading Vincent Price and flirting in Old Books…Oh, he gave Fort Lauderdale another tug. She was frozen where a rabbit once sat.

That evening, Herbert knocked on his door. "Phone call…" he said.

"Is it my wife?" Varney asked.

"No, some other lady, I think."

Varney bookmarked his page and got off the bed. Its springs readjusted noisily. He stepped out into the kitchen. Herbert was at the stove warming a can of tomato soup. The phone waited on the table with its long cord connected to the wall, stretched like a taut jumping rope. Herbert stirred his soup, pretending to be oblivious, as if all he cared about was the wooden spoon going counterclockwise.

Varney picked up the phone. "Hello?"

"Varney?"

"Yes."

"We lost Fort Lauderdale!" Sandra Van Harlow choked, then continued, "I opened the door, she saw a bunny, and off she went!"

"Ohhh."

"We've been looking for her, but it's getting dark. We can't find her!"

"That's terrible," he said, thinking as always, who names a dog Fort Lauderdale? He knew. Sandra Van Harlow, that's who. He switched the phone to the other ear. She was already talking.

"I guess you don't need to walk her tomorrow." It sounded like she was about to cry.

"Well…I don't know. It's still early. She could show up later tonight."

"I hope you're right." She was crying now. "I have to go…" she managed to say.

"Okay," Varney told her. "Keep me informed." But she had already hung up. He saw Herbert paused with the spoon hovering over the soup. "Goodnight." He followed the leashed phone back to its cradle and hung it up. Varney listened to another sound.

Herbert was using the other room down here in the basement, sort of a broom closet really. The door was shut, but Varney could hear hesitant typing coming from in there, tapping like a blind man's cane on an ice rink.

Varney was tired. He walked back towards his own small room. Vincent Price's dog was barking for him.

The next morning when Varney left his room, the kitchen windows let in sun from the garden. The windows were trimmed with crowded flowers, growing up there on the ground level. Herbert sat at the table staring at a sheaf of paper. A bowl of oatmeal looked untouched next to him.

"Morning, Herbert."

Herbert slapped a hand on the pages and lifted the sheet to wave in the air. "Look at this thing!"

Varney saw a page of terrible typing. Or it could have been some kind of code, the way words turned into numbers and dashes or blots. Then again, it could have been art. Herbert was an artist, right? A poet, or a painter, or both. Varney wasn't sure what to say, but he gave in, "What is it?"

"It's supposed to be my manuscript. But look at it!"

"Yeah, well, it's pretty bad typing, I guess."

Herbert collected the pages together and sighed miserably. "It's my own fault...I borrowed a parrot to type the manuscript...I heard great things about that bird. But you get what you pay for."

Varney had wandered over to the cupboard, opened it and retrieved his cup and a blue China plate. He was about to get his bread to make toast when Herbert spoke.

"So, you can type, right?"

"Uhh…"

"You want the job typing my manuscript?" Herbert asked.

Varney closed his eyes. He knew what this could lead to, he had an idea anyway, but as of this morning, he was out of a dog walking job. September Hill had swallowed a Schubert. Anyway, all he had to do was type—how hard could it be? It was better than looking for another job in the newspaper. He already knew from a long time ago, getting a job was all about connections, it was where you happened to be, who you knew, and then life took care of you.

"Ten years typing, right?" Herbert said.

Varney sort of laughed. "More than that, Herbert. I first took a typing class back in high school." He still remembered the desks in rows and the blonde girl who sat quietly next to him. "Maybe I could do it. My other job might be over, so I suppose I could type for you." He put a slice of bread in the toaster. "Okay," he decided. "Sure, why not."

At The Last Exit, Varney opened the binder Herbert gave him. He pulled out a stack of handwritten pages and let it stare at him. *A Little Blue Boat*, by Herbert Leopold. Varney was the only other living person besides Herbert to actually look at this manuscript. Varney was the third assigned typist, after the bird. Herbert had told him, "First, I tried out the house ghost."

"What? What house ghost?"

"Don't you know? We have one. Didn't you ever see a shadow or a motion in the corner of your eye? Hear anything strange at night? Misplace something nobody else would ever care about?" Herbert shook his head. "This house had a ghost since I moved in, for a lot longer I'm sure. Nobody ever told me the story of it. I never got an answer out of the ghost either. But it dawned on me, what's the point of a ghost wandering and creeping everywhere, why not let it help me out? So I said to it, 'Here's my typewriter, paper, all my poems…Put that ghost energy to use.'"

Varney poured his cup full of twig tea. He wrapped his fingers around its curve. He remembered Herbert telling him, "I forgot one little detail though. Ghosts can't type! There's only so much they can do in this world."

Varney took a sip of the earthy tasting tea and gave the page a turn.

Varney didn't know a lot about poetry, but as he read on he could see a golden thread running through. Herbert must have some sort of Rumpelstiltskin power, taking ordinary words and spinning them into this. He kept reading *A Little Blue Boat* while he finished his tea, each turned page finding rest in a stack on top of *The Book of Joe*.

Varney had to take the trolley and transferred onto

another one outside the city limit to get to his family's new home. He got out on Del Vista Drive under a row of oak trees. As the trolley clattered away, he stood there in the shade and stared at all the big houses with their big yards guarded by fences and gates. He shook his head in disbelief: How did his clone manage this? All the years Varney had put in and he was right back where he started, in a basement apartment. Meanwhile, look where the other him had arrived with his family in tow.

Varney had the address written down. He checked the numbers stamped on a marble colonnade. He was close. He hoped this wouldn't take long. The sidewalk ran along gardens, flowering beside the curb. They must bring a street-sweeper through every day, he guessed. The place was so tidy he felt nervous, like there was an army of butlers watching him and waiting to pounce. A butterfly bounced against the air next to him.

It turned out being pretty obvious which house was theirs though. On the other side of a white picket fence, dangling from a stately tree was a brand new tire swing, and sitting on it was Varney's pet ape. When it saw Varney, the ape stood on top of the tire and shook the rope like a washtub bass.

"Frances!" Varney cried.

But the ape had gone into full danger mode. Shrieking hysterically, Frances shimmied up the rope and clung to the branch, twenty feet above.

Varney stopped at the gate and cooed, "It's me, Frances. Don't you recognize me?" There was no doubt the creature did, its greeting routine hadn't changed. While it whimpered and shook leaves down, Varney crept through the gateway and followed the flagstones. The shaking tree was just the soundtrack in an otherwise quiet and sunny yard.

The white house seemed balled and tight as a fist ready to knock him back down the hill into the low-rent streets of town. But Varney stopped beside the doorway with its big ceramic pot of overflowing bright flowers and prepared to knock. He tried to come up with a smooth greeting, but there was the distracting yowl of Frances in the air behind him.

Finally, he just set his finger on the doorbell and pressed it.

He heard the peal of girlish bells inside.

He waited for the children's footsteps to rush at the door. He wiped a sudden tear away with the back of his hand. He should be glad they had this place, he told himself. They deserved it.

He tried the bells again and waited a half minute more, until he noticed the little blue fold of paper tucked in the door. It had been there all along and he didn't notice it. Guessing it was for him, Varney pulled it out and unfolded it.

> *V—we took the day off and went boating.*
> *Left your box in the driveway.*
> > *M.*

It was all the ache of a watering can full of ice; it could have been one of Herbert's sad haikus. Varney didn't know what to do with the cold thing, he only sighed and stuffed it in his pocket and turned from the door.

Sure enough, there was a cardboard box next to the rainspout. It was probably filled with what poured out of dark clouds, down the gutter.

There were some toys left in the cropped grass, a silver UFO saucer, a handful of farm animals, a red truck and a yellow plastic cowboy holding a gun. Varney could imagine his son playing that game, then leaving everything to go to the lake or the ocean for a boat ride.

Something hit and clattered on the rock pathway, barely missing Varney. The ape in the tree was throwing pinecones at him.

In the phone booth under the aqueduct, Varney gave Sandra Van Harlow a call. There had been some coins at the bottom of the box. Now they were lined up on the bent metal shelf in case he needed them. He listened to the phone ring. All morning long he was thinking of Fort Lauderdale. It felt like a doting chapter from Vincent Price; seeing that dog had become more than just a routine job. He just wanted to see what was going on.

On the fifth ring, Sandra answered the phone and he said, "Hey! It's Varney. I've been wondering about Fort Lauderdale."

"Oh!" she clucked. "I'm so sorry! I didn't call you? I thought I had. I called a variety of people to tell them. In my memory, I thought I did."

"What? What happened?"

"She came back to us last night."

"Really?"

"Yes! Oh, you've probably been worried sick about her!"

"Well, yeah, I guess I have been."

"She's fine. She had the time of her life in those woods."

A mechanical voice cut in on their conversation, "Please deposit five dollars."

"Five bucks?!" Varney barked. He had about a dollar seventy in coins.

"Don't worry about that," Sandra Van Harlow rushed. "You just come by tomorrow morning, Varney. Thanks for calling and checking."

"I—okay," he said and that was the end.

Another strange day…He returned the phone to its cradle and left the booth. There was a defaced poster for Accommodating Time Travel Inc. pasted over the bricks on the arch. Okay, he thought…if I have to, I will.

Even though he had his job back, Varney wanted to help out Herbert with his book. He was drawn to it like a moth to the flame. He saw its beauty, but he could also see problems, like the poems that would repeat later on with a different name and form. It would be a difficult manuscript to edit. In hindsight he would know: his future self was screaming at him to let it go. Instead, he sat there at the kitchen table with a typewriter, the manuscript, and a list of rules.

There were only two rules, but Herbert wanted to make sure Varney understood them. He had written them in block letters: ONLY TYPE AT NIGHT BETWEEN 11 PM AND DAWN and the other was ONLY TYPE BY CANDLELIGHT.

So here Varney was, all the floors above were quiet for night, and he was alone in the kitchen with the humming electric typewriter ready to go. He had to search the kitchen for a candle, finally finding one in the back of a drawer filled with tangled string, paperclips, robot parts and the other things that always lived in that kind of place. It was a tall red candle that had been used once, but not for long, probably some bachelor's long ago attempt to impress a date at this stark kitchen table. A wax tear had made it halfway down and stuck. Varney planted it in a clay candlestick holder and brought its light back to life. He guided a blank sail of paper into the typewriter and began.

When Varney stepped out of his room in the morning, there was an envelope tacked to his door. Taped on top of it was a note. The writing was unfamiliar, feminine. It was rare that anyone from upstairs would venture down here. He read her message:

This was delivered upstairs for you.

He removed her note and saw his name typed on the envelope. In the top left corner, he read Superior Genetics. Oh no, he thought, what's happened? Did his clone go on the rampage and steal a rocket to Mars? He ripped the letter open to find out.

Mr. Decker,
Attached is a check for $600.
That covers the cost of two additional clones.
Best regards,
Kay Linden
Superior Genetics

His fingers slid the note aside and sure enough, there was a check enclosed. Well, that was good news, but he sighed and looked out the porthole riding at ground level with the day. Was the world really ready for two more Varney Deckers?

That's what he wondered as he walked with Fort Lauderdale. There were four of him now, maybe more, how was he to be sure?

Fort Lauderdale was oblivious to his worries, she carried on along the path, jangling the tags on her collar, stopping to smell the weeds bunched around a hawthorn tree, then trotting on again, smiling that mouth-open grin.

What a weird dog. Varney decided he would go the library later and look for Schubert information. "Fort Lauderdale," he said, "You are one strange dog."

She gave him a quick look over her shaggy shoulder, not much, but he swore she rolled her eyes, as if he was the one being strange.

The barbed wire fence next to the path stopped and there was a way into the field on the other side. Varney liked to stop in the middle and let Fort Lauderdale's leash out all the way like someone fishing with the line unspooled. It would take a few minutes to reel her back in.

They followed their crushed path in the tall grass. Varney always checked the apple tree first. Among the leaves the apples were slowly ripening. The dog pulled him around the base of the tree, anxious to be out in the center of the pasture. It was the same every day. Fort Lauderdale knew what was coming. She would be turned and watching him with bright eyes, doing that bizarre hopping dance on her back legs, like a circus dog.

Varney looked down from the slow tree, all the leash cord was just pooled on the grass and Fort Lauderdale was standing there silently on her hind legs like a statue, with the collar held in one paw.

"Look chum," she said, "I've had enough of this routine." She sounded like Katherine Hepburn in *Holiday*. "As if I didn't try to escape yesterday, I mean I couldn't be *more clear*, could I?" She dropped the collar into the grass. "Goodbye, Varney."

It was like listening to a glass harmonica. Varney just stood there mesmerized, as she turned away from him and bounded off across the field and was gone into the woods.

That really put Varney in a difficult position. What could he do? After he reeled in the leash, pulled in with the empty collar attached at the end, what was he going to tell Sandra Van Harlow? He walked all the way back to her house and still had not thought of a logical explanation, or even a good lie.

He put the leash and collar back in their garage and stood there contemplating in the cemented room. At last he wrote a note and left it on Fort Lauderdale's kennel. All it said was: *Fort Lauderdale slipped out of her collar. I'm so sorry. Please call me. Varney.* There was a lot left unsaid, but how much did Sandra Van Harlow even know about her dog? Did she know it could talk, for instance?

Varney still had a few hours until Sandra Van Harlow would be returning to her house, maybe he could find out something about Schuberts. Maybe this wasn't unusual. Unlike poodles, or retrievers, or English bulldogs, maybe once a year a Schubert will stand, deliver a speech and run away?

As he expected, there were all kinds of dog books at the library. Varney spent half an hour just roving along the shelving, pulling some out, reading indexes, flipping through photographs, but at the end of all that time, he was no closer; he hadn't found a single clue to a Schubert's existence.

He followed the carpeting back to the information

desk and told the librarian what he was looking for.

"Let's see…" she said. She led him from the desk to the card catalog.

Varney hadn't tried that. "I'm about at the end of my rope," he said.

She pulled out a drawer and plucked through the cards. "Well…" she said, stopping, "Here's something…" She took a scrap of paper from the little box on top of the catalog cabinet. "Let's see…It's titled *My Schubert*. It's a children's book. That would explain why you didn't see it where you looked. The children's collection is in the basement."

"My Schubert?"

"That's right." She handed him the note. "Looks like quite an old book."

Varney shook his head. "A children's book."

She smiled. "You never know. It could be very useful. Besides, it's the only mention of Schuberts I could find." She slid the catalog drawer back into its gleaming wooden cabinet. "I could contact another library if you like?"

"I'll take a look at this one," Varney said and waved the paper like a butterfly. "I'll see if this gets me anywhere."

"Alright. Good luck."

"Thanks." Varney took the stairs down, passing an old man who clung to the rail like a gondola. The basement began with a big paper-maché goldfish swimming towards the children's library.

The moment he was by that fish, he was in another world. It was the Land of Oz after a dreary ride on the stairwell from Earth. He walked into dazzling color, mobiles and a flock of rainbow birds on the ceiling, all around him, imagination scurrying about the shelves like Dorothy's munchkins.

A girl passed Varney carrying a stuffed black and white dog. He thought of his daughter and son and had to wait for the raincloud feeling to go.

It wasn't difficult to find the dog books either; there was a furry mask with big white ears and a pink tongue on the end of the shelf facing him. Varney creaked to his knees and turned his head to read the titles, and there it was— *My Schubert* —painted on a tattered blue spine. He couldn't help hearing an orchestra fanfare as he reached out and pulled it free.

The book was a square blue shape, a little smaller in size than his copy of *The Book of Joe*, which he still carried with him. He was almost afraid to open the book, it looked so old and who knew, maybe it was haunted, waiting to spring at him.

Now he carried two books with him, tucked under his arm while he dug in his pocket for dollars and told The Last Exit girl, "I'd like a pot of lapsang souchong tea, please."

She whirled, filled a dented silver teapot and he paid her. "Thanks." As he crossed the floor towards his window seat, he took a snapshot view of the room. Across three long marble topped tables a group of frantic artists were making what looked like a giraffe skeleton. There were chess players who didn't care at all; they could have been orbiting the moon. Framed in the doorway to the patio in back, a couple played clarinet and guitar. Varney didn't know anyone, but he felt like he belonged. And at this time of day, his seat by the window was usually waiting for him.

He settled his bent pot with a clank on the table, released the cup handle from his finger, and sat in the greenish light cast though the ivy and glass. A street-sweeper plowed past the curb, whooshing and leaving a wet trail out there. He put his two dog books in front of him and selected the blue ancient one, opening it like a clockmaker.

My Schubert, the title page announced in Germanic calligraphy. There was no author listed, or publisher, that was it. He turned the page and his leg jumped. The woodcut illustration was the face of Fort Lauderdale! *This is my Schubert*, the writing stated underneath the picture.

Now Varney was afraid to hold the book. A slight tremble had crept into his right hand. Hard as he tried to turn the page, the book gave him that awful feeling of those old Black Forest stories, wolves starting from trees, watching children. It pulled at the page, it was like lead.

> *My Schubert can walk*
> *My Schubert can talk*
> *My Schubert will stay*
> *My Schubert goes away*

That was the last page. He closed the book. What

could he say? He dropped it onto Vincent Price and poured himself some tea.

Well, it gave him something to think about. The Schubert in the book was Fort Lauderdale alright, as perfect a depiction as a John James Audubon painting. He was halfway up the blue painted stairs, climbing the hill, when this thought occurred: What if a Schubert wasn't some dog breed? What if it *was* Schubert, singular, like Godzilla or Santa Claus? Fort Lauderdale was a one-of-a-kind myth. He stopped at the next wooden landing to think that over, sitting on the bench with the sunflowers grown next to the railing. Two bees crawled on the face of the flower, ticking it like a clock.

It made sense, he decided. No other dog book mentioned the existence of Schuberts. Schubert was only to be found in the children's section, like Snoopy or Clifford the Big Red Dog. Schubert was just another example of a less-than-real talking dog.

When the bees took back to the air, Varney got up and climbed the rest of the stairs.

Fort Lauderdale may have been a mythical creation, but Varney felt responsible when he stopped at Sandra Van Harlow's house and knocked on the door.

She read him right away. "Fort Lauderdale got away again?"

He sighed. "I'm sorry."

She let him in. They drifted to the plaid upholstered couch and he explained, "I guess the collar was too loose. She just took off, right into the woods."

He glanced at Sandra who held a tissue to her eye and nodded.

"I spent a long time calling her name, tramping around in the leaves. I couldn't get her back." As if directed in some 1950s B-movie, he looked sadly at the plush carpeting and shook his head.

"Well..." she finally spoke. "You tried your best, Varney. It was just in her nature to run off like that."

After a silence he spent staring at the gold framed photo of Fort Lauderdale propped on the coffee table, Varney asked her, "I was wondering about that... What exactly is a Schubert?"

"Oh, we just made that name up. I don't know what kind of a dog she is. Probably she's a mixture of everything in the neighborhood. We call her a Schubert as a joke."

"That's some joke...All this time I thought she was some royal dog from Bavaria. That explains why I couldn't find Schubert mentioned in any of the dog books." Then he remembered the book in his hand. He was going to show her *My Schubert*, but she was laughing at what he said. Now he was glad he didn't tell her Fort Lauderdale spoke to him. She would have been hysterical.

"Sorry," she said. "I never had anyone believe that Schubert business."

"Yeah, I'm gullible. I know...Gullible's travels."

He stood up. "Anyway, you'll tell me if you see Fort Lauderdale?"

"Of course. I'm sure she'll be back when she gets hungry."

Varney stopped in the hallway. He could have gone another three steps to the door and out, but he happened to look at the cat sitting on the railing of the stairs. It was a big charcoal colored cat with a huge smile, grinning at him. He was going to say something but he didn't.

Varney could hear the noise before he got home.

It sounded like someone beating an oar on a high-tension wire, but he knew what it was. It was that little girl on her pogo stick in front of the rooming house. What a racket. He passed her, waved his books, and started up the cement steps.

Someone was coming out of September Hill and they nearly collided. "Mr. Decker!" Herbert cried out.

"Herbert…"

They small-talked with that mechanical beating heart hitting the pavement below them. When it stopped, they both fell silent and turned to look at the girl.

She stared back. She pointed the hand not holding the pogo stick. "Mr. Leopold!"

Herbert sighed despondently. "Chloe…"

"How's your book, Mr. Leopold?"

"It's good. It's going okay."

"Don't you want to ask me about *my* book?"

Herbert whispered, "Not really," but took a deep breath and said loud enough for her to hear, "Yeah, Chloe. How's your novel?"

She smiled. "It's over two hundred pages now."

"That's really something, Chloe."

"How many pages is *your* book, Mr. Leopold?"

"Oh, my book…Well, it's poetry, so you know, poetry books are usually shorter than that." Then he pointed to the man next to him. "In fact, this is Varney. He's editing it and typing it for me."

"Good day, Varney," she said and actually curtsied. She was something: a Norman Rockwell painting, ponytail, green dress and pogo stick. "I'm writing a crime novel," she told Varney.

"Really?"

Herbert whispered fiercely, "Don't get her started!" but she already was.

"A terrible thing just happened. Jane got buried in a room under the garden. It's part of the sewers, the pipes that run beneath the town from house to house. I think she might get out, but the killer is looking for her." She put a foot back on the pogo stick. "I don't need someone to type my book though, I do it myself. That way I can revise if I need to."

"Okay, Chloe…" Herbert said. "You keep writing that book. I need to talk to Varney now. We'll see you later." He grabbed Varney's arm and pulled him towards their house.

"Goodbye, Mr. Leopold!" the girl called. "Nice to meet you, Varney!" Then with a hop she was back on her contraption, punching at the sidewalk, sending echoes down the street.

"Two hundred pages!" Herbert seethed. "Did you hear that? Over two hundred pages…I'd love to get a look at that book. I bet she's got four pages written in one of those grade school notepads. Probably ten lines to a page…" Herbert paced the kitchen in front of the sink, back and forth, from window to window like a zoo creature. "Did you hear that plot of hers? Someone's locked in a room underground?! Oh boy! She's told me a lot more than that too. It's outrageous! Utterly absurd!"

Varney couldn't believe the tantrum he was witnessing. At first he was smiling at Herbert's outburst, thinking it was a joke, but soon enough Herbert was getting genuinely furious. Trying to think of some way to defuse all that anger, Varney came up with an out-of-proportion sneeze, the kind of sneeze his grandfather would bless every meal with after dusting his plate with English hot pepper. It was loud enough and surprising enough to stop Herbert in his tracks.

Herbert stared at Varney sitting there at the kitchen table. "What is that?" he pointed. "*The Book of Joe?*" The sonic disturbance had jarred the two books out of Varney's hand and they clattered on the table.

"Vincent Price's book."

"Are you reading that?"

"Sure…" He gathered his books again. "Left off on page 81. Vincent Price is living in England. He almost bought an elephant."

After a blink, Herbert replied, "How's my book going? I heard you typing last night."

"Good…Well, I have noticed something though. It looks like sometimes you have repeated the same poem, written slightly differently…Quite a few times actually…"

"Oh…"

"But I'm just going to type the whole thing up and then we can deal with it."

Herbert gave him a peculiar stare. "Vincent Price almost bought an elephant?"

"He considered it. He got a cat instead."

With the calmness of a maniac come to his senses, Herbert mumbled lucidly, "You can't just buy an elephant."

"Welcome to Superior Genetics," a robotic woman's voice said. "How may I help you?...Say 'Schedule an appointment' … 'Find the nearest lab location' … 'More options' …"

"More options," said Varney.

"Okay. Say, 'Track my test results' … 'Get rates' … 'Claims and refunds' … 'More options' …"

Varney repeated, "More."

"I'm sorry. I didn't understand your request. Please stay on the line while I forward your call to a Superior Genetics representative."

Varney waited. He held the phone an inch from his ear while a synthesizer brayed a peppy familiar melody.

The music stopped and a human voice cut in, "Superior Genetics."

"Is this a person?" Varney asked.

"Yes. How can I help you, sir?"

"What a relief! Well, I, uh, came in there a while ago to be cloned and I just received a check in the mail today stating that there have been two more clones made of me since then."

"Yes sir. You received a royalty check."

"Yeah. I'm a little concerned though. I mean the money's good, but how many more clones of me are you going to make?"

"That's entirely up to the lab, sir. When you signed the contract, surely you read the conditions?"

"Yeah, yeah, yeah. I just wanted to know if typically there's a limit to it. I don't want a thousand of me walking around."

"That would be hard to imagine, sir."

"Not really!"

"If this is something you'd like to address with one of our law representatives, I can make an appointment for you. I have to say though, it's entirely within Superior Genetics' jurisdiction. You've handed over your rights to your clone."

"I know, I know…" Varney took a deep breath. "I was just hoping there'd be some limit…"

"Not as far as I know. It's not written in stone."

"So I shouldn't worry about it?"

"No. I wouldn't."

"Alright…"

"Is that all, sir?"

"Yeah…I guess so…"

"Thank you very much for your interest."

"Yeah…Thanks."

After that, Varney was worn out. He went to his room and lay down on his bed. The room felt very small like being locked in a walnut. He had the window open over his bed, letting in a night breeze and the sounds outside: cars, cats on the fence, and now and then voices. Next to his bed he had a little table with a lamp and his books. There was a big wardrobe which took up most of the wall. That was about it. Oh, he had a poster on the Eastern wall. It was a Japanese painting, *Cranes Flying By Mount Fuji*. That was his window to the dreamworld. As he lay on the bed, he would stare at that for a while, then reach his left hand over to turn off the lamp. In the darkness, with the outside murmuring in the screen window, he would close his eyes and picture beautiful white wings. He would put them on, give his arms a wave, feeling the air, then the lift off the ground as he flapped the wings again. The cranes on the wall would call him and he would fly.

Varney didn't have a clock anymore. When he ended up in the basement with no job to wake him up early, no schedule or places to hurry and be, he gladly said goodbye to that ticking invention. Still, there were the rare times when he would look to see what time it was, like this one, waking in the middle of the night to some strange noise. What a dream too! Some faraway girl he was young again with…Something scratched the window screen.

He opened his eyes. The room was gloomy dark. He waited and the scratching repeated, right above him. Some midnight animal, he guessed…Was it trying to get in?

"Go away!" he called.

In a moment, a voice replied. "Varney?"

He sat up. The bed responded with a metallic rattle of old rusted spring vertebrae. "Who's there?"

"Varney, it's me. The Schubert."

"Fort Lauderdale?"

The beast sighed. "*That name…*"

Varney fumbled with the thick curtains and moved them aside. "Are you out there?" Then he could see the two gleaming eyes and the silhouette in the flower bed. "What's going on?"

"I feel like a perfect idiot waking you in the middle of the night."

"What's the matter?"

"I've managed to do something completely foolish. I don't suppose you could help me?"

"Yes, of course. I'll come around to the door over there and let you in."

"Much obliged."

The phantom shadow of the Schubert left the window. Varney dropped the curtain and got out of bed. When he unlocked the back door of the house, Fort Lauderdale was sitting there, holding her front right paw off the ground forlornly. She limped on three feet down the steps into the dimly lit room.

"What happened to you?"

"You remember Androcles?" she asked. She stopped in the center of the kitchen. "My word, Varney! Is this is where you live?"

He followed her and stopped at the table.

"It's got all the warm charm of a catacomb."

"Yeah, I know. What's wrong with your paw?"

She sat and held it out to him. "A thorn…" she sighed.

He laughed. He couldn't help it.

"I know, I know. It's a thousand year old fable—I stepped on a thorn. Take a look, won't you please?"

"Alright…" Varney clicked the lamp on the kitchen table and turned the circle of light onto her. She shut her eyes tightly. "Let me see…" He took her soft paw, twisted it a little. "Sorry," he said when she whimpered, then, "Oh yeah…It's a thorn. I see it. Let me get some tweezers."

He crossed the floor to the bathroom. It was a small room, a closet really, with enough room for a shower, a toilet, a sink with a mirrored cabinet that he opened. There were some historic toothbrushes hung in there, an empty aspirin bottle, other relics and some silver tweezers. He grabbed iodine and a roll of bandages too and left the narrow bathroom.

The Schubert watched him, her ears alert, her paw still held aloft pathetically. She smiled doggishly.

Varney was careful as he could manage to be, knowing if he hurt her she would either bite him, or burn his ears with a litany of that Katherine Hepburn hot air. Fortunately, he was able to remove the thorn, dab the wound with the ancient vial of iodine and bind her paw before she spoke again.

"You needn't mummify me, Varney. This isn't *The Egyptian Book of the Dead*." She withdrew her paw and stood on it gingerly. "Yes…that's fine." She was getting used to it, padding in a circle, walking herself around the table. She grinned at him. "You've done a wonderful job. I wish I could repay you somehow."

"That's alright. We had some good times together."

"Yes," she sort of curtsied, "You're right about that." Then she pointed her long nose at the door. "Could you see me out now, Varney? I think I'm ready to try my luck out there again."

"Sure….My pleasure. Good to see you again."

He followed her up the wooden steps and opened the door to the night. She took a deep breath of it, turned her head to give him a wink, then she trotted out.

Varney stood there in the doorway a little while. He thought he might hear her howl or bark, but the city was more or less quiet on the breeze.

Of course he couldn't go to sleep after that. He went to his room, got Herbert's manuscript and returned to the kitchen table. The stack of paper watched him, holding leaves like a Venus flytrap.

The typewriter waited on the counter by the toaster. It would have been an honest mistake to roll a slice of bread in it. Varney brought it to the table and set it down.

He let out a sigh though…he wasn't ready. Earlier, he had paged through it and found another poem titled "Thanks to the Sky" repeated later as "Harvey's Return." It was a headache to sort out. He supposed his job as editor meant noticing these things and choosing the better version.

Herbert's typing instructions were pretty specific, but he didn't say anything about the television. It was a little black and white set. Who knew how long it had lived in the kitchen? On the antenna was a silver crumpled ball of tinfoil. Varney lit a candle and unwound the wire to plug the TV in. He figured, why not watch a late night movie as long as he was up? So he put it beside the typewriter. It wouldn't go on until he fed it a quarter. So he did. Twenty five cents was good for an hour. He could save time during commercials by turning it off.

Channel 12 was already on, playing a movie he recognized. It didn't matter that it was a black and white TV set, it was showing a black and white movie. The film was *Night Tide*. He saw it with his wife a long time ago, during their dating days. He escorted her to a double feature at The Neptune Theatre. They used to go there a lot. The other picture was *Mr. Peabody and the Mermaid*. Those magical days came back to him… her head on his shoulder. Sometimes he would look away from the screen, tip his head up to watch the stream of moving light above them. The theater even had stained glass windows of Neptune and a mermaid and gold faces in the walls, with eyes that glowed green during the show. Sometimes they would sit in the balcony, everything a bowl before them, the movie shining in the darkness like a pearl. Those were wonderful dreamy days and he cursed that clone, himself really, who had ruined it. The Pacific swept the shore, the music played and then the picture quickly changed to another world.

A man resembling a cheap vampire sat in a gloomy crypt with a comical bat companion hanging from the ceiling over his head. With a shrug and a wave the man said, "Well, love is strange, isn't it?" As he breezed up out of his rocking chair, his black cape flowed like a shadow and showed his name written in cartoon letters on the back of his director's chair, Count Misfit.

Varney had heard people at The Last Exit talk about Count Misfit before. He was one of those twilight cult heroes.

Count Misfit stopped before a tin bucket placed on a checkered tablecloth. The sign taped to it said: MERMAID. He pulled the flower from his buttonhole and held it over the bucket, saying, "For you my dear…"

A woman's wet hand reached up and took the carnation and pulled it in. There was a splash, then a commercial break for a used car lot.

Varney sat at the window and watched a crow on the sidewalk. It grabbed a piece of bread and took off across the street, leaving the sparrows and pigeons to hobnob and peck at the remaining seeds and crumbs that were thrown out of The Last Exit door. He had another sip of tea. He was waiting for Herbert. In his cup there were bits of leaves making slow skeins like geese in formation. When the birds outside scattered, taking loud flight, Varney looked up and there was Herbert. Sometimes the guy had a way of almost staggering, as if his feet had switched sides and caught him unawares.

Herbert entered and stood there at the door for a long moment, scanning the room. It was weird seeing him so far from the basement but obviously Herbert was in his element here. He waved at someone, saluted the table in the back where some of his poet comrades called out his name. What a showman, thought Varney. He had a pretty good idea Herbert knew where Varney was, the guy just lived for the stage. Then Herbert swung his gaze to the windows and he gave a little theatrical jump. "Mr. Decker!" he boomed.

The room went silent.

Varney held up a hand.

"Poetry has arrived!" Herbert announced. He crossed the ten feet of space and sat down at Varney's table. The café had returned to its sound—murmuring, laughing, clacking board games, a girl singing to her mandolin.

"I see you have my opus, my symphony in words." Herbert tapped the cardboard box filled with paper.

"How's *A Little Blue* going?"

"A little blue?"

"Yes, I renamed it."

"I've been typing it." Varney removed a slice from the box to show Herbert. "I'm sticking to your requirements, nighttime typing with candles, so you know progress is a little slow I guess."

"That's to be expected, Mr. Decker. I'm not paying you by the hour. Of course…" he chuckled, "In point of fact, I'm not paying you at all!"

"Well, yes, I get paid for clones so—"

"So you understand! This is for the Arts!" Herbert held aloft a statuesque finger.

"But I am having a little trouble with—I think I already told you—I'm finding as I go along that some of your poems will be repeated with the title changed, or the construction of it might be different, but it's the same poem echoed again."

In a booming voice, Herbert suddenly recited from memory. It was one of the poems from the collection. Varney recognized it, but it had been given breath, life, and it floated in the air like a mythical bird. There was wild applause from the room when Herbert ended. Even Varney found himself clapping.

"Now what would you call that, Mr. Decker?" Herbert asked as he sat back down on the bench.

"That was great."

"Well, that's one word for it. But you can't pin something like that down." Herbert took Varney's teacup and gulped from it. "See what I mean? Everything's in motion, constantly being reassigned meaning and existence."

Varney stared at his empty cup.

Herbert laughed. "So I say why shouldn't poetry reflect that too? Right!"

Varney cleared his throat to speak, at the same moment a girl appeared beside Herbert and tapped him on the shoulder.

"Are you done with my parrot yet?"

"Ahhh yes…the typist. Yes, my dear." Herbert took her hand. "The bird didn't actually live up to its billing, pun intended. However, this is my new typist. A human. You may have seen him several places at once. Allow me to introduce you to the original article, Mr. Varney Decker."

She nodded hello at him and asked Herbert, "So when do I get my parrot back?"

"Forthrightly, in fact now if you wish. Shall we go?"

"Alright," she said, eyes on him, with a smile. She didn't seem to mind Herbert at all. "Let's go." She was certainly pretty and freckled as a songbird.

"Mr. Decker…" Herbert stood up and bowed. "I bid you a good day." He placed a hand on the boxed paperwork. "Just keep typing," and he took his lady by the arm.

So let it be the way it is, okay, Varney decided as he sat in the park and finished reading all of *A Little Blue* and allowed familiar poems to walk in and out. Varney was just an office-trained typewriter put there in the night with candle and late movie glowing. He supposed he could get it done in a couple more good nights of typing. He put the lid on the box and watched the way two young lovers sat on a blanket not far away. The sun shined on them. How could he not think of Miranda and their children? Even their pet ape, if he was here, would be climbing that tree, tossing down ripe cherries.

It wasn't easy standing there before September Hill boarding house, knowing this was now his home. It's a street crowded by other houses, trees, cars parked tightly along the curb. The leaves dripped on them. His house stood there like an old boat really, its brown paint held bending walls, four stories up to a steep slanted black shingled roof. It could be a set from Count Misfit if it was filmed in black and white. Yeah…and he lived in the basement.

Varney followed the shadows already dropping onto the path. There wasn't much else he felt like doing today. What was he supposed to do? What were his clones doing? There was the one who took his job and his family and there were another two he didn't know anything about. Plus, of course, there was 'the original model' and Varney still didn't know what he was going to do.

It was Monday morning. Most people woke up on this day like the film footage of waves crashing on the shore. It was enough to cloud the sound of the word, Monday. People would just instantly groan.

When the sun wanted Varney awake, it slanted enough light through the garden leaves and the window curtains. It rested on him until after nine when he woke up. He had been in one of those weird dream cities, where his imagination and reality battled it out down alleys and over rooftops. The alarm clock used to break into that. Not in this basement though, Monday didn't bother Varney anymore.

He wasn't alone in bed. He felt someone warm curled beside him. Wide awake, he heard a contented girlish purr as she stirred along his back.

Who was she? How could she just appear like this? When Varney carefully sat up and turned to face her, he couldn't help letting out a yell. "Fort Lauderdale!"

"Ugh! *That name*," she groaned and put a paw over her ear.

"How did you get in here? What are you doing here?"

"Varney, you needn't be so flustered." She stretched the length of the bed, then crossed her paws and continued, "Varney, I had some time to think out there in the wild and let me tell you, I discovered something. All my life I've gone from door to door, master to master—that's always been the nature of a Schubert and Varney, you simply cannot run away from your nature, can you?"

Varney stared at her.

"So here I am…Home sweet home."

"Wait a minute. I can't have a—a Schubert—in my

room—and what about Sandra Van Harlow? What if she sees you with me? She lives just down the street!"

"Oh Varney, don't be such a worrywart. Honestly, I can be discreet. Besides, do you think Van Harlow frightens me?"

"Yeah, but you were her…Schubert…"

She rolled her brown eyes.

"And besides," Varney said, "look around—this place is a shoebox!"

"Then, Varney…" she sat up on the bed. "Perhaps it's time for an upgrade."

He went about the day as if he knew there wasn't a talking dog waiting for him in the dumpy basement room of a boarding house. "Varney you can better yourself," she had told him. "You don't have to settle for this rundown shanty, selling yourself to science. You had a good job. You had a home with a family. I don't see why you can't pick yourself up and start over again."

How could he explain his life to a Schubert? He couldn't. He needed some space. When he left that morning, he took Herbert's box of poetry and the portable typewriter and told her he would be back later. He had some work to finish up in town, he said.

All day he tried not to think about the Schubert, but now she was in his life and he knew she was right—his life did deserve to be better.

He supposed that was why he took along his typing assignment, so he could be finished with it. The manuscript took him the rest of the day. And there was no candlelight or midnight movie on the park bench where he tapped away until the last word. At last *A Little Blue* was done. It was time to go home.

Varney stopped at his old neighborhood corner store and browsed the cans of pet food. He chose Happy Hound. It featured a grinning dog on a bright red background. It was beef flavored, with vitamins added. On his way to the counter he grabbed a can of Chow Mein for himself.

"Long time no see," said the cashier.

"Yeah…I moved."

"You want your lottery ticket?"

"No, I—my luck's changed too, I guess."

"That's good."

Varney paid. He didn't have any reason to ever return there. He guessed it was just for old time's sake… That, and a can of dog food.

"Happy Hound?!"

Varney explained, "It's beef flavored, vitamins added." Suddenly Varney felt like he was holding a rock, covered in mud, dug straight from a landfill.

"Did you honestly think I'd be interested in consuming such a dreadful concoction?"

"I don't know what you eat!" Varney barked. "I'm sorry…All I ever did was take you for walks…I don't know what you like to eat." He sat down on the one chair in the room and wobbled. His bed rattled as the Schubert on it moved.

"Oh, Varney. You do make me laugh. What's in that other can?"

"It's uh…Chow Mein."

"Well, that's a start. Look here, why not let me give you some instructions on how to spice that up. Come now, Varney, look alive. Grab a pen and paper and allow me to tell you how."

An hour later, he brought two plates back into his room from the kitchen. Only one of them had a fork tucked into the noodles and fresh vegetables.

When Varney brought the plates to the kitchen again, there was Herbert sitting at the table, listening to a transistor radio.

"Mr. Decker!" he called out. "You lured me in here. I haven't smelled such a meal in years!" Herbert turned in his seat to get a look at the plates passing him. "Any leftovers?"

"Uh, no."

"Two plates?"

Varney set them in the sink and ran some water over them.

Herbert asked, "Who's your visitor?" He listened to dishes being cleaned. "Come on, Varney." The water was turned off.

"A friend of mine…from Fort Lauderdale."

Herbert chuckled. He turned up the volume on his radio. It was a baseball game. "I understand," he said and he stood up. "I'm just playing through."

Varney left the dishes in the rack to dry and left the empty kitchen. He opened his door and went in.

"Now that was a marvelous meal!" the Schubert announced. "What do you say we go for a nice brisk stroll in the moonlight?"

"I don't know if the moon is out. It looked a little cloudy earlier."

"Varney, you are a hoot. What are you waiting for? Put on your shoes, let's go see September Hill."

After a long twilit walk in the woods, they returned to the boarding house. Varney asked her to wait in the rhododendron shadow while he snuck downstairs to make sure the kitchen was empty. In a moment he whispered to her and she padded down the steps without a creak. He hurried her into his room and shut the door.

"You make me feel like a coed in a dormitory," the Schubert told him.

"I know. I'm sorry. It's just that, you know, there are certain rules here."

She held up her paw, "I understand. This cloak and dagger business is in my blood." She got up onto his bed and lay down, letting out a long sighing groan.

"Wait. That's another thing. I don't think we should sleep on the bed together."

"What?"

"It wouldn't be right. I'm married."

"Married?"

"Yes."

"Where's your wife?"

He sat in the chair. "She's with my clone."

"What?!"

"I know what it sounds like. I thought I could make a little extra spending money so we could take a vacation. We've never had more than just enough for bills and food, music lessons, little things. So yeah, I let Superior Genetics clone me. They paid me. I just got another check from them. $600. They're still cloning me! The problem is, the clones seem to be an improvement on the original."

With a hop, the Schubert was off the bed, to give Varney's hand a lick. She sat beside his chair. "The floor suits me just fine, Varney."

"Thank you. I'm sorry. I'm just in a strange sort of time."

"I understand."

Varney lay down on the bed. It was strange alright, but he didn't want to think about it anymore. He reached over the nightstand and turned off the lamp. He stared at the darkness overhead. Someone upstairs was walking back and forth. It would be nice to just fall asleep when you wanted to.

Then the Schubert cleared her throat and said, "Varney, did you know there are spiders on the floor?"

Varney woke up with her on the bed again. She was a dog, right? Lots of people had pets, cats or dogs, who shared their sleep. Not a talking dog though…

one that spoke like a movie star…

And it was comforting to have someone warm beside him. It made him remember and miss Miranda. He got out of bed slowly so he wouldn't wake up the Schubert and quietly grabbed some fresh clothes as he headed out to the shower.

"Mr. Decker," Herbert called from the kitchen table.

"Morning, Herbert. Oh…" he paused halfway to the bathroom. "I finished typing your book last night."

"Really? I thought your nights were occupied with other activities." Herbert winked.

"I'll—let me get your book." Varney returned to his little room.

The Schubert lifted her sleepy head. "Good morning, Varney."

He shut the door behind him. "Hi. You sleep okay?"

"I sure did."

"I was just going to take this manuscript out to Herbert."

"Manuscript?"

"Yeah. He's a poet. I typed it up for him."

"Interesting…"

"But I don't think he should know about us. I mean, we're not supposed to be—"

"Varney, you're one in a million, you really are. I'll wait."

"Thanks." He grabbed the box. "I'll be back soon."

"Mmmm," she said. She looked asleep again.

Varney slipped out of the room.

Herbert was still eating cereal.

"Here's your book."

Herbert was still chewing. He nodded and bowed and accepted the box, flipping it open to feast his eyes upon it. "Looks great…" He held all the pages and leafed through them. "This is wonderful."

Varney was halfway to the shower again when Herbert called him. "I'll hit it hard, then get the revisions back to you."

Varney stood there in the gloom of the narrow shower waiting for the water to get warmer, repeating Herbert's, "I'll get the revisions back to you…the revisions…the revisions…revisions…" until he gave up, turned the water off and stared down at his feet. He stood an inch deep in a swamp temperature pool that wouldn't drain. Maybe he could tell Herbert, "Look, I've done all I can do." Wasn't it enough to deliver the typed pages?

He bumped his knee off the plastic folding door of the shower unit, grabbed his towel off a wall hook and dried off.

Nothing was ever enough. Varney had a vision of himself typing and retyping Herbert's poems for years. The pages rushed like water through the typewriter, the poetry splashed all over the floor and filled the basement until he drowned. Quick as he could, Varney got dressed and left the closet sized bathroom.

He didn't know what he was going to say, but it

was okay. The kitchen was empty. That was fine. Now was a good time to go for a walk with the Schubert. They could get some Chinese takeout down by the aqueduct. He had no plans for the day. He felt like he didn't really know what to do about anything anyway. Who knows—it was another sunny day—maybe the Schubert would lead him somewhere?

They ended up on the banks of the lake, under the aqueduct. He was only half finished with his food and she was already done and he couldn't resist the look that her big eyes gave him. So he gave her the rest of his box of rice and curry vegetables. Varney laughed at the way she lapped the box empty. He dangled his legs off the dock; they moved the water like wooden spoons.

A dragonfly hovered and flew over the octopus-like lotus garden. Overhead, the aqueduct shook as another rush of waves from the mountain river poured.

The Schubert panted and laughed.

Everything was blues, greens, flowers, the Roman shaped architecture, water and summertime. They were fine there and could have stayed forever. He closed his eyes. Sun felt good on him.

A canoe paddling by made him open his eyes. He waved at the people. They waved back. It was so peaceful. What if this was the way it was meant to be, without empires or politics or worries? He already had a taste that he could do better after everything fell apart. He knew the Schubert was trying to help him get better.

He put his hand on her back where he noticed her fur curled. She liked that. She groaned while he scratched her. To anyone watching it looked like a photograph, like Varney and his pet dog. But if you were closer and listened carefully, you would have heard more than the cattails and wind in the willows. You would have heard the dog talking to Varney.

Her voice sounded like one of those movie stars who lived above the city, who you reached by elevator, and if you were Cary Grant she would flip for you.

It would be nice if a symphony happened to float by. Instead, two dogs appeared at a run around the corner of the path.

Varney jumped. The Schubert was on her feet as the dogs bristled about her. One of them growled slightly. They weren't much bigger than her, both sort of labs or retrievers.

"Carol! Bootsy!" A woman wearing a lime green tracksuit jogged up to them. "Don't worry about them," she told Varney. "They're friendly. Bootsy! Stop that!"

Varney stepped in between the dogs. "Nice day," he said, not knowing what else to say.

"Come on you two!" The dogs' owner clapped her hands. "Sorry to bother you," she told Varney. "Come on, dogs!" She clapped again and the three of them took off running again.

"Sheesh!" Varney said, after it quieted down.

The Schubert shook her head low and woefully. "Dogs…"

"You do a pretty good dog act," Varney told the Schubert. An old man with two children had just been petting her. You would have never known the truth about her.

"Well," she said, "I've had quite a bit of practice."

"I never would have known you were a Schubert. All those walks we went on…You really had me fooled. Let's go this way—" He pointed to an alley that was filling in with wildflowers and blackberries. "How did Sandra Van Harlow know you were a Schubert?"

She laughed. "I just went in her dream one night and told her. Sure," she told him, "it's one of the things I do."

Varney stopped walking for a moment. "I don't even know all the things you can do. So you can read minds?"

"Mmmm," she cocked her head. "That's not precisely how I would describe it. Let's see…I suppose you would say I'm able to step inside, to influence the workings of someone's thoughts. Van Harlow was easy. While she was asleep I told her I was a Schubert so I wouldn't have to hear her call me that other dreadful name quite so often."

"Have you influenced my thoughts yet?"

"Oh, Varney! I should hope so!"

"I mean—"

"No, I understand. To be candid with you, yes," she raised a paw in the air solemnly. "Last night when you were returning home, you stopped at the store to get supper. I suggested that you get the Chow Mein. I love Chinese food."

"That was you, huh? I wondered about that. I thought it was just a whim."

"You've no idea how many whims I broadcast."

They came out of the alley into a vacant lot. There was a whole field in bloom: tall grass, white and yellow flowers, a tree no taller than a broom.

"So what made you decide to stay with me?" Varney said.

"That's simple. It didn't take a mind reader to see you needed me. A Schubert doesn't appear to just anyone. Varney, I think you'll find your luck is about to change."

While Varney and the Schubert were walking beside water and green paths, Herbert was following his own map of the city. From the boarding house in the morning, he had been to the print shop, the cafés, street-front stores, a laundry, a swimming pool. He had stopped by the Food Giant grocery bulletin board, tacking signs onto telephone poles and trees along the way. He even taped one of the blue flyers to a milk truck. He had printed a hundred announcements and he made sure that all the world he passed through in his day-to-day travels would know of the Herbert Leopold event.

Varney noticed one pinned to the wooden corner

of a house on their way home. He pulled it loose of the staple so he could read it. He still needed glasses.

*Herbert Leopold reads from his new book at
The Black Spot. Tonight 8 P.M.*

A bicycle pulling a cart ringing bells went past them and the nervous Schubert bumped into his leg. "Sorry," she said.

"New book?" Varney folded the blue scrap of paper into his shirt pocket. "What's he up to? You think he means that manuscript I typed up?"

"Let's go and find out."

"Really?"

"Sure." But then she quieted as a woman carrying a big paper bag went by them on the sidewalk.

"I don't know…" Varney said when they were alone again. He started them walking. "I guess I should support Herbert though…"

The Schubert, trotting along beside him chirped, "Say, I've got an idea! Let's make a night of it! I've got an awful craving for stir-fried vegetables. Maybe even some dumplings!"

Varney shook his head. "All I have is some change. We'd have to go home and dig around for some money."

"Nonsense! We'll make do."

"Really? Is finding money one of your abilities?"

She laughed. "Varney, you don't seem to understand. You could have all your dreams come true if you wanted."

They joined the boulevard. There were more people around. To fit in, they had to turn into a man walking his dog. A block from The Orient restaurant, Varney tried to act unsurprised when he noticed something in a pile of windswept leaves. It was a twenty dollar bill just sitting there.

The sun was setting when Varney and the Schubert showed up at The Black Spot. It looked like the bay below and every window and bit of metal that could shine was lit on fire. There were people silhouetted on the sidewalk in front of the café, standing around the doorway or sitting at the two little tables, talking, laughing, a girl was singing.

Inside, The Black Spot turned into a ship. The wooden walls had portholes. There was black netting draped across the back where an enormous steering wheel centered a small stage.

Varney and the Schubert moved through the crowd and found a small round table painted like a compass dial. The Schubert scooted underneath, next to Varney's feet.

Looking around, Varney recognized some people from The Last Exit. They were Herbert's friends, but it took him a moment to spot Herbert.

Herbert wore a blue three-piece suit. He had a flower in his lapel and a bright plastic Mardi Gras bead necklace. He must have felt Varney's look because he turned from the sailor he was talking to and gave Varney a wave. "Mr. Decker!"

Varney held up his hand and waited as Herbert navigated to his table.

"Mr. Decker. I'm glad you made it."

"Yeah, I saw one of your flyers today."

Herbert held out the typed manuscript. "I thought I'd give it a test drive."

"Good," Varney smiled. But as he glanced at the top curled page of the manuscript he saw handwriting and marks stitched all over it. "You've been making some revisions?"

"I made a few changes. There were some things I didn't like here and there."

A bell clanged. A huge bald man in a long black heavy coat was holding a white rope on the stage. He rang the bell again and roared, "Ladies and gentlemen…" The room quieted down to just the sound of the recorded waves and seagulls. "The Black Spot has an event tonight…"

"We know, Jerry!" shouted an old woman seated close to the stage. A large red and white dress tented over her like a tablecloth.

Jerry glared at her. "Alice knows…" he crookedly grinned. "Tonight we have the greatest poet in this city of ours. Herbert Leopold is here to read from his new book!" He put a hand on his brow to scout the crowd for Herbert. "What's the title, Herbert?"

Still close to Varney, Herbert called, "*A Little Blue Goes a Long Way!*"

Varney coughed or choked suddenly and the Schubert jumped. Everyone else was applauding though, as Herbert made his slow way towards the stage.

Jerry continued, "So you ready? Here he comes, everyone. Herbert Leopold!"

Herbert patted Alice on the shoulder and leaped onto the stage. Jerry shook his hand and left him alone to the crowd. As it quieted down, Herbert held his pages aloft again. They flapped like a dove's blurring white wings.

"Before I get started, I want to call to your attention…I want to thank my editor and typist, Mister Varney Decker. Varney, stand up and take a bow!"

Varney reluctantly complied. He waved to the room and sat back down while the applause died.

"Hey, Sara! Could you bring Mr. Decker some tea? Sara, are you here?" Herbert spotted the waitress and pointed her way to Varney. "How about some tea for my editor? Thanks. Okay…This, as I mentioned, is *A Little Blue Goes a Long Way*. We're going to get it published as soon as Mr. Decker types the revisions. So I'd like to dedicate the first poem to him for all his diligent work. This poem is entitled 'The Community of Fish in the Drainage Ditch.'"

The room had calmed to only the soundtrack of waves in the speakers, as Herbert began to recite. It only took a few lines before Varney shut his eyes and shook his head. He realized it had happened again. Herbert had renamed the very first poem and so it went from there. It was great poetry though, if you didn't know, if you weren't the one who had to type it, and retype it, and try to hold each poem pressed like a living butterfly to the page of a book.

When the last word floated off the stage, Alice was the first on her feet, clapping her thin hands and booming out praise. Everyone else joined her. The reading made Herbert a glowing lightbulb in the middle of the room.

Varney was on his feet too. He could feel the Schubert pressed close to his leg. He put his hand down to scratch her furry head.

"Hey landlubber!" someone close to him said; a man in a pirate costume. "You can't have a dog in here!"

The Schubert couldn't completely hide under the little compass table. Her long face poked out.

"Oh," Varney said, "She's my guide dog. I need her."

The pirate waved an invisible sword.

The Schubert mumbled, "We should go."

"Okay." Varney left a dollar on the table and they were gone.

Outside, the night had dropped. The round windows of The Black Spot lit the sidewalk in front and Varney thought he ran into a mirror.

One of his clones faced him. He wore a tuxedo coat, tan colored corduroys and brown wingtips that looked like they had walked across America. "Oh," the clone said, startled.

Varney was the first to recover. "I was wondering when I'd bump into one of you—I mean one of me. The city can't be that big."

"He looks just like you, Varney!" the Schubert said.

"Well, almost. We have a different tailor."

The clone stared at the animal next to Varney. "Is that a talking dog?"

"No," Varney said.

"But I heard it talk. I saw its mouth move."

"This isn't a dog. This is a Schubert," Varney explained. "She's my friend."

"I've never heard of a Schubert before."

"Well, how long have you been alive? A couple days? There's a lot to learn. What are you doing here anyway? Do you know Herbert too?"

"No. I don't know anyone here. I came here to read. There's an open microphone at 9. Anyone can read."

"You wrote something? Poetry?" Varney looked astounded. It seemed these clones were all reflections of him and his world, only they succeeded where he failed.

The clone had a notebook in his shirt pocket. "I've been writing a novel. It's called *A Homemade Dictionary*."

"A novel?"

"Yes. It's nearly finished. Actually, my agent is trying to get it placed at Seahorse Publishing."

They heard the bell clang inside The Black Spot and Jerry's voice. The lantern over the door blinked.

"I should go in…I still need to sign up. You want to hear me read?"

Varney shook his head. "No. We need to get

home."

"Well, if you'd like we could meet for coffee some-time. There's a lot to talk about."

"Yeah, I know. Maybe…"

The clone paused in the doorway. "Okay. I'll see you sometime. Hang in there. Oh…" he waited an-other second. You could hear someone muttering on the stage. "Thanks for the life."

Back at the boarding house, Varney lay on the bed with *The Book of Joe*. He held it propped on his stomach, but he couldn't read. "I can't believe that clone wrote a novel. And he's already got a publisher. He's only been alive a few days!"

"He must be a real go-getter," the Schubert said. She was curled at the foot of the bed and sleepy. She yawned.

"Must be…See, that's what I'm trying to figure out about these clones. They must come with some of my talents, but they just do things so much better than me."

"Do you want to write a novel, Varney?"

"I don't know…If I could…I sure don't want to go back to that office job."

"We could write a book together, Varney. Oh, they're great fun to write! I've done it before. One of my caretakers quite some time ago wrote a book with me."

"This one, right?" Varney pulled it off the bedside table. "*My Schubert?*"

"That's the one! It was a bit plain as I recall. It was a book for kindergarteners. The pictures are flattering though."

There was a knock on the bedroom door, followed by, "Varney? It's Herbert." Varney sat up. He returned the books to the table and took three steps to the door.

"I hope I'm not interrupting you," Herbert said through the door gap. "I just wanted to give you the manuscript with the revisions." He held the stack of paper towards Varney.

"Okay, Herbert. Thanks. That was a great—" but he froze up as he stared at the first page of the manuscript. He fanned through it. Every page had been scribbled all over. The white background with typing had turned into a painter's tarp. "What happened to it?"

"It's much better now."

"But it's totally different."

"Revised," Herbert corrected.

"I would have to retype the whole thing!"

"It's only the second draft."

"I can't do it," Varney told her. "I can't even look at it again. He changed names, titles, the structures. It's going to drive me crazy! It's like changing the blueprint from a blender to a helicopter. And Herbert said this was only the second draft! Can you believe that? As if there's going to be more! I don't want to do this anymore." Varney tossed the manuscript onto the little table.

"Listen, Varney. It's too much work. Tomorrow you tell him you can't retype it again. For heaven's sake stop thinking about it tonight. It's late. Come to bed."

"You're right." He sat down on the edge of the bed. The mattress sank as all the hidden ancient coils and springs screeched beneath his weight. "Herbert's going to flip when I tell him…"

Varney switched off the lamp. "You should have seen the way he went off at this little girl who told him about her book. He's got a lot of anger. Just look what he did to that manuscript—that could be my face tomorrow!"

"Oh, Varney. You're being melodramatic. He can't expect you to retype that book all over again."

"But he does!"

"I think you're worrying too much about it, Varney. You've done your part. Let him find someone else. Now let's get some sleep."

Varney lay there in the dark. He listened to the curtains shift in the breeze coming through the screen window, then he smiled. "I remember my wife Miranda used to talk like that whenever I had some problem at work…I wonder what's happened to her…" He turned over and pressed his face deep into the pillow.

With the Schubert's help, Varney worked up his courage until he was able to carry the manuscript out of his room, into the kitchen. He was hoping Herbert would be there, at the table with the radio or a bowl of oatmeal, but the kitchen was empty, striped with the bars of sunlight coming in. He took a deep breath and continued to the stairs, going past the door to outside, following the creaking steps up to the third floor.

Varney knew Herbert lived down the hall. It wasn't hard to pick the right door. One door had a postcard of a panda bear, the other was scarred and plain and the last door had the blue flyer from last night's reading taped to it…Also, a photocopy of some old wooly-looking poet. Varney guessed it could have been Herbert wearing that 19th century beard and shadows… The same eyes on fire.

Varney was close enough to knock on the door, but now he felt like leaving the book and bolting. No, he knew he had to go through with this…it had to be done. There was opera music playing in the room.

Varney shut his eyes and rapped on the wood below The Black Spot announcement. He heard something clang. Another couple seconds, Varney heard footsteps approach the door and it swung open.

"Mr. Decker!"

"Hi, Herbert."

"Come on in…"

At the end of the room was a window, a plant growing and a record player spinning opera. The square of ceiling above sagged with a draped blue sheet that looked like a parachute. There was a mattress on the floor and a cluttered bookshelf, a suitcase with a row of melted candles on top. Varney stopped in the middle of Herbert's room.

"So, I see you brought the manuscript. Do you have questions, comments?"

Varney thought of the Schubert talking him calmly through his decision. "I'm bringing it back to you, Herbert. I'm sorry, I can't type it again. I wish I had time to, but I have to get a job. I need to—" he set the manuscript on a table covered with handwritten notes, "I need to do other things right now."

"I understand," Herbert told him flatly. "I don't want to take up all your time."

"Thank you," Varney let out a sigh. "It's been driving me crazy! I didn't know how to say it, I'm so glad you don't mind."

Herbert stared at the table, the papers, where all his handwriting scattered and piled.

Varney felt a flower turn awful in that silence, watching Herbert who turned into a woodcut again. "I…" Varney tried. "I don't know, maybe we can look for someone else to type it."

"Don't worry about it," Herbert said quietly.

The opera, the blue waves above, Varney felt like he was on a sinking ship. His mouth was full of water.

The Schubert took him for a walk. She said he needed it. The morning sun lit the green canopy of oak leaves.

"It was bad," Varney repeated. He hadn't said much else since leaving the third floor.

When they got to the blue stairway, the Schubert sneezed as she led the way, her body slanted steeply from her nose to her tail.

"I wish I could just start this morning over again."

Varney stopped himself, grabbing the handrail. "I should go back and tell him I'll type it. What's so bad about retyping it? That's all I did at my office job every day. Type, type, type."

The Schubert snorted. "Come on, Varney. You're not going back there. I left a note for him in the mailbox."

He let go of the handrail and followed her. "What note? What did it say?"

"I told him there's an octopus at the aquarium who can type 90 words a minute. All he has to do is pay her in sea urchins."

Varney smiled.

The Schubert pulled over on the landing to rest. "I must say these stairs are most awkward for me. I feel half-ready to tumble head over heels at any second."

Varney sat down on the bench and closed his eyes. "So I'm off the hook," he grinned. He took a deep breath of the August sunlight summer and sighed. The hill crept down with flowers and houses and telephone poles into trees and the town grown to the blue water bay. "God, that's a good feeling!" he said. He watched the swallows dart across the vacant lot.

When they started walking again, he felt light as a balloon.

The Schubert stopped at the door to Fuji's Five and Dime and looked up at Varney. "I'll wait here while you go in."

"Am I getting something?"

"Are you acquainted with those yellow lined notepads?"

"Yeah, sure, we had a cabinet full of them at my office. You want one?"

"We need two of them, Varney. We've got work to do."

"What sort of work?"

"We're writing a memoir, Varney."

Varney groaned, "Oh no, not another book…"

It was in the air, it couldn't be denied, and Varney really felt like it was destiny when the Schubert stopped at the newspaper dispenser.

The headlines were right at her eye level. "Varney!" she cried out even though there were other people nearby. "Is this the girl you were talking about?"

He leaned over to look. "Teen Writes Blockbuster," he read. He got closer. "Holy cow! That's her alright. Chloe Flores…Herbert's going to go berserk!" Varney dug in his pocket for change and bought a copy, folding it under his arm. "We have to go somewhere and read this."

They were halfway down the block when Varney started to laugh. He couldn't help it. He was imagining the sidewalk in front of the boarding house and he saw Chloe and Herbert with pogo-sticks. Herbert was fumbling, stepping on, stepping off, and turning the contraption around in his hands while Chloe was laughing, bounding higher and higher and singing like a bird.

They were at The Last Exit when Varney first became suspicious. He and the Schubert were alone on the patio, she was sitting under the table narrating and he was writing it down on the yellow pad, and Varney had just finished a chapter when he looked up before he turned the page.

Framed in the café window, someone was looking out at him, scowling at him as if Varney was out there pulling the leaves off the tree.

Varney turned the page, looked at the window again and the person was gone. It wasn't a good look he got from them—Varney was concerned—but the Schubert had already started to talk again and he had to hurry his writing.

For the next three days they stayed in Varney's room while the Schubert told her story. They only left the boarding house occasionally, for walks in the fresh air woods of September Hill.

The room was filled with the smell of Chinese takeout delivered twice a day to their door. The little white boxes with pictures of dancing cranes nested in the wastebasket in the corner.

Varney still worried each time he stepped out of the room that he would run into Herbert in the kitchen, or on the sidewalk, or on the steps, but there was no sign of his neighbor. Varney and the Schubert were in a world of their own and the yellow pages filled up with writing.

On the morning of the fourth day, Varney held the

Schubert's completed manuscript in his hands—held it like it was some golden museum artifact—and after he placed it in the drawer of his bedside table, he announced, "Let's go out and celebrate!"

Varney decided to take her to The Showboat Theater, a white wedding cake of a barge parked on the weedy lotus blanket creaking slowly into the green lake's edge. It had seen better days and you could tell, walking on the sloping deck that it probably didn't have long until it sank. But the lucky stars were still shining on it that day.

As for the Schubert and Varney, maybe not… Feeling full of their book being done, walking the lane towards the lake, laughing, the Schubert talking away, they didn't know they were venturing right into a trap.

They passed the house with the aviary in the backyard. They both loved that place. When it was summer, you could hear those tropical birds singing from a block away. Even the everyday birds who lived around there would come to the fence and branches to sit and listen.

Of course they slowed for that, anyone would, and as they turned the corner around the tall thistle guarding the sign post, they were taken by surprise.

Someone threw a noose around the Schubert and three people grabbed Varney. It was so far from what they were feeling a moment ago, it was easy to pull them into the back of a van waiting at the curb.

Varney landed on the wheel well and the van was

thrown into gear. The Schubert was held down opposite him. He looked at his captors and recognized one of them from The Last Exit. "What do you want?"

"You're a traitor to poetry! After today, the name Varney Decker will be the new Benedict Arnold."

They all poured to the left side of the van as it took a fast corner turn.

The Schubert was next to him. She tried to tell him something with her eyes and he tried to answer her.

Varney knew the place they were taken to. It wasn't where he expected—some back road outside of town, against a barn covered with blackberries—they were in the parking lot of Jalopy Wash, next to a hedge of blue hydrangea.

"Get out!"

With his hands tied behind his back, Varney was pushed onto the asphalt, to stand there while everyone piled around. The Schubert came out next to him and was pulled over to a rhododendron and tied to its limb.

"You're not going to like this, Mr. Decker. You made yourself a powerful enemy."

"What did I do?"

Varney was shoved and fell into a rusted, blood-red wheelbarrow.

What could he say?

A switch was thrown. The wheelbarrow was moving on a track. Varney could only watch himself like a cartoon hero as all the carwash machinery started and a rainstorm formed in front. Over the roar and spray, Herbert's gang was chanting William Carlos Williams' infamous red wheelbarrow poem and the hot water was beginning to dot him, but Varney wasn't worried at all. Like a movie star, he knew he would be saved at the last second.

Imagine a little red boat digging its bow into Hokusai's woodcut painting of that big Japanese wave. The wheelbarrow filled with hot water and the tide rushed up Varney's legs then suddenly all the blasting sound of the carwash was turned off. The ocean fell onto the cement floor and pooled away into runnels.

The Schubert was barking and Varney heard footsteps and he could turn a little, enough to see himself approaching.

"Hello friend," his clone said and started to untie the roped up wheelbarrow. He was still wearing the same tuxedo jacket.

"How did you know I was here?"

Varney's clone sort of chuckled.

Varney knew the laugh, but it had been a while since he used it himself.

"They've been talking about it for days. I guess it's one of their trademark vendettas. They call it The Red Wheelbarrow." The clone pulled the last rope free of Varney.

"They're gone now," the Schubert announced, trotting up to the edge of the wheelbarrow.

"I'm pretty lucky you came along," Varney told his clone. He stretched and extended his hand. "Now it's my turn to thank you."

"My pleasure," the clone shrugged. "Actually the Schubert here did all the work. Once I untied her, they took off running."

"Thanks to you too," Varney bowed to the Schubert.

"Think nothing of it. That was some celebration, Varney."

They left the red wheelbarrow where it stopped, dotted with rain and no chickens in sight. Varney, his clone and the Schubert stood there in the Jalopy Wash parking lot trying to decide what to do.

Some sparrows were splashing about in a puddle. The day was warming up.

The clone stared around the carwash, at the neighborhood scene, the leafy trees, the hovering dragonflies, the rooftops and the big flock of white clouds to the south and he said, "I feel like an astronaut who just landed here."

Varney nodded.

"I don't have much more time though."

"What do you mean?" Varney asked.

The clone gave that laugh Varney remembered. "I don't know how much Superior Genetics told you about clones. It's probably in the fine print somewhere. Clones don't have a very long life span. Those birds live longer."

The sparrows splashed in the puddle.

"Do you know how much time you have left?" Varney asked.

The clone looked at his copper dial wristwatch. "Two hours."

The Schubert moaned and Varney repeated, "Two hours…" They were both caught in that thought… Only two hours of life left seemed so strange and awful to them.

After another laugh—the clone allowed everything so easily—he said, "So there's something I'd like to do while I still have time."

It seemed like a strange thing to do with so little left of your life, Varney thought at first, but once they got there, rented the paddles, lifejackets, and set the silver canoe upon the crackling green water, it felt perfect. They got settled in the hollow shell with Varney in the bow, the Schubert behind him and the clone in the stern. The shoreline left with hardly a sound.

They weren't in a hurry. Varney dug each stroke in, brought the wooden blade out and watched the swirl of water it left indented in the lake, before he cut into the surface on the other side of the canoe. They didn't go more than a couple hundred feet offshore when the clone spoke up.

"I guess I'll bring some sort of last memory or experience imprinted with me when I leave here." Like a last photograph, the soul retains an impression. "That's what I'm guessing anyway. When I saw a postcard of this lake, I thought that's where I want to be in the ending moment."

The canoe was drifting by itself.

They were each watching something silently.

Varney had his eyes on the little silver diamonds dropping off the tip of the paddle.

The Schubert rested her chin on the gunwale.

The clone was mesmerized by the sunlight sparkling on the water ripples. "That other clone of you, the one who's living with your family, he'll be gone at the same time as me. All the others too…We all go together. Then the mold will be broken, so to speak."

"Where's he going to die?"

"You're in luck actually. Not at your house. He chose to go into the city. So you can go back home."

"Yeah, right…And back to my old job and nobody will be the wiser."

The clone laughed. "You won't have to worry about money. I finished my book. I won't get to see it published, but that's happening soon. My agent seems to think it will be pretty popular. I tell you because you'll be getting the royalties. I have nobody else and you were the one who gave me who I am." He looked at his watch, but nobody noticed. He almost whispered, "I can leave this beautiful world knowing I've lived and done some good."

The lake was so peaceful, the sky so blue, the trance Varney and the Schubert were in was only interrupted by a hushing, pouring sound in the silver hull behind them. When they turned around, the clone as they had known him was gone. A bucketful of gray sand lay in a pile where he had been.

Varney paddled the canoe back to shore. He tossed the two lifejackets and oars onto the beach. The Schubert hopped out and watched while he pulled the boat out of water. They walked quietly to the counter to return the gear.

"Where's your brother?" asked the girl.

Varney pointed at the lake. He didn't feel like saying it was his clone and his clone had turned to sand. Varney had spent ten minutes gathering the remains and scattering those ashes onto the water while they drifted. How could he explain that? He just told her, "He went off swimming."

"It's a nice day," she said. She hung up the jackets again, stacked the paddles and while she was in the shadows, Varney and the Schubert walked away.

They didn't talk all the way back on buses and trolleys, and walked silently to the boarding house. It was dark. A late summer evening was pressing a bright orange sun deep in the leaves overhead.

Varney was glad Herbert wasn't in the kitchen. He didn't feel like witnessing whatever their conversation would be. "Thanks for the carwash," was all Varney wanted to say anyway. He opened the door to his room and really all he wanted to do was lie down on the bed and sleep for a week, but the Schubert broke their miles of silence.

Standing there on the olive colored carpet, she

said, "Varney, the time has come. We've written our book, your clones are gone, it's time to move on."

"You mean leave here?"

"Pack up what you can carry and let's get out of this steamer trunk." She waved a dramatic paw at the cramped room.

"And go where?"

"Back to your family of course."

"Oh—I'm not so sure…"

"Varney, listen to me. The whole strange dream is over. We've written a fine book together. I'm quite sure it will be as successful as your clone's. You're ready. And furthermore, I'm certainly not spending another night here!"

What life he wanted to take with him, he fit into two cardboard boxes that he could carry. The rest of it, clothes, some books, whatever things that didn't matter anymore, he brought out to the alley and threw in the dumpster. When the room was emptied of all but the furniture and the Japanese birds flying on the wall, he stepped out of there and shut the door.

It was easy to leave, even with the boxes in his arms. He felt he had joined those cranes at last. Mt. Fuji, hello!

By now it was nighttime. Varney was on the city sidewalk, just a man carrying two cardboard boxes, with a dog walking beside him. Someone could have taken pity on such a sight. Before he reached the next corner, someone did.

Was it just good fortune, or was the Schubert magically spinning that big green car their way?

Whoever or whatever forces were at work, a finer miracle couldn't have appeared.

It was a 1959 Cadillac. The lights of the city shined in its chrome and the door was painted with gold letters, Count Misfit.

The Count himself, dressed in his television uniform, leaned across the wide seat and opened the passenger door. "You look like you need a ride," the late-night voice of B-movies called.

Varney laughed. In that fantastic moment of seeing this, he had recaptured from his clone that old face he owned. "Yeah, sure!"

The front seat was wide enough for Varney and his boxes, and the Schubert had room to curl beside his feet.

"What's the story?" Count Misfit asked. He eased the big green bow of the car back into traffic. The street bent around them, picking up speed. It was like driving through phosphorescence.

Varney told him the story from the beginning. The Count circled the blocks, crisscrossed the sturdy piers of the aqueduct, and drove beneath the gondola pylons, all around the park, like a bat hunting above the neighborhoods.

"Well…" Count Misfit said at last, "That sounds like one of my midnight movies brought to life." He nodded, "You know, I've got a contact in the movies. If you could turn that into a script, I could send it off to her."

The Schubert gave a laugh. "We've already written a manuscript."

The Count nodded heavily, "Alright. That's great." They were paused at a red traffic light.

"It's in uh, one of these two boxes," Varney said. "I'll dig it out when I get home." He sighed nervously. "I don't know what that's going to be like…It's getting late, I guess."

"No," the Count started them moving again, "The night is long. See that?" He pointed at a neon sign, blue and green with a red rose glowing in the middle. "The Quartet Flower Shop. I know the ladies there. We have to get you prepared before you go home."

The Schubert's eyes twinkled in the passing streetlight sodium arc.

After the flower shop, with a mixed bouquet cargo in the back seat of the Count's car, they stopped on Holly. The department store was still open. That was the Schubert's idea. "Even I'm getting tired of seeing you in those same clothes," she told Varney.

Varney left them waiting in the Cadillac. He saw himself reflected on the big pane of glass in the storefront and, it was true—he looked like a worn-out clone of himself. The electric door opened and he went inside, following the manikin's pointed arm to the corner where all the suits were hung. He had music to stroll to, a familiar tune by Cornelius Barter that had been turned into muzak. Like a beehive in the rain, wet violins wrapped around it.

Varney didn't want to spend too long searching the hangers. Besides, he had a pretty clear picture of how his clone had dressed. He found a suit in a charcoal blue, grabbed a white shirt, a thin black tie, and hurried on to the shoes. He got a good pair. They looked like two ravens.

He paid for everything, and was transformed in the bright yellow lights on the sidewalk outside. The Schubert put her head out the open car window to stare at him.

Count Misfit drove them to Del Vista Drive, parked under wide chestnut limbs, let the engine idle and the music play. It was quite dark as he turned the spread of headlights off and The Spaniels sang on the radio.

"Is that the house, over there?" the Count asked.

Varney nodded, sighed, "Yesss…" He sat and watched it. All three of them did.

The windows were golden. It looked like a steamship anchored on the lawn.

"They're waiting for you," the Schubert told him at last.

"Okay," Varney said. He put out his hand. "Thanks, Count." They shook hands. "You came along at just the right time. I guess I better do this." He reached over the Schubert and opened the passenger door.

She hopped out and waited for him.

Grabbing his cardboard boxes, Varney got out and stood there in the neighborhood atmosphere.

"Stop by the station sometime," Count Misfit said. "Tell me how things are."

"I will. Thanks again." Varney shut the wide door, muffling the song.

With all the ease of a shadow lifting from the ground, the Cadillac poured away, red taillight coals dwindled, and it turned on Del Vista curving good-bye.

"I'm glad it's ending this way, Varney," came the voice from the soft grass. "It's been an adventure I'll never forget."

"You're bowing out too?"

"Now Varney, you know as well as I do, it's in my nature. My Schubert will stay, my Schubert goes away." She took a couple steps. He heard her nails click on the pavement. "You can't go on holding those boxes forever, Varney. Someone will think you're a statue. Goodbye."

He couldn't even put the boxes down to give her a hug.

The chestnut tree moved with the wind.

So there he was, alone but not alone, all he had to do was go to the house and in.

CONVENIENCE

I saw in their eyes something I was to see over and over in every part of the nation—a burning desire to go, to move, to get under way, anyplace, away from any Here. They spoke quietly of how they wanted to go someday, to move about, free and unanchored, not toward something but away from something.

—John Steinbeck, *Travels with Charley*

Chapter 1

Art Barker watched down the rust spotted, dented hood, aiming for a little fuzzy light in the distance. There were stars all around him, but by now he knew the way, even without the navigation on. His radio was half-static, half-Bing Crosby, and he absent mind-edly gave the dial a tiny turn. The sound didn't come in any better, but it was okay, he was lucky to get any music in these wide open spaces.

Before the song was over he could see the yellow light getting clearer. He braked. There was a neon sign spelling Convenience above the little square of tar where it was always nighttime. He glanced at the red numbers on the dashboard digital clock, not because he had to be there on time, it was a force of habit: he was the boss of Convenience.

He swung the Corolla around behind the store and parked it next to the big black garbage bin. The wall had been half painted with a rising jolly-faced sun. One of his employees had started that. Art wished he could remember the boy's name. He hated when that happened. While the engine cooled, he stared at the big smile. The rest of the wall was not unlike his Co-rolla; rusted metal, bolted together. Art could picture the tall lanky boy painting away. He really liked that kid; he was a laugh to have around and Art wasn't really surprised when he said he was giving his two weeks to go join the circus. Art was happy for him. He smiled just thinking about it. If anyone could still run off and join the circus it was him.

Art reached across the seat and got his lunchbox, unlatched the door and slid out, giving it a kick to close it. The Corolla clanged and hissed. Off in the distance, in front of the store, he could see the steady dotted lights of traffic zipping past. Every once in a while one of them would careen off the path, to come buy cigarettes or gas, candy, beer, or some Pop-Awake for the long distance driving. Convenience was in a good place for catching traffic, but business had been better before Ray's Culver City opened.

Art turned the corner, passing the windows displaying posters and advertisements, when he suddenly yelped, "Cal!" That was the boy's name, Cal, the sun painter who left for the circus never to be seen again.

Art was glad he remembered that. What a relief. With a smile, he approached the front door. The memory of Cal's name almost made the teenager appear here again; Art could see him on the roof, up in the antennas, rigging a trapeze with the stars overhead.

Chapter 2

The store was well lit with bright colors, four double sided fully stocked shelves that ran to the back wall, and a glass fronted cooler filled with shiny beverages and packaged meals-to-go. As Art entered, he passed the postcard stand and caught sight of Viranda standing behind the counter, dusting the television. She turned at the sound of the door chimes.

"Hi Viranda!"

"Hello!"

She kept things nice. She was a good find, but she had graduated high school, summer vacation was almost over and she would be moving on. He noticed she left her book *Travels with Charley* like a little tent open facedown beside the cash register.

"Art, it looks like the road sign isn't working again." She pointed at the TV screen above, and sure enough it showed a view of deep space.

"Oh drat!" he said. "Well…I guess I better go fix that…"

She sat back down on the stool in front of her book. She smiled, "I'll watch for you." She pointed at the televised stars.

"Okay…" Art was out the door again. Every week, someone was turning the Convenience sign around. That's why he attached a camera to it, so he would know when it happened. He had his suspicions, he had an idea it was someone at Ray's Culver City, maybe one of their greeters, or maybe even Ray himself. It wasn't hard to imagine Ray Culver braking his silver and white Cadillac Primo X-Press beside the Convenience sign and giving it a good spin around. Then guffawing, hopping back into his car and shooting away. Art hadn't caught the culprit on film yet. It was like fishing. It would happen sooner or later. Whoever they were, they were stealthy.

Chapter 3

Art let the Corolla's rocket engine idle while he fiddled with the seatbelt. The dashboard trembled, an odd harp-like plucking came from somewhere. It was about time to get a new car, but he hadn't won the lottery yet. Actually, after doing the taxes this year, he had just barely come out ahead. $61. Not a lot he could do with that.

He flicked a couple switches then levered the car into reverse. The view of Convenience backed away. It was weird to see all the years of his working life just a floating gas station in space, but that's what it was. A little satellite, a store sitting on the middle of a round parking lot tarmac like a teacup on a saucer.

With a clunk, Art pushed the lever into forward gear and accelerated towards the thin ray of shimmering light that was the highway. He would be merging into it soon.

On the radio, the orchestra faded and the announcer asked, "Ladies and gentlemen, how will The Shadow defeat his enemy this time? In a few moments we will continue this exciting story, but meanwhile motorists, remember this—the next road you travel on may be perfectly safe when dry, but deadly enemies when wet! Don't take chances motorists, especially when you can now get a tire that will stop you quicker, safer, on a wet pavement than you've ever stopped before."

Art couldn't help laughing. It had been years since cars had tires. But he loved being so far from Earth that the radio waves were only now washing over this part of space. Wherever he went, he tuned in a radio to pick up the signals of that far-off America. It was a hobby of sorts. Back at Convenience, Art had installed an antenna on the roof to catch the music and programming drifting by. He would spend his evenings listening, sifting through, and though he never told anyone, he was collecting all his favorite moments, the comedies and beautiful songs.

Chapter 4

Art ran a line around the cleat, tying the Corolla to the ten foot ball of green turf sprouting with wild flowers and the tall Convenience neon sign. NEXT LEFT blinked in red.

The rocket engine gave a cough. Art's car dragged the sign clockwise so it faced the zipping traffic. He waved at the camera mounted on the top of the letters. If Viranda was watching the TV she would see him. He untied his car. The sign looked great, but he knew he'd be back sooner or later to turn it around again.

A month ago he planted seed packets all around the globe. He sat admiring the flowers for a bit. There were daisies, dandelions, buttercups, little blue and purple ones he didn't know. Only a hundred feet away ran a steady stream of rocket cars and transports.

Chapter 5

When Art returned to Convenience, there was a van parked in front. He knew who it was: Art expected Steve Vines twice a month, bringing samples of the latest fads from along his route. Whenever Steve showed up, Art was sure to be talked into buying something absurd. Funny thing is, sometimes they sold. Those Martian rocks that flew when you hummed to them sold out in a week. Other times, they were just ridiculous, or worse, merchandise that Art's store couldn't sell no matter how hard they tried. Once he had to drag two boxes full of Achilles Feathers into his car and dump them in an asteroid field. He didn't feel good about that but he couldn't give them away. Then of course there was the postcard stand that stood right next to the door. That had been a Steve Vines deal. It was stacked with pictures of Florida: its beaches, the Everglades, Disney World rides, Tomorrowland, Cape Canaveral, alligators, mermaids and pelicans. All the icons, all beautiful postcards, and it seemed like a great idea at the time to put that postcard stand by the door, but after what happened to Florida…it was too sad a reminder.

So, as Art parked for the second time today, he wondered what was waiting for him behind that half finished painting of the sun.

"Alright," Art said as he pushed the door open. "Where is he? Where's the salesman?" Actually, he was a little surprised. He expected to see Steve standing there at the counter with a lemonade on the house, regaling Viranda with some far-fetched story.

"He went out to the van. Look what he gave me!" Viranda lifted the necklace off her blue smock. It looked like a string of living butterflies.

"Hey, that's nice! I bet we could sell those."

"Sorry, Art. He only had one." She let it rest back on her. The wings were fanning all around her.

Then the screen door batted open and Steve arrived. "Mr. Barker!" he announced. He carried two stacked big flat boxes. The rattling sound of glass came from them as he entered and set them on the counter. Steve wore a blinding yellow suit. He quickly extended an arm to shake Art's hand. "How're things?"

"Everything's fine."

"Still holding onto those Florida postcards? Smart man. Those are collector's items now." He grinned and placed a hand on the top box. "Have I got a treat for you guys! Are you ready for this?"

Viranda looked excited. Art tried to appear nonplussed, with his hand resting on a shelf, tapping a bag of canary seed.

"Let's have us a look-see…" Steve said. He turned to open his boxes and Art read the lettering inside the sun-shaped logo on the back of Steve's bright yellow jacket: Official Sunlite Salesman.

With a tug, Steve unfolded the cardboard corner.

Viranda gave a yelp and covered her eyes. Art was shielded by Steve's back, but the whole room had turned white.

"Aahhh!" Steve cursed as he fumbled to close the box. "I forgot! I forgot! My fault! I thought I had that box on the bottom." He rubbed his eyes.

The room was filled with bubbles, or so it seemed to Art, but at least he could still see. Viranda had the heels of her palms pressed against her eyes. "Oh my God!" she mewed, "I can't see!"

"Don't worry my dear," said Steve. He reached a hand towards her, knocking down the pencil holder. "It's just temporary, this happens all the time. Well, no, that's not true, we were supposed to be wearing sunglasses for this. I forgot to hand them out. Mine are still in my pocket. Don't worry though, we'll be able to see just fine in a couple minutes."

"What the heck do you have in that box, Steve?"

"They're harmless really. This shouldn't have happened, it's quite incredible." His hands flapped across the counter, thumping like fish against the boxes. "I brought you two dozen. I forgot how bright that many are!"

"What are they?"

"Oh, they're all the rage right now. You wouldn't believe what I could get for them on the open market. Everybody's gotta have one! They're miniature suns! I know a guy who collects them for a firm out of Bristol. One of these is all you need for lighting." He forced a laugh, "But two dozen is a bit much, wouldn't you say?"

"I still can't see…" Viranda whimpered.

Steve tapped his watch as if he could read the dial. "Don't worry, five more minutes."

Chapter 7

A half hour later, Viranda and Steve were still sitting in folding chairs in front of the counter, still unable to see. You wouldn't have known it though, Steve was happily building some longwinded account of his travels and Viranda seemed content listening. Art had been out twice to sell gas. He figured he was pretty much running the show. In fact, the way things were going, it wasn't hard to imagine leading Steve Vines out to his van at the end of the day and saying good-night. Viranda was luckier, one of her parents would always pick her up from work.

Finally Art had to interrupt Steve's monologue. "Do you think we might want a doctor's opinion on the eye situation?"

"What? No! We just happened to receive a larger dose than ordinary. It won't be long now." He touched his closed eyelids. "I'm starting to get something. A little texture…some gray plaid."

"Well, I'm a little concerned. Viranda, do you want to call your parents?"

"Oh come on," puffed Steve. "We don't want to alarm them. Honestly, she'll be fine. Listen, I brought something that will cheer you guys up." He got up and stood there for a listless second. "Art, I wonder, could you get it from the van for me? My sight isn't one hundred percent yet."

Art shook his head. "What is it this time? A carnivorous necktie?"

"No, no. You made a joke! I like that, Art. A little comedy relief. Actually, there's a gift in my van, I'm presenting it to your establishment as a token of my respect and a humble apology for this temporary un-anticipated error on my part." He reached into his yel-low suit pocket and took out his keys. "Would you do me the favor, Art? It's a smallish wooden box…" he motioned his hands in a square shape, "Behind the seat. The box says Burton on it."

Chapter 8

Art carried the wooden box at arm's length as if it was Pandora's curse. It was a little bigger than a shoebox, but heavy. There was a copper latch on it keeping it closed. "Are you sure we don't need sunglasses or any other kind of protection before we open this?" Art asked.

Steve Vines made a sour face and touched his heart, as if wounded there. "Arthur…This is a one of a kind wonder." His eyes circled the room like rolling marbles. "The market value of this object is immeasurable."

"Burton…" Art said, reading the crude lettering written with cramped pen strokes on top of the box.

"Open it!" Viranda said. "You'll have to tell me what it is though."

"Alright…If you say so…" Art flicked the latch so the hinged cover of the box could be opened. But he hesitated—he didn't entirely trust the look on the blind salesman's face. He thought he could take a quick look, a glimpse. If it was dangerous, or a swarm of bees, he could slam it shut. Art was ready, but he was saved by the bell ringing behind the counter. A car had run over the air hose in the lot, someone had pulled up to the gas pump.

Chapter 9

It was a white station wagon replica, a 1967 Pontiac Tempest. There were a couple fishing poles visible in the back.

Art didn't like to admit it, but he knew a lot about cars. He stocked a whole row of the magazine shelf with *Space Rocket, Chariot, Light Speeding, Racing Monsters* and others. The Pontiac Tempest wasn't in those magazines, but he knew it, it was a popular model for families. Sure enough, there was a seven year old boy in the backseat. He held a toy alligator up to the window. In the front seat was his father. He had a brown Labrador retriever's head. "Could we get a half tank please," he asked Art.

"You got it. Nice car."

"Yeah," the dog-man chuckled. "You see a lot of these?"

"Fair number." Art took the cap off the fuel tank.

"We're going fishing. They released some brook trout over on Thompson Street creek."

Art nodded. "I heard about that." He popped the cap back on. "Hey, you guys want a couple lemonades? On the house?"

"Oh yeah! That'd be great!"

Art smiled. "Hold on a minute." He left their car and walked across the lot, up the wooden steps and opened the screen door.

Viranda and Steve were waiting for him.

"I'm starting to see a little now," she said.

"That's great! Miraculous!" Art stopped near her,

"How many hands am I holding up?"

"I can't see *that* good yet!" she admitted.

Art grabbed a couple lemonades out of the ice barrel.

"Did you open the box yet?" she asked.

"No. It's on the counter behind you. I'll be right back and open it."

"Good man," said Steve.

Art went back outside. The boy was watching him. Art could hear the boy's father telling him, "This is our lucky day!"

Chapter 10

"Okay, here we go." In one fast and unstoppable move, Art reached across the counter and opened the box. The thing inside was already talking.

"Entrepreneurship is an interesting subject for me. I wouldn't claim to be an expert on it, but on the other hand I was a practitioner of it."

"What is that thing?!" Art cried.

Burton went right on talking, "I thought I'd give you a brief background, and really what I want to do is provide a baseline engaging in startup organization. The entrepreneurial process is for people who are willing to explore. It involves risk dealing with ambiguity. It's about using skills creatively and organization, to really be able to help society by taking an idea and turning it into an innovation—not only an idea but a sustainable one. The sustainability of entrepreneurship is taking this innovation and saying this will be a long term innovation to benefit society."

While it continued to yammer, Steve Vines interrupted, speaking over it, "I got Burton from a man in the circus. Actually, I paid for him. Modesty prevents me from revealing the price. As you can tell, Burton is a perfectly preserved head. He's quite alive, although the definition of life may be in question. He'll go right on talking like that all day if you let him."

They listened. They couldn't help it.

"Even though the thinking of entrepreneurship tends to be very fast, when I talk about creating value, it can be economic or social. It's economic in nature, tangentially related to the economic realm, people are buying or engaging their services."

"This is a terrible, sickening present," Art said.

"Entrepreneurship is not necessarily about generating a branding concept. For example, the automobile, or what you may call the horseless carriage, had its beginnings—"

Viranda laughed. "I like Burton!"

"An entrepreneur who is successful creates value for society by exploiting that difference, being able to exploit that value to one's benefit."

Steve grinned, "Thank you, my dear. With your permission, Mr. Barker, deed of ownership has been transferred to your charming employee."

"Certainly I would argue that it's really about seeing things in a new way, okay, seeing a different pattern, taking what you already know and looking at it a different way. Everyone has that ability. It's true some people were born to be entrepreneurs, but everyone can think of something in their own life. Now whether that relates to—"

Art put his hands over his ears. "It's completely awful! I've had enough!"

Burton continued, "So what sort of people work as entrepreneurs? I would say all types! It's a 24-7, 365 type of thing. You can't do an 8-5 punch the clock, you have to pursue it all the time," rambling on until the top of his box was shut and latched.

Suddenly, it was so quiet you could hear the hum of the cooler in the back of the store.

Art shook his head ruefully. He admitted, "I'm tempted to run this thing out to the asteroid field."

"No!" Viranda held up her hands. "Come on, Burton's mine now."

"Well, I never want to see it again. I want it out of here. You can bring it home and see how long it lasts there."

Viranda held the box protectively close to her and laughed.

Chapter 11

"It's inherently ambiguous, I don't pretend to understand turning ideas into innovation, but you need to ask yourself, does it hang together as a story? Is it sellable? Can it be moved into a sustainable environment? Is there value in it? Does it generate the benefits that outweigh the costs? Whether that value is recognized, will people value it enough to accept that proposition?"

Art screamed, "Viranda!"

She was laughing. Her father was laughing too.

"Will their investment be valued for the long term and will the marketplace accept it? Operationalizing that benefit into an organizational structure, what I want to point out, is that except for the funding, there's really no difference. You are engaged in the functional equivalent, the process of cross-functional, carving out time and creating a structure that allows for—"

It took her that long to shut the box and Art was about to throw a lemonade at it.

"Sorry, sorry…" she was still laughing as she finally got the Burton box latched. She held onto her father's arm. Even though she promised Art that she could see again, she kept a hand tied to her father and walked with him step by step towards the door. "I'll see you tomorrow," she called.

"I hope you're seeing sooner than that." Art watched Viranda's father open the door for her. "And don't bring that Burton-thing back tomorrow!"

Chapter 12

Well, he could only hire help until suppertime, then he was alone. It was quiet. Art gave it another hour. That was enough for a day.

Behind the counter, he reached up in the air and turned off the TV that clicked off the lights on the highway sign. There was no reason to be open when it was this late. Anyone around should be flying home for the night, wouldn't you think?

Art cleared the cash register, pressing the key that started churning out a paper trail of all the sales for the day. While it poured out its scroll, he removed all the money and stuffed it into a white burlap bag. He waited for the receipt to unroll, then tore it off and put it into the emptied cash drawer. He carried the bag to the back of the store. He knew his way in the dark. He opened the door to the cooler and went into the cold.

Over in the corner was where he put the bundled bag of coins, bills and checks. He covered it with an upside down cardboard box of Moxie. Who would guess that's where he put a day in the life of Convenience?

It was freezing. He didn't want to stay in the cooler a moment longer.

Back in the dark storeroom, he went behind the counter to get a glowing jar off the shelf.

Chapter 13

The jar was filled with fireflies. Their light mumbled around the smooth glass beneath his hands.

Art held the jar with his arm while he opened the front door, stepped out and locked the store behind him. The square CLOSED sign rocked in the window.

Unscrewing the jar lid, he held the glass up to the stars. One by one, the fireflies tracked out. They would flit about the parking lot of Convenience, and by the time morning shift started, they'd be back in their jar to roost for the day.

Art set the jar down on the cement curb. It was easy to lose sight of the fireflies amid all the whirls and glitter of outer space, but he liked knowing they were there. It was an old fashioned touch of Earth.

On his way to his car, he knocked on the parked van and said, "Goodnight, Steve."

A muffled voice replied, "Goodnight."

Chapter 14

Art caught sight of his home and yawned. The fifty foot replica of the Eiffel Tower blinked a red light from atop it as he slowed the engine of his Corolla and guided the car toward the opening garage door.

He had a nice crop of dandelions going. Every time he returned from work, more of them had popped up all over the sphere he lived in. He had tried other things, vegetables, berries and a tree, but nothing did as well as dandelions.

The car glided into the garage and the door folded down behind, shutting out space. He listened to Dorothy Lamour finish her song before he switched off the radio and clambered out of the rocket.

A single lightbulb hanging from the ceiling illuminated the sparse room. There wasn't much to see, the gray walls were left unpainted. It was only a landing bay for rocket storage.

Art's footsteps echoed him over to the orange painted door. As he opened it, the projector was activated and the room he stepped into was instantly transformed. It went from a bare, round chamber, with pipes on the wall, a wardrobe, and a hammock slung in the middle, to a beautiful vision of the world he left behind. The hallucination was complete, down to the smell of ocean and the feel of walking on sand. He was on a moonlit beach. His hammock was pitched between two palm trees.

Art kept his house programmed to Fiji, 1372 A.D. He didn't think he would ever tire of this setting. He gave a deep thankful sigh as he approached his hammock.

Chapter 16

Thousands of miles from their planet, suspended out in space like mobiles, there were other little houses like Art's, and cities and farms, all connected by aqueducts and roads. Then there were the things that appeared alongside the roads, like gas stations, casinos, circuses and stores. Almost everyone had been deported off Earth while repairs were undertaken on the abused planet. It had not been easy to leave, but it was obvious it had to be done. Earth had to heal. Art was a boy when he left, though he still had a memory of looking out the oval back window of their rocket Beetle, watching home fall away. When they arrived, his father started Convenience on an empty stretch of highway. Meanwhile, they adapted to projectors and rocket ships, until they began to feel they would never see their natural planet again. Spread out in a flotsam of tiny dots in space, they waited to go home.

Chapter 17

Art woke up in the same place, to warm morning sunshine and the rhythm of the surf not thirty feet away. He lay there in the hammock sway, not quite ready to get up, just watching. The blue sea sparkled with the new sun, and the yellow line of sand ran along the shore towards the far corner of the island.

Then he did get up, in such a hurry that he nearly fell standing up. Way down the beach there was some white thing moving. Art walked quickly towards it, even though he was only barely out of dreams. What had the projector conjured up for him? He didn't think Fiji was inhabited during this era. He wanted to be alone. The projector dial had been set on Fiji for weeks and he had never seen anything but birds and sea life. It was predictable, repetitive, it was programmed that way, as serene as a Mozart record.

Now he knew what it was, but he couldn't believe it. His bare feet stopped in the sand and he stared. The creature had noticed him too. Art could see its black nose pointed and its black eyes watching him back. It was a polar bear.

All around him was a tropical island—what had happened to his Mozart chamber music? Someone with a lobster claw had hit the chords of a Gibson Les Paul.

The polar bear seemed just as interested in Art; its long nose was smelling the air. Then it began to move in Art's direction.

Even though this all took place in a room no

larger than thirty feet domed around, Art found himself petrified with fear, especially as the polar bear picked up speed and was running. There was always the potential for danger when you were in projection. Art had heard about people who never left their program alive, apparently dying while in there. That was rare of course. More common was a simple spectral error where the projection was incomplete, allowing a window of your real room to show through. A cement square in the middle of a fantasy. That was annoying and had to be repaired. Everyone relied on their projection, otherwise where was there to be? A hollow shell of concrete floating in outer space.

There didn't seem to be anything imaginary about this polar bear, kicking up clouds of sand on the run. It was almost upon him.

At last, Art gave a yell and turned around, bolting as fast as he could. He passed his hammock and dived for the nearest palm tree. Attached to it was a silver box with a red button marked STOP.

Chapter 18

Art was listening to another music that was not riding on radio waves a hundred years old. He held the phone a few inches away from his ear, far enough to hear when the screeching would stop and he would be taken off hold. It was some current pop hit, sung with the fad-affected phrasing of an atropaceous polypod.

Viranda's book was on the counter next to him. She was outside fueling a car.

Art pulled the book over and stared at the cover. *Travels with Charley.* A man and a dog and one of those little wheeled trailer trucks they used to drive. There was a yarn strand sticking out. That was her bookmark. She was about halfway through the book. He meant to ask her what she thought of it. The top edge of the pages was stamped with Alameda Public Library. He wondered how old the book was.

The door opened and a bicycle wheel entered.

D announced himself as he rode into the store, stopping next to the postcard stand. "You won't believe what I have…"

"Hi D," said Art.

The old man got off the yellow Schwinn 10-speed bicycle. He held up a bony finger that looked like it was made of newspaper.

"I'm on the telephone, D."

"That's okay. Give me a minute, where'd I put that?" He looked through the boxes and packets attached to his bicycle.

The door opened again. This time it was Viranda, returning. "Hi D."

Art asked her, "How long have I been on hold, Viranda?"

"You're still on hold?"

"Yeah…" Art could hear the terrible racket in his phone fading like a tractor tearing up a vinyl field, then becoming another so-called song.

"Wow!" Viranda said as she came around the counter and sat on her stool. She picked up her book. "You should send them a telegram instead. What's D looking for?"

"Something he has to show me. Hey, what's the story with that book of yours?"

Viranda smiled, "Oh, you know. I like to go to that antique store, Trident Import. Last week I found this big wooden apple crate. I thought my dad would like it. Then I looked inside and it was full of library books, all the same title, *Travels with Charley*. Each copy is from a different library. One of them is from Paris!"

"Holy Mackerel," Art said.

She turned the book around and opened it and pulled a card from a slot on the inside cover. "See, they would stamp this card to tell you when the book was due." She pointed her blue painted fingernail at the little stamp marks, "June 8, 1953…May 3, 1957… Oct 31, 1957…July 13, 1958…Dec 9, 1960."

"Here it is!" D said. "It was in here…" From the depths of his zippered backpack he removed a black bowling bag. Like a cartoon stork, he relayed it to the counter and set it down with a clunk. His hands were trembling, hovering over it.

Chapter 19

With a shaking hand, D reached into the bowling bag and pulled out a tin can, silver with grooves around it, then he reached back in and took out a similar one. They sat beside each other on the counter.

D's mouth was open slightly, revealing a grin of yellowed jagged teeth.

The can on the right jiggled, clanking lightly as it spoke, "Greetings, Earth people."

"Is this the convenience store you spoke of?" the other can rattled.

"Yes, yes," D practically cackled. He pointed at the cans and told Art and Viranda, "Lady and gentleman, allow me to introduce our two alien visitors." Behind his thick lens glasses, frames patched with white tape, D's eyes seemed to bounce like dice.

"Uhhh," Viranda said.

"I'm Art. I'm the owner." Art started to put his hand out, as if the can-looking creatures could shake it, then he reconsidered. "Viranda works with me."

The aliens twisted a little from the top, in bowing gestures. "Your ambassador has a proposition," a tinny voice came from one of them.

Art raised his eyebrows. "Ambassador?"

"They mean me," said D. "I explained to them that I come here every day."

That part was true, Art thought. D appeared each morning to get any leftover day-old sandwiches. He would stay for a while, sometimes an hour, carrying on about the government, conspiracies, rumors, or whatever else had him knotted up, worked up to unwind. Viranda managed to more or less ignore D. Art felt two ways about him. Some days he wanted to toss him out the door on his spindly bicycle, other times, he got a weird sense of entertainment. Plus, the guy was quite old and lonely and what else could he do but ride his bicycle to the nearest outpost?

"I found these fellahs in my backyard last night," D explained.

"We are conducting studies," they clanked on the counter.

"We got to talking," D said, "and I—"

"This one seems to never *stop* talking," one of the cans clinked.

D held up a hand defensively, "Now listen boys, I'm just trying to help you."

"Did we hurt your feelings?"

"Did we make you feel bad?" the other grated.

D's head bobbed to the side. "I'm alright. I appreciate the apology."

"We did not apologize."

"Yes," D said. "Well, you could. It wouldn't hurt to be a little respectful to someone who is working on your behalf."

"Okay. We are sorry."

D nodded.

Viranda had gone back to reading her book.

Art gave up on the telephone and hung it up.

Chapter 20

A couple hours had passed. D was gone, but he left the two aliens on the countertop. They had been quiet since the old man rode away. All they wanted to do was observe an Earthling establishment. Not that there had been much action. There had been cars to refuel, some people came and were gone, after buying the sorts of things Convenience sold. Art sent a telegram. Viranda read her book. Time passed.

Around 3:30, a robot staggered in the door. It panned the room with its scanner, then gave a jump. It had four legs. It looked like a wooden chair, one that had been knocked around, and after a long life of weathered, battering servitude it had found its way out the door of a secondhand store, through four years of Robot Academy, into an illustrious career in telegram delivery. One of its legs dragged as it approached the counter where it stopped, cleared its amplifier and announced:

"You have a message from Professional Projections."

"Good," Art said. "Fire away."

"One of our representatives has been alerted to your situation."

After a long moment, the robot shuffled backwards from the counter and began to hobble away.

"Uh, thanks," Art said, adding, "When does that mean my projector will be repaired?"

It was too late for an answer though. The robot had clambered out the screen door, its message had been delivered successfully. It was getting back on its rocket sled to shoot away to the next job.

"Well...." said Art, "I guess I'll find out..."

Chapter 21

Just before closing that night, Viranda's father parked their Lincoln in the lot and came inside to fetch his daughter. As she gathered up her jacket and book, he waved a couple squares of paper at Art and said, "I've got a present for you."

"Oh really?" Art was draining the last of the black syrup out of the coffee Sylex into the sink.

"Mote Disby came in to buy apples for the Drive-In and he gave me some free tickets for tonight's film. Would you like a couple?"

"Good old Mote Disby..." Art sighed. Mote used to stop for gas at Convenience. He even had an order for refreshments that he would pick up a couple of times a week. Mote used to give Art those passes to the Drive-In regularly. That was before Ray's Culver City was built. It had been a while since Art had seen Mote. Art thought over the offer. It didn't take him long. It was Friday, what else was he going to do? Sit at home and wait for Professional Projections to show or not show, or go to the movies? "Sure I'd like to go. I only need one though, it's just me now."

"Alright then." Viranda's father smiled. He passed Art a ticket. "Hope to see you there."

"Yeah thanks, Marvin."

Viranda waved at Art from the doorway as she and her father left. The headlights of their car illuminated the window and the rockets pulled them back across the pavement.

Art sighed, alone in the store, or so he thought.

"You haven't got a date?" one of the tin can aliens asked him.

Art jumped.

"Did we hurt your feelings?" the other can rattled.

"No," Art blurted. "I'm fine." Truth is, since his wife had turned into a moth and flown off, he was turning into a lonely human being. If he wasn't at the store, he was submerged in his 1940s radio broadcasts, or else drifting in projection.

"Why don't you invite us to the Drive-In picture show?"

"Yes," agreed the other alien.

Art gave a slow blink. "Oh, alright…You can come."

Chapter 22

It was pretty amazing to be out in space listening on a radio wave to that America long ago, still alive. The only time he turned the dial down was when the news came on. Art knew enough about history to see where they were heading. There was no way for him to reach back, tap on Jack Benny's shoulder and warn him.

"Okay," he said, during that lull in music, "Why don't you tell me your names. We never did get properly introduced."

The cans were standing in front of him on the dashboard. The one on the left responded quickly, "Rick."

"No," the one on the right rattled, "*My* name is Rick!"

"Correction. *I* am Rick. I said it first."

They were both clanking furiously, as if the car was driving off-road.

"Hey!" Art took a hand from the wheel to separate them. "Take it easy. Why don't I call you Rick 1 and Rick 2?"

"No!" they chanted.

"It was my idea!"

"Incorrect! It was mine!"

Art tried again, "Okay, okay, let's see…How about Rick 1 and Rick A? One begins numerically and one is alphabetical."

If they had the ability to glower at him, the two shiny cans were doing that now.

"That is ridiculous."

"Utter foolishness. My name is Rick."

They were back at it again, clanking viciously on the dashboard.

Art put his hand on one to separate them and gave a yelp. The alien was red hot. Art could have poured water in it and brewed tea. "Listen…I don't mind if you're both Rick." Anyway, close as he was to them, he couldn't see any difference between them, why not let them both be Rick? "Rick…" he said, pointing fingertips at one, "and Rick."

While they stood on the dashboard glowering, Art turned the radio back up and thankfully Frank Sinatra was there, crooning love to the moon.

Chapter 23

Art was hoping to find a Professional Projections repair truck parked at his home, but no such luck. The Corolla glided into the garage and stopped beneath the lightbulb. With the aliens tucked under his arm, Art paused at the orange door to make sure the projector on the other side was still deactivated. He didn't want to open the door only to be mauled by an arctic predator that shouldn't exist.

Even with the switch clicked off, he only pushed the door an inch, ready to shut it fast.

"I had a little trouble last time I was here, Rick. My projector gave me quite a scare. It looks okay now…" Art shoved the door with his foot. There was no sign of a polar bear. Still, he entered the room on edge, tensed to run.

"Nice place, Art."

"Picturesque."

He was sure they were mocking him, but their flat voices were always pitched at the same grating tone. "Well, it's a lot better with the projector on. Here, let me set you down, I'm going to check my phone messages." He put them on the table that folded out from the wall and picked up the phone receiver. "Nothing…" he said. "No messages."

One of the Ricks said, "Awwww," with all the sympathy of a cartoon villain.

"Nobody called you," Rick's shadow responded.

As Art's arm came down with the phone, the Ricks chimed, "Uh-oh." The phone hovered near them like a hammer. "I think we hurt his feelings," Rick squeaked.

Art wasn't listening though. He wasn't even looking at them. His attention was on the cement colored room that circled all around them. It was like a big clam had swallowed a hammock, a wardrobe and them. Without projection the place was a prison cell.

Chapter 24

Nothing was too far away. The Big Screen Drive-In could be seen from miles, a blue drop in the stars that soon filled the Corolla windshield. He slowed and joined the line of cars waiting to go inside.

The red car in front of him rocked back and forth

with teenagers. The line crept towards the ticket booth that was moored next to the airlock gateway, crowned with a twirling halo of searchlights. Blue neon letters BIG SCREEN danced across the tall white painted wall with the clear dome overhead reflecting suns and planets.

Art read the Now Playing sign: *Jackson Ferocious* and *Better Than Earth*; it was a double feature. He searched his pocket for his ticket and found it. The way he left the house—nervous about his projector repair, sticking a note on the door, taking along the two can aliens who by now were really getting on his nerves—what nerve he had left was frazzled.

The teenagers' car roared through the gate ahead of him as Art paused by the ticket booth. Behind the glass window, the robot spun its Clark Gable head around and a blonde Marilyn Monroe faced him.

For a moment she stood there wearing a three-piece suit, then that turned around and the robot wore a sparkling red dress. She spoke into the microphone, "One ticket, sir?"

"I already have a ticket," Art said. "It's a gift from Mote."

"Lucky you," she smiled. It was hard to believe that lurking on her other side was Clark Gable.

Art handed her the ticket. "You get dizzy from all that spinning around?" he asked. You would think that even a robot would tire of that all night long.

She shrugged and gave him another smile. "That's showbiz." She tore the ticket. "Enjoy your evening."

"We will," the Ricks buzzed at her.

The Big Screen Drive-In had been meticulously recreated from plans of the old outdoor theaters popular in the 1950s and 1960s. Art drove with the windows open, letting in all the sounds of car radios and laughing, kids running for the playground in front of the stage. The whole gigantic grassy field of the place was like a farm sprouting parked cars in shiny rows, all pointing like flowers towards the movie screen glow.

An usher with a lantern waved Art's Corolla down a weedy aisle. The car bounced over a pothole. The little aliens on the dashboard squealed and tipped. "Sorry…" Art muttered.

Down the row, a teenage girl with a lantern rocked the orange light towards an open spot.

Art avoided a patch of daisies, hit another bump, and turned the steering wheel into their spot beside a metal pole. "Here we are," he said and shut off the motor.

The Ricks scooted closer to the windshield, almost touching the glass, while Art reached outside and grabbed the speaker. It was connected to the post by a thick black tangled wire. He hooked the speaker onto his half opened window.

When he turned the speaker on, a commercial for Ray's Culver City barked against a frenetic tempo. Art quickly spun the dial off. He was satisfied watching out the window. It was such a faithful reproduction of that dream-gone-America he really felt dropped back in time. The energy of the place had transported him to 1953, in his Chevrolet, waiting for *Robot Monster* to start. Even so, he also knew this reality wouldn't have had to exist if those people could have stopped building atom bombs, exploding them, making war and otherwise carelessly polluting their planet.

A car pulled in next to them. Art could see the family of kangaroos inside. As the sedan shuddered and turned off its motor and headlights, the doors were already opening to let out three bouncing children. Off they went. Well, Art thought, that wasn't something you'd see in 1953.

Chapter 26

The crowd in cars loved *Jackson Ferocious*. Every once in a while, a horn would go off and another in another row would agree, and Art could hear the laughter echoing around. Sometimes the Ricks clanked appreciatively too, but Art was having a hard time with it.

The film was about a TV program that would search for an unknown artist. They found a guy spending his life making little books that nobody read. All of a sudden, he went from being a shadow to a celebrity, as they bombarded him with praise and honors and fame. Then they told him it was all a joke, everything was being filmed for their television show.

It wasn't over yet when Art's telephone started to ring. He grabbed the receiver from the console and said, "Hello?"

"This Art Barker?"

"Yes."

"I'm from Professional Projections, I'm at your house now. Where you at?"

"Oh great. I'll be there soon."

"Yeah, well, how soon?"

"I'm at Big Screen, it won't take long to get back. I didn't know if you were coming or not."

"You put in an order, didn't you?"

"Yes, but I never heard back, I didn't know when you would show."

"Are you going to watch the rest of the movie?"

"No!" Art was already turning the key, starting the

motor, "I'm on my way."

Chapter 27

It had not been easy dragging the Ricks away from the film. They were furious, and all the way back home they griped at him, about his driving, the condition of his car, his navigation skills, even the clothes he chose to wear. He had to turn off the radio when they started in on Charlie McCarthy. If they were in a better mood, Art thought, they'd probably befriend Edgar Bergen's wooden ventriloquist doll—after all, they were birds of a feather. So, even though it wasn't very far, the drive was a relentless experience until Art braked at home; a dome surrounded by grass and dandelions.

A tan colored minivan was waiting for them.

Art led the way into the garage, parking as close to the wall as he could, so the van could fit in too. Much to the delight of the Ricks, the side mirror scraped and snapped off against a duct.

"Hah!" Rick guffawed.

By now Art had no idea why he didn't just heave the two of them off into the abyss. Instead, he got out of the car and left them in there.

The van was stopped right behind the Corolla. Rust spots covered its grill.

Art waited for the repairman to get out.

The guy was taking his time, that's for sure.

Behind Art, he could hear the Ricks. They sounded like hail on the Corolla windshield.

The van door opened and a boar with tusks stepped out. He was stuffed in blue overalls. The nametag said Chom Andyson. His bristly hand clutched a tool case. He glared at Art. "I get paid by the hour, just so you know."

"Okay, okay." Art led him the way to the door. "I shut the projector off." He laughed weakly. "I got a little scared."

Chom grunted.

They went into the house. Not a bit of Fiji was in sight.

"So, what'd you do?" Chom wheezed at him.

"Nothing. I had my projector on all night as I always do. When I woke up, it looked the same as ever, except way off in the distance I saw something different. A dot."

"What kind of dot?"

"A white dot."

"Hunhhh."

"So, I walked closer to investigate. I guess it would have been over in that direction. Anyway, you'll never guess what it was."

"I don't guess," Chom said.

Art nodded. "It was a polar bear!" Art paused, waiting for a reaction from Chom, who just stared at him.

"People see all kinds of things that aren't there."

"Yes, I'm sure that's true. This one was hungry though, it chased me all the way to the STOP button. I've heard stories about people dying in projection—now I know how it could happen."

Chom shook his thick head. "People die in elevators too." He puffed as he took a screwdriver from a pocket. "Where do you keep your box at? Never mind, I see it." Chom waddled over to the hammock and put a hand on the switch box mounted to the pole. He unscrewed the panel and tossed it on the hammock netting.

"Do you think you can fix it tonight?"

Chom gave him a haughty look, "I won't know til I look at it." As Chom pressed a switch, suddenly they were on a beach in Fiji. "Is this your last projection?"

"Yes."

Chom chuckled as he looked around himself. "This is it?"

"Yes…"

"So where was your *bear*?" Chom grinned at the

last word.

"I'll show you."

Art took him out of the palm tree shadows, onto the beach. The shallow ocean waves curled and splashed a few feet away. "Way down there…" he pointed.

Chom set his toolbox down on the sand and with a grunt looked through it for something. A pair of binoculars. He popped the lens caps off and peered through. His breathing was as loud as the surf. "Over there?"

"Yes. It was just a white dot, then it got bigger real quick."

"Yeah…" Chom returned the binoculars to his toolbox and walked back to the palm tree. Art followed along in the bumpy sand.

"Could you see anything?" Art asked.

Chom ignored the question and punched the button on the tree. They were back in a bare room.

"Home sweet home," Art said nervously. "I've heard stories of people getting stuck in their projection."

"Not true." Chom was attaching a transistor radio-sized device from his toolbox, plugging it into the box. It began to make a ticking sound.

Art shuffled uneasily.

Chom snorted. "Oh yeah…" he said. "I'm going to have to blow away your profile."

"What?"

Chom was pressing buttons on the device. "I have to rebuild the entire system."

"Oh nooo…"

"You really did a number on it."

"I didn't do anything! I woke up in the morning the same as ever."

Chom grinned at him, all teeth and bristle, "Maybe you got some enemies."

"No…Not that I know of…"

Chom laughed at the look on Art's face. "Well, someone or something out there sure doesn't like you."

Art stood there listening to that thought.

Chom was disassembling the box, sawing the room with his whistling breathing.

Art didn't like the idea of enemies, and someone or something, as Chom put it. Who could it be? He supposed Ray's Culver City wouldn't mind seeing the end of him and Convenience. But would Ray set him up with a killer polar bear? Art was barely getting by with the store. Was there someone else out there?

Art was winding up like the rubber band of a toy airplane until, when there was a scratch on the door and it unlatched and fell open, Art let go with a yell and jumped a foot in the air.

The two small can-sized Ricks entered the room. They tipped and clanked, moving towards him.

Chapter 28

"How did you get out of that car?"

They came clattering into the middle of the room and stopped, the lights blazing on them.

"We're not helpless," said Rick.

"Correct. We know how to open a door," the other chanted.

Chom held the projector box with its wire hanging loose like a plant ripped from the soil. He stared at the Ricks with an actual real look of amazement. "Hey, I know you guys! You make movies, right?"

"Correct."

"Guilty as charged."

It was as if Chom had been pulled into sunlight, he changed that quickly. "I saw your movie at Big Screen last night. It was awesome!" Chom had become a radio beacon of sunshine. Art barely recognized him.

"Wait!" Art stammered, "You guys—Rick—you're directors? You made that film we saw tonight?"

"The one you walked out on?"

"Killjoy!" They were buzzing like beehives.

"Oh brother…" Art mumbled. "I hope I'm not in a movie right now."

"Fat chance," Rick scoffed.

"Boring," the other concurred.

"Yeah!" Chom piped up. "What are you hanging out with him for anyway?" Then he brightened again, "You should follow me around if you're making a movie."

"Interesting offer."

"Worthy of consideration."

"Go ahead," Art told them. "Don't let me stand in the way."

Chapter 29

Before they left, Chom installed a temporary projection, one that would hold together long enough for the replacement unit. "You'll like it," Chom had promised. "It looks like your other one, like a calendar page."

The Ricks loved that, they had found a star in Chom, and they seemed excited to get out of Art's world to where the action was.

It was Friday night. All Art had lined up was a hammock.

Once they were gone, Art examined the projector box. It was made of cardboard, with a matchstick sized switch. Art flicked the switch up, towards the penciled word ON. The lighting in the room blinked, the speakers yelped with feedback, then he was standing in a pleasant green orchard.

His hammock was strung between two apple trees. The light was a pale green in the leaves. Some fireflies sent signals far off into the rows. Near him, a paper lantern gave off a sleepy candlelight.

Chom was right. It was beautiful and calm as a calendar photo.

Chapter 30

A branch over Art popped with pink and white apple blossoms, new small green May leaves and a blue sky beyond. He stretched and his body rocked the hammock. It was a perfect morning awakening in the trees. He watched a little bird hop along its branch. The hammock swung as he moved his legs over and planted his feet on the grass. Did he miss Fiji and its sand? A little, but this was nice too. Every month or so he would change the projection; it was like traveling, living all over the Earth.

He listened to the bird songs and the breeze. He thought he wouldn't mind holding onto this setting for a while, standing up, stretching, looking around. It had its own charm, and Art probably would have stood there in the projected apple orchard longer if it wasn't for the intrusion of a bell ringing. It made the whole place he was standing in a dream and not real at all.

The bell sound was coming from the outside world. He reached over to the tree trunk the hammock was tied to and he shut off the projection.

Suddenly the trees were gone.

He walked towards the doorbell. He was expecting to open the door and see those Ricks out there like a pair of shoes. Instead, he opened the door to a salesman.

A stocky fellow stood there, tan three piece suit, with a big suitcase in each hand. He set them down and tipped his hat. "Good morning, sir. I'm Steve Collins. Don't let the getup put you off. I'm on the level."

"Can I help you?"

"It's not like that," Steve said. "I want to help you. See, I have a superb supply of what you might call freshwater friendship."

"What?"

"Allow me to elucidate." Bending down, Steve flicked open latches on the suitcases to reveal thin rows of shelving built inside filled with sparkling little jars of tropical fish.

He stood back up and straightened his lime green tie, grinning at Art. "Presenting Collins' Fish Carnival!" He could tell Art was interested. Yesterday, a woman had chased him away with a moonbucket. This was going to be easy. "Also, every sale includes a free inflatable fish bowl."

While Art looked at the fish, Steve quickly blew up a packet which became a clear hollow ball.

Art said, "How much are the goldfish?"

"A mere 98 cents." Steve beamed. "It's said that they can tell your fortune too."

"That comes with the bowl?"

"It surely does."

Art was reaching in his pocket as Steve continued, "However, a goldfish is not going to live a long happy life in a fishbowl this size."

"It won't?"

"No sir. This bowl has been tested and approved only for the beta breed."

Art stared back at the rows of fish.

"They're down there in the lower right corner."

"Oh…Okay…Those are nice." Art set a finger on the glass jars. "How much for this blue one?"

"Yes, that's a fine specimen. That fish is $10."

"Ten dollars!"

"You couldn't ask for a better fish. That beta and this bowl are made for each other. I wouldn't be a bit surprised if that beautiful fish right there gave you five years of companionship and camaraderie. Why, for every penny of your original investment, you'll reap endless hours of—"

"I think I'll just go with a goldfish," Art said.

Steve sighed. He was crestfallen. You could almost see the steam hissing out of him. He handed over the inflated fishbowl but he stopped himself before he grabbed a jar from the suitcase. "I'm sorry, it's just that I feel responsible for every creature in my carnival. The thought of a goldfish in that bowl…I just know I won't be able to sleep tonight. If you could only dig a little deeper and find it in your heart to buy—"

"Look Steve. I'm a businessman too. I know this game. You're doing a great job, I'm impressed. Really. I just don't want any other fish but a goldfish. It's that simple. If you don't want to take my 98 cents from me, I can live without it. Besides, what I'm really saving up for is a duck."

"A duck!" Steve Collins crowed. "Why didn't you say so? Out in the car, I've got—"

"I'm kidding!" Art held up his hands. "It's a joke! I'm joking."

Chapter 31

At Convenience, Art left the goldfish on the counter beside the jar full of fireflies. That was the only light in the dim store. It was still early morning. He had time to do a chore. He locked the door again and walked to the back of the building.

Twice a month he emptied the garbage bags from the bin and drove them out to the dump. Personally, he kind of liked the trip, he even looked forward to it. Believe it or not, going to the dump was sort of an adventure for Art.

He was whistling as he put the bags into the trunk of his Corolla, filled it and got behind the wheel. The rocket started with the radio playing the Duke Ellington Orchestra.

Listening in to that long ago America, Art supposed he would get to hear the steady change happening on the radio as the world went from the blues to rock n roll. But that was years away on the dial. For now it was still jazz, Jack Benny, and buried away in the waves, there was the war.

Chapter 32

Art's car was stopped in line behind a pickup truck filled with blackberry vines. The big pile of them shook like a trembling beast as the truck idled, waiting at the booth. First they weighed you going in. They gave you a ticket, then after you dumped your garbage they weighed you going out. Simple arithmetic—you got charged for what you left behind—it was genius.

The blackberry hedge twitched and moved through the gate into the dump, giving Art his turn.

He stopped at the red light and rolled his window down.

A woman with long straight blue hair leaned out of the booth to pass him a plastic tab. "Household items?" she said.

"Just general garbage," said Art. "From the Convenience store."

"Alright. You can go straight ahead."

Art smiled. "Thanks." He put the weight tab on the dashboard, the same spot where the Ricks had been not so long ago. Good thing they weren't there now, he thought, they would have been terrified of this place. He passed a corral filled with dented rusting cans.

To his right, he saw the blackberry truck off on its way to a hole filled with leafy tree limbs, vines, and grass clippings. A scarecrow was waving the truck in.

Just as the lady had told him, in front of Art was a cement ledge. It was painted with yellow and black stripes. It ran along the edge of a vast field of garbage. Some seagulls kited above, others stood on piles, shrieking, or crept along out of the tractor paths.

Art slowed to let a loader grumble past, then he parked next to the bee-colored wall.

He got out into the fumes and noise and opened the car trunk.

One by one he took each bag, heaved it to the ledge, stood on the steep edge, looking down at the jumble of all their unwanted things: TVs, bedsprings, lamps and boxes and bags like his, ripped and spilling open. Each one tossed made a crash as it joined the tide below. He needed another moment to take it in.

Far off, a yellow bulldozer pushed a smoking wave.

Once the dump was full, it would be cast off to drift to some other part of space and another dump would start over again.

Chapter 33

Viranda worked on Saturdays too, but she came in later. When she did, she spotted the goldfish right away.

"Ooh! Where'd you get him?"

Art was moving things on a shelf. "This salesman showed up at my door when I was still barely awake." That was one of the problems living without that pink and blue birdsong sun coming up sky—morning could be at any time. "He tried to con me into a fish that costs ten times more, but I got that goldfish. And…" Art pointed his hand, "He threw in a free fishbowl. Not bad work, huh? That's called the art of salesmanship, Viranda." He returned to shelving, smiling.

"Yeah," she said. "That's all Burton ever talks about."

Art yelped. "You didn't bring that thing, did you? I never want to see that talking head again!"

"No."

"Or hear it!"

"Relax, Art! I left him at home in our kitchen."

"Hmmm," Art said. "I hope he doesn't fall into a pot of soup…"

"Art!" She was seated at the counter on her stool with her book next to the goldfish bowl.

"How did you like the films last night?"

She shrugged. "They were okay."

"I left early. The repairman called halfway through that Jackson movie."

"Oh yeah. Is your projector fixed?"

"No. But at least I got rid of those aliens."

She gave him a concerned look. "What happened to them?"

"The repairman took them. It turns out they direct movies. I guess he's hoping to be the star of their latest film: *The Projection Repairman*...."

Viranda laughed. After she turned on the TV set, she said, "You better look at this."

Chapter 34

It took Art a few minutes to get to the roadside beacon.

Someone had covered the ground with penguins. They were all around the signpost.

He couldn't tell if they were toys or alive. They weren't moving. They might be sleeping. "What do I know about penguins?" Art thought.

Surprisingly, while he landed next to the ball of green lawn with the blinking neon Convenience sign, the penguins didn't scatter the way he thought they would.

They were just watching him.

As he hopped across from the tethered car, one of them fell over beak-first into the grass. That made him pretty sure they were stuffed animals.

One stood right by his foot. Art reached down and touched the penguin, finding it to be plush and soft. He concluded it was a toy.

He felt like a fool, but there was nothing else he could do.

Art went all around the grass picking up penguins, making a pile of them to cart off in his Corolla.

Chapter 35

Art and Viranda had exhausted the topic of the beacon sign, the penguins, who could be behind it, and why was someone doing this? Etc. They even wondered if the penguins had something to do with the polar bear, even though, as Viranda pointed out, they were Earth creatures who lived on opposite ends of the pole and anyone with the vaguest knowledge of Earth animals wouldn't make that mistake. And maybe that was a clue! But then who truly knew that much about the wildlife of their home planet anymore. It was fading like a dream, only kept alive by stories and movies made by tin cans.

When the mail came, it gave Art something new to think about.

He pushed the bills aside for now and focused on the Zearz catalog. It was filled with house designs, kits you could order and build on your living sphere. Of course Art was quite proud of his wildflowers, but for some time he had been entertaining the thought of putting a nice house on the lot. Nothing too much. Something with a tower and a telescope.

He stopped on a page and he stamped his finger on 1923 2ST3.

"I found the one I want," he told Viranda. Wouldn't it be great, he thought, to get out of the dome into that!

She came near him to see. "Which one?"

He tapped his finger on it, "This one. Model 1923 2ST3."

"Sounds like a phone number."

"It's also called The House of Usher."

"Hmmm," she said.

"House of Usher…" he echoed. "Why does that sound familiar?"

Viranda shrugged.

"I've heard that somewhere. I think."

"Usher is probably the architect," she said. "They all have pretty weird names. Our lake-house is The Spruce Goose."

"Yeah. It just seems so familiar."

"That must mean it's meant to be. The House of Usher is awaiting you!" she said dramatically.

Just as her words were launched into the air like paper kites, the screen door opened and Chom Andyson let himself in.

Art only knew Chom Andyson for an hour or so but it was obvious the projector repairman was a changed man. He walked into the room with none of his usual swaggering. His voice had become a meek rasp as he stopped before the counter.

"Hello?"

Art stared.

"I…uhhh," Chom cleared his throat with a fragile cough, "I was hoping that I might be able to return those two cans…"

Viranda almost said something.

Art smiled. They must have really given Chom a rough time, the poor guy was actually humbled.

Chom clenched his bristled hands.

"I thought you and Rick were pals." Art knew it wasn't the nicest thing to say.

"Look Mister Barker, I'll have your projector installed this afternoon if you'll take them back! I'll even upgrade your system. I'll—"

The screen door bolted open and Chom Andyson froze.

Behind him, scraping their way towards him, came the Ricks. One of them held a little camera. It made a soft whirring sound like a moth on a window.

"Got it!" Rick said when they arrived at Chom's heavy boots. The camera stopped. "Hey, give us a boost up there will you, Chom."

Chom shot Art an almost tearful look, then down he went to the floor level and back with a Rick in either hand. He set them on the counter and took a backwards step.

The two Ricks shuffled forwards and both of them tipped in surprise as they caught sight of the goldfish bowl.

"What's that, Art?"

"You think you can replace us with that reptile?" the other Rick sputtered.

Viranda put her hand over her mouth.

"It's a goldfish, Rick," Art told them.

Rick scraped a little closer so his reflection was silvery on the glass. "Well, I don't like the look of it."

The other Rick took some film of it, then said, "We've grown tired of Chom."

Chom winced.

Rick continued, "Did we miss anything interesting around here?"

"I went to the dump…" said Art, then he had a wonderful idea. He smiled. It was perfect, it would get Rick off Chom's hands and maybe solve a mystery for Art. He said, "Rick, how would you like to catch a crime on film?"

They stared at him for a moment, then turned to confer with each other in their squeaking patter. After a few seconds, they turned back to Art with their answer.

Chapter 37

So here he went again, leaving Convenience, driving with the Ricks on the dashboard. It wasn't something he hoped to relive, but if they could catch the culprit on film, Art felt their time together would have been worth it.

Art saw the Convenience beacon sign coming into view and tapped the brakes.

A Rick was filming their arrival.

The green ball of grass and flowers rolled into view. The neon blinked its message for the rockets shooting by. Fortunately no more penguins had been added to the little round moon. Art's trunk was already full of them. What was he supposed to do with them all?

The Corolla coasted up and Art parked, tying the car to the cleat embedded in wildflowers.

"This is it," Art said. If the Ricks were expecting a better line from him, they didn't say so. Rick didn't stop filming as Art opened the door, took them in hand and transported himself to the beacon. It was like a lighted buoy floating in a black sea.

Art had already explained the scenario to Rick and they decided all they needed was a good place to hide. The weedy flowers and grass grew about half a foot thick, deep enough to camouflage the cans, but Art said, "What if I hid you on the sign? Whoever's coming out here probably wouldn't notice you, and that would be a good clear shot for filming." There happened to be a perfect spot in the corner of the sign's frame where they would fit right in with the corroded metal.

Somehow the culprit had been able to avoid the stationary camera Art had installed, but with two living creatures blending in, on guard and filming, it couldn't go wrong.

Rick decided, "It is a good place."

"Yes," agreed the other.

Art gave a look over his shoulders to make sure he wasn't being watched, but in the deep pool of outer space you can't be sure. It must have been an old Earth reflex. He quickly put them on the sign and was pleased with the way they looked. If he didn't know better, he never would have known they were metallic can-sized aliens with a camera, making a film that very well might include a pest caught in the act.

"Oh," Art said. "What if they come from the other direction, behind the sign where you can't see? Should I put one of you on that side?"

Rick said, "We won't miss it."

The humming little camera was pointed at Art.

"Okay," he held his hands up. "You're on your own. Should I stop by later tonight, or tomorrow morning?"

"Tomorrow," the Ricks replied. "Goodbye."

Art said, "Adios," got in his car and left them blending in to their surroundings.

Chapter 38

"I wouldn't like to be stuck out there," Viranda said, staring at the TV from her perch on the stool. "How boring."

"They're film makers," said Art. "They're used to this. They edit out what they don't need."

"Still, being marooned on a sign for a whole day doesn't sound like much fun."

"I'll check on them in the morning. They'll be fine. If we're lucky they'll have it all wrapped up." He glanced at the TV and watched the chord of rocket traffic bolting past.

Viranda said, "Whoever's doing it is pretty crafty."

Art nodded, "I know."

Chapter 39

Convenience mostly catered to a car driving in, or a bicyclist like old D, someone getting a newspaper or an ice cream. It was a small store and didn't expect to earn much, so how did Art Barker manage to keep the place open? For the answer to that, follow the orange rocket trail of his Corolla to midtown, where he went on his lunchbreak.

He took a left turn on Holly Street and parked next to the bank. He grabbed some coins from the glovebox before he left the car. He locked the door and stood beside the parking meter.

For each coin he dropped into it, the little wired catapult inside of it pulled back more. He gave it ten minutes just to make sure. Sometimes the bank had a long line; if he got stuck and time ran out, he didn't want that catapult flinging a pellet at his car. Depending on the mood of the vicious contraption, it could shoot paint, a stone, or a phlegmy gob of acid that would eat a hole through your car.

He left the meter ticking and followed the flowered cement pathway.

As he approached the bank's black tinted glass doors, all the flowers on their tall stalks turned to film him. He tried not to notice them. The doors flicked open like the chittering wings of a beetle and he entered the cool temperature. His feet were instructed electronically where to walk, taking him to the five people waiting in line. He also tried not to notice the syrupy muzak version of an atropaceous polypod pop song. It would look suspicious if he covered his ears, he would just have to clench his fists and get through it.

There wasn't much to look at. The walls were gray marble. He was aimed for a dark wooden textured counter where a row of tellers monitored transactions. Behind them, where he couldn't see, the functions of the bank clicked and scuffed like tap shoes.

Art kept his hand bent, watching his feet. It was interesting to see the carpet move and pull him as the line stepped forwards. If he resisted, the carpet fiber would knot around his feet and tug. He imagined that someone trying to rob the place would be thrown to the floor and smothered in a carpet ball like the tar-baby—not a very pleasant thought.

When the next teller was ready, the carpeting delivered Art to the counter, planted him there like a scarecrow.

"Hi," Art said.

"Hello," the teller smiled. She wore a purple orchid in her hair. It could have been a camera, but it looked so real. "How may I help you, Mr. Barker?"

"I need to sign my deposit statements over to my account."

"Oh yes," she said and turned to type. "Let me retrieve those for you."

While she was doing that, Art noticed the day calendar positioned on the counter. Above the grid of days was a very familiar sight. It was where he slept last night, a beautiful orchard full of apple trees. He even recognized the spot where his hammock was strung.

He reached over and unclipped the top of the calendar photo so the previous month flipped down. It was Fiji! White sand, palms, blue sky and sea. It was just what he longed for and remembered. Carefully, his finger strayed over the photo, to a tiny white dot on the sand, across the bend in the beach. He tried to rub it off, but it wouldn't disappear. If it was only a flaw in the photograph that would be okay, but what if it wasn't? What if it was that polar bear?

"Here you are, Mr. Barker." The teller snapped a white folded paw of paper onto the counter.

Art could feel the carpet tightening on him, no doubt sensing his sudden change in mood. "I—" he coughed, "I was looking at your calendar, sorry." He flipped the orchard over the tropical scene.

"That's alright," she said. "We still have some complimentary calendars. They're free to our customers."

Art hid his flustering, opening the folded paper, using the fountain pen tied to the counter to sign on the dotted line. He glanced at the page with the big number in the thousands printed on it. His father's life work, his legacy, amounted to quite a lot of money that Art received as a trust fund payment every month. It seemed only right that Art put that fortune into Convenience. His father had spent the other part of his life working there, stocking shelves, ordering supplies, pumping gas, getting by seven days a week. Art didn't have the heart to see it fail. It was just a lucky thing that his father had that other income to pass on.

Chapter 40

It was hard to believe Art's father spent so many hours devoted to that task, while the rest of his day was making sure Convenience stayed afloat. Art knew that after a long day, his father would lock himself away when the rest of the family went to sleep. Art didn't know how his father could do it. He couldn't understand the drive behind it. It had to have been a vision.

At some point, on a day that would change their family fortune, Art's father went to Trident Import and returned home with a box. The store was filled with boxes that had been packed with Earthly treasures, but it took a certain sort to want to go in that cavernous mysterious warehouse to take your chances on some relic taped in a box you couldn't open until you paid. Viranda went there sometimes—her box of Steinbeck books came from Trident—but Art never had the need to go there. It seemed to him that what you got there could curse you in a way, taking over your life somehow. And didn't he already have his fill of that with Steve Vines?

That box Art's father bought certainly turned his world around. There were nine crumbling movies inside the box, the last known copies of an ancient black and white series made on Earth, during the years 1949-1957. Realizing they were falling apart as he watched them, Art's father transcribed them and turned the dying films into bestselling books for homesick, nostalgic Americans.

Chapter 41

Ma and Pa Kettle (1949)
Ma and Pa Kettle Go To Town (1950)
Ma and Pa Kettle Back On the Farm (1951)
Ma and Pa Kettle at the Fair (1952)
Ma and Pa Kettle on Vacation (1953)
Ma and Pa Kettle At Home (1954)
Ma and Pa Kettle at Waikiki (1955)
The Kettles in the Ozarks (1956)
The Kettles on Old McDonald's Farm (1957)

Chapter 42

Art drove back towards the store with his new calendar on the seat next to him, listening to Peter Lorre in a radio play, when he found himself pulling off the road to go check on the Ricks. It was a good thing he did too.

At first, the beacon resembled that cold-looking white dot on the bank calendar, then, as Art neared, he could see the reason why.

There was a white cloud hovering overhead, sending a flurry of snow below it, as it moved in a slow orbit around the beacon.

"Oh, come on!" Art groaned.

The sign, the flowers, everything was covered in a thick blanket of snow and it looked like the cloud would keep going.

Art slowed the Corolla up close and rolled down the window. It was a gag cloud. Of course he knew about them—you could buy them at Ray's Culver City. You could also buy rain clouds, or hail, wind, or rainbows.

He put the car in park and leaned over the backseat looking for the long rope he kept back there. At least there wasn't a lightning storm circling his beacon. He thought of the article he read in the paper just last week about a teenage joker who blew up a mobile home with one. He found his rope and quickly bent its end into a lasso, then he dragged the coil out the open window.

The cloud was just as peaceful as a sheep and it let

him catch it easily.

With the cloud tied to his car, Art gave it a good pull and released it free into space.

He watched it tumble away, still making snow, going, going, gone.

Chapter 43

Art put the car in reverse and returned to the snowball beacon. He knew the place to park, but it took him a while digging around in the snow to find the cleat, so he could tie the car up. He rubbed his cold hands together before he could use them.

The sign was a slab of white. It was smooth with snow, but he supposed the Ricks must be under there somewhere.

His shoes crunched pleasantly on the fresh snow, singeing his ankles with each deep step.

"Hello?" he called.

No answer. It was a steep mountainside, frozen like

a photograph buried in the snow. Art stopped next to the covered sign and brushed at the corner spot where he left one of the Ricks.

Little avalanches rilled to the snow on the ground. He reached his hand into the soft cold and felt an even colder curve of metal alien. He grabbed Rick and pulled him free, leaving a spot where it looked like a mummy can had been entombed in white sand. He turned Rick upside down and dumped out the snow.

"Rick?"

The alien didn't answer him. He set Rick at his feet and hurried to reveal the other one on the sign's other corner. Rick's twin was in the same condition.

Art felt awful for them. He carried them close to him, back to the car, stumbling in the snow.

They were so cold he took off his coat and wrapped them in it, putting the nest of it on top of the calendar, driving faster than an ambulance for the store.

Chapter 44

As Art rushed from his car, carrying his bundled coat, the first thing he noticed was D's bicycle leaning next to the screen door. "Hi," he could see himself telling D, "I just froze the aliens."

D must have known about this. He did possess some peculiar abilities, waiting just in the doorway as Art reappeared in Convenience.

D let go with a wheezing laugh. "What's the hurry?"

Art flopped his coat onto the counter between D and Viranda. They both stared at him as he tried to explain. He didn't even know how to say it, he opened and closed his mouth like a fish in the air. Instead, he unwrapped the jacket and showed them the Ricks.

They lay on their sides, looking for all the world as dead and recycled as a couple of soup cans.

Fortunately, D knew what to do, or acted as if he did. Like a stork flapping into motion, he was around the counter, past Viranda, where he grabbed the Sylex full of hot coffee, spun to the counter and in the next moment he was pouring the coffee out, splashing it over both the Ricks. Then his gnarled hand stood them up and he poured the last of the steaming black coffee into them, filling them to overflowing.

All of this didn't help Art's speechlessness.

It was Viranda who had to break the shocked silence. "D, are you sure that was the right thing to do?"

D was going to say yes—he heard about it on the late-night radio when they had a whole segment on alien CPR—but the second he started to speak, the Ricks shuddered violently, showering the counter with coffee.

While Art and Viranda jumped backwards, D shot his hands to them and flipped the Ricks upside down, pouring out the rest of the coffee. With his trembling hands, D reset them upright on the counter. Viranda was already busily cleaning up with towels.

"What do you think?" said D with a gust.

The Ricks trembled, as if a train across a backyard was rumbling by. One of them made a sound suspiciously like life, a cough, and the other agreed with one of its own.

D was beaming a crooked smile. He slapped both hands down on the counter on either side of the Ricks and announced, "Welcome back from the dead!"

Rick moaned.

D laughed.

Art finally mumbled, "I'm sorry, Rick. I sure didn't expect it to be dangerous for you to be out there."

After a sneeze, a Rick said in a raspy voice, "Your coffee is terrible."

The second Rick continued, "The worst in the galaxy."

Chapter 45

Art was glad they were okay, but he was happier to see them leave in D's backpack, the way they started out.

"Do you think that will make it into the movie?" Viranda asked. She was standing at the screen door, looking across the neon lit parking lot, watching D pedal away.

"Good question."

There was a blizzard of static on the TV. Art knew he would have to stop at the beacon on the way home. He had to bring a shovel to clear the snow.

It had been a busy day. He hadn't exactly gone looking for intrigue, but it found him anyway. Maybe the Ricks should have stayed filming him after all? He glanced at the antique electric Moxie clock with its shimmering Lisbon Falls waterfall background. It was almost quitting time. He hoped for something just as peaceful as that tranquil scene of idyllic Earth water that fluttered on the clock like a mirage.

Actually, there was a place he liked to go, an old abandoned dome. Someone had wanted to build on it long ago, but they never did and now it was overgrown. He called it the vacant lot.

"It's hard to believe they make comedy movies…" said Viranda. She returned to the counter and sat next to the goldfish. "Neither Rick seems very funny."

"Their films are probably plotted on a proven scientific formula," said Art. "People like them because they know what to expect. Audiences have seen it so often before." He grinned. "Yeah…I don't see how Rick could make this into a movie though. Who knows what's going to happen next?"

"I do," the goldfish said.

Viranda almost fell off her chair.

The words had left a rippling tremor on the water's surface.

"You…do?" said Art. He leaned closer to the bowl.

The fish told him matter-of-factly, in a rich baritone brogue, "You'll soon be paying a visit to Ray's Culver City."

Chapter 46

"I knew it!" Art repeated for about the fifth time. "Didn't I tell you, Viranda?"

She rolled her eyes.

"I'm giving you an extra pinch of food," Art told the goldfish, as he peppered the water. "We've been talking about Ray's for a long time, haven't we, Viranda? I knew he was behind all my troubles!"

"Now wait a minute," said Viranda. "The fish only said you'll be going there. That doesn't have to mean anything more."

"No, I've got a feeling I'm going there and something will happen."

"Ooh!" she said with her hands hovering in the air mystically, "Maybe you'll buy a slice of pizza?"

Chapter 47

Not two hours later, Art was eating pizza at Ray's Culver City—not because of Viranda's prophecy—everyone knew that Ray's had the best pizza—but since he was there, how could he refuse? Anyway, he knew if Viranda happened by, she would tell him, "I told you so!" and give him that look. He sprinkled some more hot pepper flakes across his pineapple, green pepper and dried tomato slice. It was going fast.

He had to admit, Ray's had it all. Art was just in one little window of it, looking out on the vast refueling lot, wondering how many hundreds of Conveniences could fit inside Culver City. Cars and trucks, like little magnetized toys, crept up to the rows of gas pumps for automatic service, then they buzzed away. And most of them came back around to the hive, for the shopping or entertainment inside.

"It takes your breath away, doesn't it?"

Art dropped his pizza crust as he gave a jump, turning to see the wide man in the blue and white uniform standing next to his booth.

Ray tipped his huge white cowboy hat. "Hello, Art." He put out his thick palm for a handshake. "I haven't seen you for a while."

Art gave Ray's hand a pump and Ray asked, "How's the pizza?"

Art shrugged, "Everyone knows you have the best."

Ray chuckled. "It's not just the pizza, Art. Look around! Culver City specializes in quality, all kinds of quality."

Art couldn't look at Ray's smile any longer. He was sure the heart beating in the man was no bigger than a hummingbird's.

Ray must have felt the sudden drop in temperature for he leaned in a little closer over the table and said it simply. "What brings you here, Art? I mean besides the pizza."

"Well, Ray," Art started and he pictured his poor beacon sign and the battle that ravaged over it, now scoured by snow. "I guess there appears to be a little rivalry between your place and my store."

"Little," the big man chortled, "Very little indeed, Art." He laughed. "However, I suppose like a pea under the mattress of a princess, your store does cause me some aggravation."

"Enough to sabotage my beacon?" Art couldn't believe he said it. So much for tact.

Ray wasn't even slightly affected though. "Let me explain my philosophy," he said cooly. "I am a provider. I am here to serve the people, that's what I do. Whatever they want, they come to me to get it. And you, with your little store, well, it's like a pebble dropped in a clear pool. It muddies the water. I don't want to sound greedy, but people don't need the competition anymore. They can get everything they need right here, and at a cheaper price too. It's all about convenience…which is a funny choice of word, isn't it?"

"My store is a family tradition," Art replied. "We were here before Ray's Culver City, we have a loyal clientele who depend on us. We—"

Ray interrupted, "Now, I know you've picked up a few stragglers and malcontents over the years. Enough to form a parade? Enough to pull a wagon? I'm not sure what silly notion compels you to go on, but let me assure you, you're doing the people a disservice. And I'm sure your father's memory, not to mention the small fortune he left you, would be better applied to something more worthy." Ray pushed his cowboy hat back an inch and tapped his forehead. "Think about it, Art. Take a stroll around Culver City and observe. Talk to the folks you see. I don't need to freeze you out. Nobody needs your Convenience anymore."

Chapter 48

When Art left Ray, he did go for a walk, on the revolving balcony, past specialty shops opening door after door. Below him were the reflecting pools stocked with whales and the African savannah yellowing around the next corner. It was a never ending game to stun the senses.

Yes, Ray's Culver City was amazing alright and everyone was carrying bags, but more and more Art was feeling it was too much. There was too much of everything—it went beyond what people needed. This walk was making it all the more clear that Ray's was probably exactly what went wrong back on Earth… There was no need for this much.

He felt like stepping up on the balcony and shouting it out loud, "Our needs are simpler than this! It's not about buying more gadgets and gizmos! This place is a lie! You'll only want more!"

Chapter 49

Oh, there were a lot of things Art would say up there on the balcony, but generally he was a pretty quiet guy and talking wasn't always the easiest thing for him to do. After his epiphany, he went back to his car, his old Corolla, waiting for him in the parking lot surrounded by the new chrome-covered rockets everyone else drove.

Who were these people? What were they thinking, driving these things to Ray's Culver City? The longer he stayed, the more he felt Ray's beefy laugh blowing hot air. Self-doubt was creeping its way back in already. There was some truth to what Ray said. Art was only keeping Convenience afloat with the Kettle Trust Fund. Was he just throwing it down the drain?

Art unlocked his car and quickly got in. Convenience was only a short drive away. He grimaced as he started the engine. On top of it all, the pizza had given him indigestion.

Chapter 50

Art discovered the vacant lot the day after his wife turned into a moth. When he found out she was gone, he went looking, though his looking only took him this far before he realized there were endless bright dots of light for her to fly to.

There was a Cyclone fence that bent wearily around the lot like a chain metal wave of scales. He simply let himself in where it was ripped apart. His feet and legs were brushed by the tall yellow grass.

He didn't know the history of this place—that was the nature of vacant lots—it was always someone afterwards who found them. Whatever they used to be was gone and even the ruins of a cement foundation, a stooped tree, an old tire swing with rope as thin as a spider web—it was all part of the silence.

Art felt like an enormous clumsy bird as he tried to behave respectfully here, twisting the flowers aside, not meaning to make a sound walking.

He crept to the spot where a polished greenish stone broke free of the ground, folded his legs under him and perched on the rock. He looked across the tops of the grass and weeds bent by a breeze that had been left behind too, then he closed his eyes and listened.

Chapter 51

The sound of a jam jar lid unscrewing, lifting off from glass, and the fireflies tipped out into the dark parking lot air. A couple of them crawled softly on his arm before they flew.

Art watched them join the clamor of the stars. He had been in such a rush to get to Ray's Culver City, he forgot to let them out. So he had to come back to Convenience. He knew they liked their freedom every night. Anyway, now that he was back, he liked being here.

This place was a part of him, his memories and family, he couldn't bear to think of it drifting off into a silence like the vacant lot. So he kept it alive. So what if there were only a few people coming and going? Convenience was what Art wanted it to be.

He opened the screen door and went inside to the familiar smell that sat on wooden shelves, that ticked out of the Moxie clock, that lay ripening in the apple barrel. The long day had come to an end, there was nothing more to do, so Art unhooked the cot from the wall behind the counter, stretched out and was asleep in less than a minute.

Chapter 52

As much as Art wanted to sleep through the night, it wasn't to be. About three hours later, like a dragon breathing, gusts of red, yellow, white, orange, blue, woke him up. He almost fell off the cot, forgetting he wasn't in a hammock on a beach in an imaginary Fiji.

A Roman Candle was going off in the parking lot. That was another thing you could get at Ray's Culver City. Fireworks. Art made it to the door knowing his way in the darkness of the store, unlatched the hook on the screen and was out on the porch to see the last sizzling pop.

He peered out into the gloom around the store's platform and caught a glimpse of a black car tearing away, red tail lights twinkling like the eyes of a bat.

A wisp of smoke curled and vanished from the dead firework. Art walked over to it.

The bright paper covering the tube had mostly burnt away. He kicked it over and rolled it, looking for some message written on it. He wouldn't have been surprised to read *Get Out of Our Town At Sun-up*. Wasn't that just the sort of cowboy thing that Ray would write? It seemed to be, but fortunately there was only the burned remains of the word Roman. Art gave it a good kick so it skittered and tipped off the edge of the platform on its long journey through outer space.

It was gone, but it left a scorched flower mark on the pavement.

Art turned and went back inside.

Chapter 53

After tossing on the cot for a while, Art gave up. He couldn't fall asleep again, at least not yet.

He went to the counter and turned the TV on.

In a moment, a picture formed.

Thankfully it was a picture you could hang on your wall. Cars were going by once in a while, peacefully. He could even see the edge of the beacon was green again, snow free. It was good to see, but not exactly entertaining. Art reached up high to the set and turned the channel to see if a show was on.

There was.

In a small room, cluttered with electronic equipment, the camera zoomed to a man seated before a panel full of blipping lights. He started pressing buttons, pulling levers and turning dials, using both hands like a piano player's tantrum. All that motion caused the dial on the control panel to push all the way around into the area marked with stark letters: Mind Control. It was set in motion.

Up from that basement room, up through the dark nighttime house, all the way past the window lit on the second floor, shades drawn, crawling with the rainspout along the gutter, by a black cat sitting on the roof, to the chimney and climbing those bricks, following a thick vein of wire to the top, where a thin cloud of smoke ghosted out, further up a metal post, all the way to its end, a fan of aerials.

Whatever was going on underground was transmitted to a signal shown on the TV screen as ghostly white rings spreading across the city map, fading out only where the forest and countryside formed, crumbling like sand on the window of a farmhouse where a woman slept in a moonlit room.

Then the movie cut to a studio set, a hat rack stacked with glowing candles standing next to a cardboard coffin. The lid opened with a loud creaking sound effect as words covered the screen, a couple letters backwards…Count Misfit.

From deep in the coffin, the top of a ladder appeared, leaning, and up climbed a gaunt vampire wearing black cape, white shirt missing a button.

"Hello friends." He paused there on the ladder with a tired wave. "I was watching the movie down in the cellar." He pointed a thumb downwards as if the ladder extended a hundred feet below inside the coffin.

"You'll never guess who I'm watching the movie with… Let me just go down there and bring them up, then you'll know."

Count Misfit slowly descended out of sight.

There was distant thunder and a wolf howled. The camera shifted uneasily. Black tree branches grew up the walls of the Count's room, strung with little Christmas lights. An open window showed a cartoon full moon.

The ladder trembled with Count Misfit's return. He balanced a silver tea tray on one hand. Two tin objects rested on it.

"Oh no!" Art couldn't help but say out loud. It was the Ricks. Or a couple of cans that looked just like them.

Count Misfit almost smiled, he couldn't help it. "In case you didn't guess, on the show tonight we have the directors of this very movie you're watching."

The camera moved in on the Ricks.

"Greetings."

"Hello."

Count Misfit said, "Can I just ask you a question before we return to the movie?"

"Yes."

"I suppose."

The Count continued, "The end of the movie is such a shock. Can you tell me about that? It looks like footage from another film."

"That is correct."

The other Rick piped up, "We found some old film at a yard sale."

Count Misfit nodded and turned to the camera to explain, "In case you haven't seen the film yet, I'm going to tell you what happens." He shrugged, "I'm going to spoil it for you. The villain of the film—"

"Dr. Biocal," both Ricks chirped.

"Dr. Biocal, I'm sorry. Dr. Biocal discovers an unknown radio wave he can use to put people into a hypnotic state. It works only as far as the radio beacon on his roof, so of course he wants to boost the frequency. He goes into the city and finds the tallest building to transmit from. Great idea, by the way."

"That was dependent on the stock footage we acquired."

"Right," the Count nodded. "So he climbs to

the top of the skyscraper, connects wires to the radio antenna up there and is about to transmit when this enormous gorilla appears! The gorilla is carrying a woman, there are biplanes circling him, shooting at him. That ending came out of nowhere!"

"It came from a yard sale," Rick buzzed. "Super 8 footage."

"We had to film entirely in black and white to match that giant ape footage."

"Okay," said the Count. "I wonder what that other film is. Do you know?"

"No idea."

The other Rick said, "That's all that's left of it. We used all we had."

"Well…" Count Misfit shook his head, "It's an incredible ending. So let's get back to your movie now and see it happen."

At 6:30 AM, Art woke up to the sound of newspapers thumping on the porch. He had ten papers delivered. They usually sold out by noon. The morning started from there and slowly proceeded, quiet, a few sales, some cars came and went, then D was at the door, leaning his bicycle on the post outside.

D tottered inside, his arms wrapped around a cardboard box. "I got a goodie to show you," he told Art.

"I don't want to see a head in a box, or tin cans that can direct movies."

D ambled over to the counter and left the box on it. "Take a look. You tell me."

Art, wondering what Ray's Culver City would do with D, sighed and looked into the box. "What is that?"

D laughed. "Don't you know?"

"Another outer space entity?" guessed Viranda who had also taken a quick look.

"It's a pelican," D told them. "It's a bird."

"Where did you find it?" asked Viranda.

"It was in a tree near my house…Must have been blown off course. The problem is, he's weak and looks hungry, but I have no idea what to feed it."

"Hmmm," said Viranda. "Strawberries?"

They stared at the bird and wondered. D said, "I suppose…"

"Well," said Art, "There's one way to find out." He left the counter and went to where the fruit was kept. He soon returned with a green pint of strawberries.

"I guess it wouldn't hurt to try…" He offered the pint of berries to Viranda.

"Thanks," she said. She picked a ripe one from the top and lowered it near the pelican.

It only blinked.

Viranda waved the berry in front of its beak, but it didn't do any good. "I don't know…" she decided. "I could be wrong about pelicans."

"Maybe it's not a pelican," tried Art. "D?"

"It's a pelican alright. I used to be a real bird enthusiast when I was younger. I still remember. You can ask me about swallows, terns, auks, I can even distinguish an avocet from an egret," D said proudly.

"You just don't know what they eat," Art said.

"That wasn't my specialty."

"Okay, okay." Art tapped the box. "I have an idea. Viranda, if you don't mind watching the store, I'll take a trip to the library."

"You want me to watch the store?" she said.

Art moved around the counter. "Hopefully they still have books about birds."

"I'll stay here and keep the young lady company," said D.

Viranda gave Art a look, though Art just waved at her anyway.

"I'll be back soon."

Chapter 55

There were always elm trees standing there in front of the library. Art parked next to them and got out into their shade and walked to the door. The pathway was speckled with light and shadows moving in the breeze. It was a nice day, he almost hated to leave it and go inside.

It was okay though, it was just as calm inside. There were desks, shelves, with a counter to the left of the door. Nobody bothered him as he came in. He could have been some leaf blown by the wind.

He went to the library once in a while, so he wasn't in another world. He knew the way to where the books about birds were shelved.

There wasn't much there. *Make Way for Ducklings*, *To Kill a Mockingbird*, a movie called *The Raven*, a record by The Byrds and some folded paper manuscripts. Art stood before that weak shelf display wondering, was this really all that survived and stayed alive for people wanting to find out about birds? Of course in this time birds didn't really exist. Earth was off limits, everyone lived in outer space. If a bird appeared out so far, it was like the fragile creature from a dream had appeared. All he knew about them was they used to sit on the branches around you and sing beautiful songs.

He didn't see anything about pelicans and he felt thankful when a librarian appeared.

"Hi," he said. "Do you work here?"

"Yes," she said. "It looks like you need help."

"I'm looking for information on an old Earth bird called a pelican. I don't see anything here."

What a look she gave him. "You're really lucky!" she smiled. "We just got a donation called *The Pelican*, a sound recording."

"What are the odds?"

"Good!" she smiled again. "I haven't heard it yet, but it might have what you're looking for."

She showed him the way to the listening booths at the back of the room. The wall had six glass doors. The librarian carried the record into the narrow wooden booth and set it on the turntable. "There you are."

"Thanks," Art replied.

She scooped up the record someone had left behind, "Spaceman" by the Phil Ochs Orchestra. "Tell me what you think."

Art nodded to her and shut the door. He flipped the switch to start the sound.

The vinyl scratched and crackled as it spun beneath the needle, then an ancient croaking voice began to speak.

"What a marvelous bird is the pelican…His beak can hold more than his belly can…But I don't know how the hell he can!"

That was it. More scratching, as the needle made it to the middle ring of the black disk, and the record stopped.

Art was a little stunned.

He listened to it again, the same flinty message winched up out of the sea on a rusted chain.

He left it on the record player, stepped away from

the booth and gave the librarian a wave.

"How was it?" she asked.

"Uhh. It's not really what I was hoping for…Is that all you have on pelicans?"

"I'm afraid so. We do have a good book about mockingbirds though."

"No thanks." He was about to go, then he paused. "Oh, you know what? There is something else I'm curious about."

"Certainly."

"I was thinking of ordering one of those Zearz houses from the catalog. The house I'm interested in is called The House of Usher. I don't know why that sounds familiar to me. Can you tell me what the name is from?"

She opened the thick book on the desk, flipping pages, turning them backwards, forwards, slowing, running her finger down the fine print. "I don't see any House of Usher listed in the library records. That doesn't mean it didn't once exist. We lost a lot of information on the trip from Earth. Some things may never be recovered. I often refer people to Trident Import. They may have heard of it. Of course, you could try Zearz. They must have a good reason for naming their product The House of Usher."

"Alright, thanks," Art said. He knew it would be a long shot. He glanced at the shelf that held all the world's knowledge on birds. It seemed pitiful, searching for the meaning of words that sparked some vague recollection. That was it. People were only supposed to know what they knew.

Chapter 56

When he returned to the store, he was surprised to see the pelican out of the cardboard box, shaking out its big purple wings, and nesting comfortably on the counter.

Viranda waved at Art. "We fed him! We figured it out!"

"She did," D said. "She's a very smart girl."

"How did you know what it eats?" Art put his hands near the pelican. The bird was so content it seemed to be smiling.

Viranda said, "By deduction. I looked at its webbed feet which I suppose makes it a water bird. Then I thought of the things that live in water that this bird could eat."

"So much for strawberries," said Art.

"Yes," she laughed. "That was way off. But when I tried feeding him fish, he came to life!"

"Three cans of sardines!" D beamed. "Still looks hungry too."

"His beak can hold more than his belly can." Art was about to recite the recording, then he stopped. "Hey…Where's my fortune fish?"

Chapter 57

After D and his pelican left, it got busy for a while. Art went out to the gas pump four times. Finally he decided to sit on the porch and watch the parking lot from an overturned wooden apple crate.

The pavement had been cobwebbed with white seed fluff drifting across space from cottonwood trees, who knows how far away. The breeze swirled them across the porch floorboards, pushed and piled them into corners like snow.

Art brushed some of the fluff off his blue pants as he stood. A car waited at the pump. It wasn't a car you saw very often, but one that Art knew of course. It was a Fiat, a 1970, or late 1960s model.

He was halfway to it, into a blizzard of the cottonwood, when the driver's door opened and a clown stepped out. Art froze. The snowstorm passed around him. The clown stepped next to the pump, making room for another clown getting out. Then another one slipped from the tiny car.

When there were eight of them waiting, Art walked to the red painted Fiat.

They stood around on the little cement island like bright strange flowers, stretching, shoving each other, going through their clown routine. One of them was assembling a trombone.

Art said, "Hello," as if it wasn't so strange to have the parking lot overrun with clowns. He shook hands with the nearest clown. Actually, he shook a hand in a thick white glove. "That's quite an act, getting all of you in that little car."

"Oh, there's more," the clown said. "We left the elephant in there. Should I bring her out too?"

"No. That's okay. We just got rid of a pelican, I don't need any more animals. Thanks though. So, can I help you with something? Would you like your car refueled?"

"Actually…" said the clown. "Our car never needs refueling." He patted the hood affectionately. "The magician did some work on it. Now, BZZZT, it just goes and goes."

Art whistled. "That can't be good for my business."

The clown waved a floppy glove at the pump, "That's right, gas is the past. But I'll tell you what we would like. Apples!"

"Oh. I've got those. Picked fresh."

"Yes, yes." The clown nodded and the bird on his hat fluttered its wings. "We were also wondering if we could give you one of these for your store window." He reached in his coat and pulled out a rolled up poster.

It unscrolled to show an elephant holding a woman waving a flag, unfurling with the words: Circus! "That's Jacqueline," the clown sighed. He handed the poster to Art while he slipped his other glove under his coat lapel and made it beat like a heart beneath the cloth.

Art said, "Sure, I can put this in our window," adding, "You know, one of my employees works for a circus. I'll be right back."

The clowns seemed content just to be out of the

Fiat. Two of them were gathering cottonwood snow-balls and tossing them at each other.

Art went inside, got some tape and stuck the poster up next to the Moxie neon sign. Then he remembered the apples. He gathered a bunch into a paper bag and went back out.

That same clown with the canary on his hat brim was waiting for him, only now he had a jokey tele-scope pointed at Convenience. A big eye was painted on the lens.

Art asked, "Is the circus coming here soon?"

"Yes indeed." He put his white glove against his mouth and admitted, conspiratorially, "We're the ad-vance guard, scouts for the circus. We look up high," he pointed the telescope up at the ring of stars, "and we look low." He directed the telescope to a snowy ball on the pavement.

"I got you some apples."

The clown tucked the telescope under his arm and bowed low like an admiral.

Art passed him the bag. "They're free."

"Many, many thank yous," the clown told him with another nautical bow. He held the bag out for the rest of his crew. They made a clown scene bump-ing into each other, falling over, grabbing for apples.

As Art was turning to go back to the store, a "Pssst!" turned him back. The clown with the apple bag held one of them up to the Fiat's open window and called, "Jacqueline!"

The other clowns watched in staged surprise as an elephant trunk snaked outside, searched like a periscope and plucked the apple away.

Chapter 58

Towards the end of the day, as things started to slow down, Art told Viranda she could take off early if she wanted to. It was summer, so of course she did.

There wasn't much more to do. Art looked around the place. It was quiet.

The TV was the usual scene of the rocket road and Art didn't want to take the chance of running into those cans on another channel. He liked to think of them buried in the basement of Count Misfit's coffin. That was a good place for them.

It was so quiet, lonely, it occurred to him what he was missing, and he pressed a button under the counter.

The screen door let in the sound, the drops tapping out there, the breath-like hiss in the air. It was raining. He turned the dial under the counter and watched the rain become a downpour.

Rain hit the pavement and bounced, everything was turned silver by it and the smell of all that raining flowed into the store like a cool river all around the room, turning corners and swirling around Art. He loved it. How could he have forgotten how much he loved the rain?

He could see the tomato plants out on the porch dancing, there were puddles forming little oceans, the gas pump shined with a polished wet light.

Then, slowly, Art spun the rain dial and gradually the falling water turned off. The miracle
was over, but not really.

It was a silent, beautiful painting out in the Convenience parking lot, and then a robin began to sing.

Chapter 59

There had been so much going on the last week, he got so out of touch with his old ways. There were six days of radio waves stored, waiting for him to go through. Six Days in 1943. He used to consider it his duty, that he was saving part of America's past before it drifted off forever, even further off into outer space. Was he getting lazy about it, or was it just not so important to him anymore? Anyway, maybe it was okay to let it blow on by. That's what the people did back then, creating all those songs and stories for the radio, letting go of them like the cottonwood tree.

He turned the radio off. The singing of some woman stopped. At least in Convenience her voice was still riding that wave beyond, finding other stars, other ears, maybe another Art out there, light years beyond, or just around the corner.

Chapter 60

Before Art left Convenience for the night, he paused at the postcard stand. It was filled with Florida. He gave it a little spin. The beautiful tropical dreamland. When the Americans left Earth, they tried to take Florida with them, peeling it off the planet, pulling it into outer space with them like a rare bright postage stamp. It would have been a wonder, a floating gem, but it didn't get far. It got wrecked, crumpled and scattered into billions of pieces, making a coral ring around the moon.

And here he was with a postcard stand full of Florida, slowly turning the metal rack. It squeaked with a crying sound until he made it stop on a green field full of orange blossom trees.

It was time to go home. Hopefully it was safe and sound.

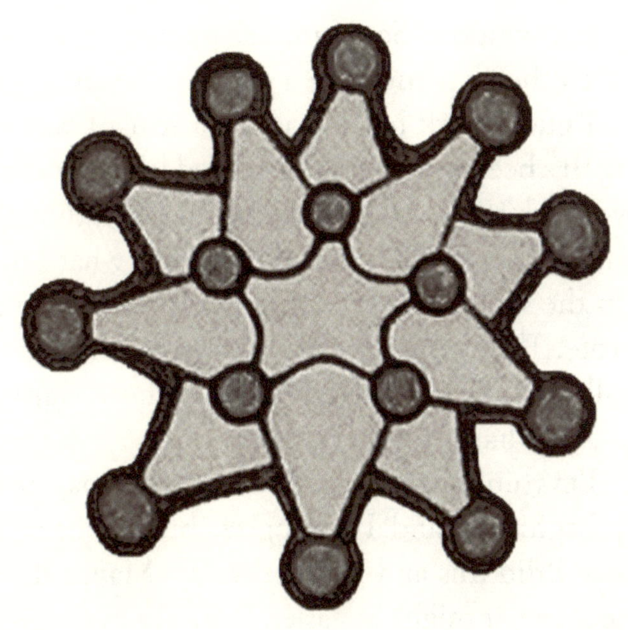

MOSS TEMPLE

I'm trying hard to find the time and peace of mind to tell this story. I spend the long day at work then it's a long walk back home where my typewriter is set up by the window. Sometimes I just sit there tired and watch the glass turn like a painting becoming night.

I guess work has produced a sort of wall to writing. It's been growing dull colored bricks and is spread over with ivy. Now I'm making an effort though. How can I call myself a writer if that's not what I'm doing? On the shelf above me, there's a row of seven books I wrote. This is the start of a new one. I have no excuse really, it's all been locked up in my head waiting.

But I have stopped already.

I'm thinking too much. Sorry. This may be a choppy beginning and I apologize, but it's been a while since I did this and I do feel rusty. Maybe if I just set the scene, it might be easier. Sometimes the words just need a push…I'll describe something, anything to get it going.

First, there's my typewriter. The sound of this clacking machine will be the proof that I'm getting something done. It starts and stops with ideas and misfires. I'd like to say something more about my typewriter. It's made of sky blue metal, smallish in size, my hands can nearly cup it. It's a model made years ago, probably for children. It makes a great sound like the little shoes of a rabbit.

Every word sits on the white rolled paper, waiting to become part of a sentence. Right now I'm watching that word I typed, *rabbit*. Even as I type, sometimes my eyes will go back to that word, watching it move as I continue to press the keys. And then, when I flick the silver return lever, the whole page jumps, taking the rabbit and the other words up higher. It's like a white field of snow pouring from the typewriter. That rabbit is making its way north. Look at him go.

I actually think I'll try writing a throwaway sentence like this one just so I can feel the whole thing happening. Imagine writing a whole novel that way, not caring what's being said, only creating for the thrill of the typewriter sensation. What kind of writer would I be then? I guess this would be a typewriter manual.

Much as I like my typewriter, I feel that I've already said too much about it and I'm nowhere near the novel that I hoped for. I'm just circling it like a moth. I feel a little dismayed spending such precious time describing a typewriter. I do apologize. After all, it's not the only machine in the room.

There's another one that I suppose might be considered a little more interesting.

Yes…I guess that's a good way to start…I'll tell you how I got my robot.

It's a short trip on the ferryboat from the reservation, across the water to Lemon Island. The sun was shining in a blue sky, the water was blue too and a few seagulls followed along in the air expressionlessly.

What else was there to do but sit in your car, look out the window, and feel the humming buzz of the motor flywheel shake the whole ship? Darren Birch had some money stuffed in his shirt pocket and he waited for the ticket-taker to come stand by his car and hold out her hand.

It cost thirteen dollars to ride across the channel. $13 wasn't exactly a bargain, but there was no other way over. Darren kept his hands on the wheel, fingers curled over its smooth shape. It felt like he was driving over the creasing waves. But for 13 dollars, he wondered if he could have filled the car tires with helium and floated across.

There was a rap on his window. A woman stood there with her hair flying around her face. "Thirteen dollars."

"Yeah, right." He paid and watched her scribble out a receipt ticket. Just over her shoulder he could see the approaching dock of Lemon Island.

He took the receipt and put it on the dashboard, where it riffled with the dried flowers and drawings his children made. They were at school today. His wife was at work and actually he should have been too, but he had called in sick. Sick…the thought still made him smile. It was a beautiful day, floating in a blue sky, and he was on a boat to go look at a robot.

The car started with a rattle as all the parts gnashed together and Darren put it into gear, driving up the clanking ramp onto the cracked tar of land. He liked Lemon Island. He liked the yellow flowers that grew on the edges of the tar like ripe fruit. He wondered if that's how the island got its name. A beautiful sight captured in time, it reminded him to be grateful that he was off work, out in the world and free as a bird. Each day there was something he needed to do. It was easy to get so wrapped up in your job, and the daily tracks you travel on, that you could forget every day was actually a unique miracle you need to be thankful for. Always find something to replay when the day is done, something to guide you, as if life's long corridor would be dark without them. There was always something. Knowing what that might be may take a sort of poetry, but that came easy to Darren Birch. Poetry was his goal in life. For despite working ten hours a day at the Moss Temple, he considered himself a poet.

Roland Traffic lived about a mile from the ferry landing. There were a couple steep hills jacked out of the ground like a rollercoaster ride, fir trees and cedars on either side of the road, and then Darren was slowing for a left turn onto a gravel road.

He parked beside an old red truck. It seemed to be guarding the barn that cupped its long cedar walls around Roland's studio.

Darren stepped out onto the grass. Birds were

singing. All across the field there were sculptures, some of them shaped like flowers with tall silver stems, some of them were wooden windmill-things. The grass lay itself down to form a narrow path to the barn.

Before he got there, Darren was stopped by a square pool of water on the ground. Its edges were marked by smooth black stones and there was a white sign that read: Sky Window. Darren let his gaze loosen and suddenly the water was a blue mirror reflecting white clouds. He walked around that hole of sky in the grass and got to the door on the barn.

An old bell awaited him. A string attached to it hung in the air. It would become a sound as soon as he pulled it.

It was a steamship ringing far out in the night, tolling to a water flock of foggy sheep. The brass tone held balled in the air like a yellow apple. When it faded, Darren waited, listening to the meadow birds. He thought it possible that Roland wasn't in his workshop; he was always busy, he could be anywhere on the island.

Then Darren heard something that wasn't a bird song. At first it sounded like cake pans in the barn, then when they got closer to the door they seemed like garbage can lids, clapping on the wooden floor in there.

The noise stopped.

The door handle turned and as the door opened, Darren was facing a tin man.

Although it was a mechanical man it just wasn't possible to see him as not human. He looked like a big solid-shaped person who had been dipped in metal wax. He wore a rusting pair of overalls, with a metal cap tilted atop his head. He may have seen better, shinier days, but he was still quite a sight. The robot's faded golden eyes seemed just as surprised to see Darren. A smile formed the corners of the metal mouth and spoke softly as summer bicycle wheels, his voice gently wording, "You must be Mister Birch."

The robot led Darren into the barn. The place was filled with a great breath of air like a dirigible. Darren stared all about in wonder. There was a giant metal sign reading HERALD, leaned against a wall. Long boards were lain down with steel poles and pedestals and all the other odds and ends Roland Traffic used for sculptures. There were also the tools, saws and welders, and it looked like a furnace on another wall. "Watch your step," the robot warned. They were almost there. A square room had been built in the middle of the barn, set up like a garden shed. It had a closed door with pebbled glass like a movie detective's office. The robot reached out a purring arm and tapped.

Darren had to admit he was much taken with the robot. When he had met Roland on the mainland a couple weeks ago, Darren told him about his job and how it tired him day after day. Then, with his hands cupped around his tea, the old man replied, "What you need is a robot. You should come out and see me on the island. I have one for you." The robot was made for hard labor, even his overalls uniform and cap gave him a look of some strong New Deal builder of dams and skyscrapers. He would have been happy under a jalopy, or hoisting the blade off a thresher caked with farm mud.

Roland Traffic looked electrified. His white hair stood on end, giving him the look of a somewhat stooped dandelion gone to seed. The wrench he held in his hand, the navy blue overalls oiled by work, he had been busy in this little room in his barn.

The robot fit himself in the doorway and Roland patted his shoulder.

"Thanks, Jeffers."

The robot made a contented sound like a Sunday morning coffee percolator.

Roland greeted Darren and asked, "What do you think of Jeffers?"

"He's an amazing machine," Darren said with a smile.

"No, no, no," the old man said quickly. "Jeffers isn't a machine. He's my brother. He's ten years older than me, he's my older brother."

"Oh, I thought you made him for me."

"No, my father made Jeffers. My father built Jeffers to be my companion and to help around the farm. I can't imagine him away from here. Anyway, I couldn't send him out into today's America. He has no idea. He still thinks there are airships and calliopes." He patted his metal friend and asked Darren, "So, are you ready to see your robot?"

"Yes, of course." Darren was looking all around the room—tables, the projects in process, shelves hanging wires like waterfalls. There was even a fish tank. But he didn't see anything else like Jeffers. "Did you make me a robot?

The old man shrugged. "I would say it made itself. Here…" He took a black cloth off of a jar on the table clutter.

It was a normal canning-sized jar. It could have held peaches. Instead, there was a cloudy looking fog inside. The old man picked it up and held it towards Darren. "Take a look."

Darren reached out. He didn't know if it was going to be freezing to the touch, but the glass felt no colder than a book. He stared at the contents of the jar. A piece of cloud, or whatever it was, spun slowly like cotton candy. It was a dreamy color of gray sky.

"Watch carefully," said Roland.

When it happened, fast like a splash of paint, Darren jumped and almost dropped the jar. A face looked back at him.

Roland laughed. "Spooked you!"

Darren returned the jar to the table. "What is this?"

"That's your robot!"

"That thing's a robot?"

"Robots don't have to be mechanical. This is a new design, you could say. You don't have to be afraid of it, Darren. Just wait until I open the jar, then you'll really see your robot." His hand trembled over the top of the jar, clutched around its edges and turned the lid off.

For a moment the raincloud stayed inside.

"It's alright," the old man clucked, "Come on out."

He tapped the glass and there was a sigh as the cloud began to climb out.

The wispy thing flowed in a thick coil, out of the jar, in an arc to the floor. Feet formed, then legs, a body, arms and a head and soon a sulfurous looking person stood beside Darren. It was a sort of person, but there was something ethereal about it. Forms and light in the room almost glowed through it, like holding an agate stone to the sun.

A few minutes later they were outside. Roland had convinced Darren to take the robot. The three of them stood beside the barn looking across the grassy field planted with sculptures.

The robot waited beside Darren and stared with eyes round as teacups. It wore a strange assortment of clothes, a vest and a flattened hat, old and worn as a circus performer.

"I can't believe you built him," Darren said. "He looks like a ghost."

Roland put his hand up, "He only looks like a ghost. He's designed that way. There are a lot of people who feel the same way you do about their jobs. This is a reflection. Ghost-like."

"I guess you're right," Darren said. "It's just a little creepy—sorry," he told the robot next to him. It made no response, it seemed to be watching across the flow of the land, on into the beyond.

Roland crept onto the grass. Before him was all his museum. His fingers spread out and read the ground.

He stopped in a few steps and pointed down. There in the lush green, white petals grew.

"What do you think of that? They put up those petals like circus tents. I've been keeping an eye on daisies as they grow. It's like looking at a map. They make cities, cluster around each other, and as you follow their line, they go over here, growing another city. A hundred years ago it was like that. Across vast distances, train lines were crossing the country, stopping at towns along the way. Before you knew it, the land was filled with roads and lights at night. I wonder if they have miniature telephone lines and highways going between each other too, with tiny airplanes you can't even see."

Roland took a breath and seemed done with his daisy lesson. Beyond him stood the big metal flowers he made. "Well," he clapped his hands. "Let's find out if your robot can pass your job requirements. I'll be right back."

Darren and his robot watched the old man return to the barn. Jeffers stood sentry at the door. Darren still preferred that robot. That's what a robot was supposed to look like.

When Roland came back, he carried a rake and a cardboard box full of paper scraps. He stopped halfway to Darren and spilled a pile of leaflets on the grass. It looked like a small hill of snow. Roland left it there and approached Darren and his robot and held the rake out.

Darren knew it was an historic moment, like that painting of George Washington in his boat with everyone else pulling him along.

Darren's robot floated over to Roland. Its legs blurred. When it moved it was like the wind pushing leaves.

"Here you go," said Roland. The rake disappeared from his hand and floated from him towards the lawn where the paper waited. "There you are," Roland turned to Darren. "Look at that."

Darren had to admit, the robot was ready for his job. All you needed was a rake and the hours to stick to your work. For years the country had been in a war economy. It meant that's what everyone was doing. It was normal to feel that way, creating an air of fear and hopelessness and all the more reason for poetry.

The older people could remember when it wasn't that way, and every once in a while there were glimpses of it, raindrops, little windows when it was different.

"And you're sure it's okay, I mean legal, for me to send the robot to work in my stead?"

"Oh yes," Roland nodded. "You just show them these papers." He passed Darren an old yellow envelope. "This is Jeffers' documentation, but the laws are still applicable I'm sure. Before the latest wars started, there was a real push for these workers. Legislation was passed. Robots were supposed to do all our labor for us. Jeffers was one of the first models. This one of yours is the most recent model. It's the only one of its kind actually. This is the prototype. But I see a day when there will be a lot more."

Darren wondered if he ought to try and coax the robot back into its jar for the journey back. He still wasn't used to it and he knew other people would be taken by surprise by it. It sat there in the car seat next to him like a pale deep-sea creature—a sort of jellyfish person—almost pulsating with the light coming in the windshield.

The car engine was rattling, but Roland seemed reluctant to let them go. He stood next to Darren's open window with another thing to say. "Would you look at that," the old man pointed across the field. Some of the sculptures clanked and turned in a breeze.

Amongst the others, Darren could see a copper colored fish statue. It was moving slightly too, its body changing. Now he could tell the scales were made of umbrellas and they were slowly beginning to open.

"It's going to rain," Roland said.

"But it's such a nice day."

"You wait," Roland smiled. "That fish is never wrong."

It was a quiet return to the city. All the way to Goodweather Elementary…across the sparkling ocean water, the miles of road and hurried freeway, on into the crowded neighborhoods…the robot hadn't said a word. Darren hummed, broke into words sometimes, and wished there was still radio to listen to. The little black radio slept in the dashboard. The airwaves had been silent for years. For old time's sake though, every once in a while, he would turn it on to listen to the static. His new robot was silent the same way.

Darren found a parking spot below a lush green tree. Birds were singing up above the tin roof, strung in the leaves out of sight. A bee tumbled along the windshield.

"Alright!" Darren said, "We're here!" He tapped the steering wheel. He looked at the weird shape next to him. No, he still wasn't used to it. Him. The robot. "Maybe you better stay here, while I get Leo…"

The robot didn't mind. He seemed to be counting something invisible.

"Okay then. I'll be right back. Sit tight," and surprising himself he brushed the robot lightly on the shoulder. It was like touching the cheek of a girl.

Darren stood beside the curb. He listened to flagpole clinking. There was a painted yellow stripe on the tar. He touched it with his toe. A pebble moved. A crowd of other parents, mostly mothers, were also waiting, either standing there like him, or talking to others. Underneath it though you could feel the ticking tocking of the clock…They were all there to see their children again.

At 3 o'clock, there was a click and the school bell rang. The front doors popped open like a birdhouse and they all flew out. Their sound was like a shining river.

Darren loved this time. Maybe it was his favorite

moment in life. It was all the rarer for him to be here, as he was usually at work. Work could take everything away from you: it stole moments like this, whatever you loved to do, and took you from the people who meant the most to you. He wanted to hold this moment like a photograph.

All the boys and girls streamed from the doors, all happy and laughing and looking around, and then Darren saw Leo.

The little boy wore the blue coat they got at the Value Village.

Leo was looking for him too. When he saw his father, he waved. He left his friends and ran. The little boy came to him and hugged him. He felt like a nest full of hummingbirds.

"How was your school day?"

"Good."

Darren took hold of his son's backpack and carried it for him. There was a yellow salmon patch sewed on it. His son was in Salmon Grade. Their classroom was filled with aquariums and pools and the floor where they cared for the fish had a winding stream between the desks. Their studies began in the first year when the salmon were lettered. To learn the alphabet, the ABCs were written on the underwater sides of each fish. The boy's heavy backpack was bound to be full of fish information.

Darren kissed top of his son's head; a warm spot of sweet smelling hair.

As they walked to the car, Darren tried to find the words to explain what was waiting in there.

"I got a robot today," Darren said.

"What?" the boy said. "Why?"

"He's going to help me. He's going to work for me at the Moss Temple."

"Is that him in the car?"

On the other side of the street, in their car parked under the tree, the cloudy robot sat on the passenger seat.

"Yeah, that's him."

"What's his name?" Leo took hold of his father's hand as they crossed before the stopped traffic.

"You know what? I don't even know his name!" Darren took his keys from his pocket. "I never thought to ask." Then, quieter, he added, "Actually, I'm not so sure if he can talk." Darren rapped the hood and said, "We're back!" He opened the back door for Leo.

The boy stood there staring at the robot apparition. It turned and stared back and smiled. It waved the pale frond of its hand kindly.

Leo crawled into the back of the car. "Hi," he said. He sat behind the driver's seat.

"This is my son, Leo. We were talking on the way back here…" Darren got behind the wheel and shut the door. "I realized I don't even know your name."

The robot's face shifted from a smile to a worried expression. It touched its mouth and signed an x over its lips.

"Oh, you can't talk?"

The robot nodded.

"That's what I thought." Darren started the car and reversed carefully onto the road. "That's alright though. At the Moss Temple, you don't really have to talk. It's just work. You'll see. We'll go there tomorrow morning." He joined in with the other cars leaving the school. A bright yellow bus wheezed by like a whale.

"Hey robot," Leo said.

It turned its head owlishly.

"Can I give you a name?"

The robot nodded at Leo. Darren watched his son in the rearview mirror.

"Can your name be Bugs?"

The robot's teeth again gleamed in a smile. Clearly the name was good with the robot, or Bugs, as he would now be known.

Darren smiled too. He thought about the name as he drove. Bugs was a good name for a robot. He thought of those creatures toiling away on the edges of sidewalk, making nests and roads and colonies.

The car turned down a side street and slowed as they neared a tall billboard. "There's Mike!" Darren pointed at the man way up in the air. Mike stood on the ledge of the sign with a paint roller. Darren slowed the car. They rolled up to the shadow of one of the tall silver billboard legs. "Look at that…" Darren said.

Mike was fifty feet above them, holding a paint tray in one hand and using the other hand to roll on a milky colored wave. He was painting a swimming pool scene, with children playing in the water. There was a lot of blue and white in it. It could almost drift off the sign and melt into the sky. The picture was nearly complete. In the center was a boy holding a rocket bomb above his head. He had a fierce expression. There weren't any words on it yet. For now it was still art. This was Mike's job to paint scenes like this for the Department of Propaganda. The big red letters would be put on last. All over the city, on billboards, on streetcars, buses, posters on walls and signs on windows, were the war reminders. Mike moved oblivious to their watching. He was like a bee on a flower, dipping for more color.

The car arrived at his daughter's school when the bell had already rung. Some of the students were still wandering about under the walkway eaves. They wore the baggy overalls that were in fashion. Darren parked next to a cardboard jalopy and cut the engine.

"There she is!" Leo piped up. He thrust his arm between the front seats to point.

Edith was walking towards them. She walked watching the ground in front of her, barely in the world, a lonely teenager. She did look up just before she reached the car, in time to see the front passenger seat was already occupied. The robot made a weird sort of wind-like whirr. Edith almost stopped, then continued to the back door where she got in beside Leo.

"That's Bugs!" Leo chirped. "He's our new robot."

Darren turned in his seat and said, "Hi Edith!"

"Why do we need a robot?" she said.

Darren started the car and explained. "Bugs is

going to help me with my work. So I'll have time to write."

Edith huffed. "Why don't you get me a robot? So I don't have to go to school."

"Uhh…" Darren steered them through the compound gate. The iron arm popped back in place behind them. "How was school today?"

"The same."

"Are you still making canteens?"

"No," she said. "I don't know." She let her bag fall beside her feet. "Why can't we share Bugs? I'm sick of school."

"I know," Darren said. He couldn't blame her. That school was really no different than his job. All they did was study codes, camouflage, and make the routine weaponry for the war. Everything was about war. How could anyone be happy with that?

"I named him Bugs," Leo said, breaking the silence.

When they arrived home, their pet monkey scampered to the door. He carried an armful of shoes. It was his habit to gather them all in a pile and like some duty-bound butler with a screw loose, bring them to his masters at the door.

"Hi Zombo," Leo said.

The monkey chattered, dropped the shoes and stepped aside.

"Move, Zombo!" said Edith.

Darren tapped the monkey on his little red cap.

"Hey Zombo. Is that all the shoes you could find?" He tripped over a sandal and caught the edge of the washing machine.

Zombo bowed a few times and scampered after the children. He wore a bright scarlet suit with gold braiding and shiny buttons. He could have been a tiny bellboy in one of those old Manhattan movies.

"What's for dinner?" Edith called from the other room.

"I'm hungry!" Leo agreed.

Darren stood in the kitchen like a scarecrow for a moment, with his arms pointed woodenly at the cupboards. "I'll see what we've got. I just got home too, you know."

The monkey stood beside Darren's legs, holding out an empty bowl.

After they had eaten the contents of three packets, Darren regarded the pile of dishes beside the sink. He didn't want to have those plates and pots sitting there when his wife got home.

"Oh for God's sake!" he suddenly slapped his forehead. "Did you kids let Bugs in?"

There was silence in the other room. He left the kitchen to check on them. His daughter was deep in the sofa cushions, the soft cloth had consumed her so only her face showed, listening to her headphones. His son was playing his game, also oblivious to the world. Zombo sat in his little rocking chair. He gave Darren a dull, blinking look.

Darren sighed and hurried from the living room. He couldn't believe the robot had been in the car all this time! How long had it been since they got home? A half hour? At least! The screen door bounced behind him on the way out to the driveway.

Bugs remained in the front seat. It looked like someone had drawn a chalk picture of him on the glass.

"Bugs!" Darren called. He stopped next to the window. He couldn't tell if the robot had turned itself off, or run out of batteries, or had just, like a person, fallen asleep. He tapped gently on the window. "Bugs?"

Slowly, the robot's eyes opened. It registered the dashboard in front of it—the colorful children's stickers, the dried flowers and the mess of coins and things in the open glove compartment. Then its gaze turned towards Darren.

"Hi Bugs," Darren said. "I'm sorry we left you out here." He opened the car door. The breeze of outside air shook the dried flowers and the lank pale legs of the robot.

"It's just that you're so quiet," Darren apologized. "And when we get home, the kids are so…" he paused to open the house door for Bugs. The robot moved like a shadow across the cracked cement towards the doorway with Darren. "Unquiet. And after I herd them in, I have to make them food and do the dishes and feed Zombo. I'm sorry, you just got forgotten in all that rush."

The robot floated inside, over the discarded shoes and then into the kitchen where it stopped and waited for Darren.

"Bugs is here!" Darren called to the kids in the other room.

The only sound from that direction was the rustling of a little red suit as Zombo stirred and came their way. When he turned the corner by the bookshelf with the rubber tree and hanging vine, he froze and put his tiny hands to his mouth in fright.

"Zombo, this is—"" but that was all Darren got to say. The monkey flew from the room like his long tail was on fire.

Bugs took it in stride. Nothing seemed to ever bother this robot. He found a spot in the corner and stood there like a lamp.

Time moved on. Darren, Leo and Edith spent a half hour searching for Zombo, but the monkey seemed to have vanished.

The streetcar rattled and slowed just past their house. Its windows glowed caterpillar yellow as it let a rider off.

When Lila got home, Leo ran to her, "Mommy!" and jumped around her. They were all happy—even Bugs picked up on the excitement and sort of buzzed, lifted off the ground like a balloon.

After she was seated next to Edith with a warm

bowl of food, Darren pointed to the robot in the corner and told her the story.

"Tomorrow I'm taking him to work to show him the ropes," Darren said. "I'll show him how to do my job. When he's got it down, I can come home."

In the middle of the night Darren woke up. His sleep had been the same bad dreams. He sat up. His wife was crunched up on the far side of the bed, wound tightly in most of their blankets.

He swung his legs over the edge and padded out into the hallway. Usually Zombo would be there, asleep in his little hammock, but there was still no sign of him. They had spent another half hour before bedtime looking to no avail. Why had the monkey been so afraid of Bugs? Darren wondered. Of course the robot was a bit odd, but surely nothing to go running from as if your life depended on it.

Darren passed the doors to the children's rooms and returned to the dark living room. He whispered, "Zom?"

What he saw instead made him jump. Like a black balloon, Bugs was curled up in the corner of the ceiling above the TV set. "Bugs?" he said.

The robot uncurled like a spider and slowly descended the wall, back to the floor.

After Darren showed the robot how to rest for the night in a way that wasn't so disturbing, he got Bugs seated on the couch and turned off the lights. Back in their room, Darren lay under the thin sheet and couldn't fall asleep. The sheet felt like a spider web. His nighttime thoughts just wouldn't let him be calm, he couldn't help worrying about the robot he had brought into their home. Roland Traffic hadn't really said anything about it. Why couldn't Darren have Jeffers instead? That was how a robot was meant to look and behave.

Finally Darren tossed onto his right side and tried to recapture some of the blankets from his wife. He managed a corner of the Afghan. He yawned. Anyway, he knew it would be morning soon. There was nothing he could do at this hour. It was either worry or dream. Somehow he fell asleep.

The alarm clock woke him up.

The rest of the house stayed asleep while Darren bumbled about in the dim orange light of dawn. Usually Zombo would appear for a little while, or at least Darren would see the monkey in the hammock, an arm covering its eyes.

The robot trailed Darren to the door where Darren paused to put on his shoes and coat. He also carried a green bag with his lunch in it and a notebook.

They stepped outside. It was raining very lightly, enough to fuzz the skin like a wet cat brushing over. Darren thought about taking the streetcar, but that would cost a dollar and then he didn't want to hassle with the driver over fare for Bugs. Did robots ride for free? Was there a rule in place for that? Besides, Darren didn't usually carry money anyway. It would be okay, the rain wasn't bad. A walk would do them good.

The Moss Temple looked like a postcard. The rainwater on it made it almost glow. "There it is," Darren told Bugs. They stopped for a moment on the other side of the street to appreciate it.

The city was built and cluttered all around the pagoda-shaped temple. It stood on its own little plot of land. There were alleys on either side, reaching back to other streets, with electric lines draped overhead. On the left side was a little grocery store, followed by more doors, apartments and stores. To the right of the temple was a car mechanic shop. The big garage door was open. A sedan was hoisted in the air.

"See all that moss on it?" Darren said. "My job is to remove it from the temple. Pile it in the wheelbarrow, then empty the moss into that big container over there. That gets dragged off every Friday. They refine it and use it to make bombs." Darren sort of laughed and shook his head. "I don't know, whatever is in that moss is strange stuff. It only grows on the temple. It gets harvested every day and it always grows back. During the night I guess…" A cab tore past them in the road. "You ready for work now?"

The started on the roof. Darren showed the robot how to use the rake, how to skim it without too much pressure applied across the ceramic tiles. Bugs got the hang of it quickly. In fact, he seemed suited to the job. He was so light, ethereal, there was no risk of him breaking those clay roofing tiles and he walked fearlessly, right up to the edge, to sweep all the moss off. It seemed that even if Bugs did fall he would float like a leaf to the ground.

With both of them at work, they were on to the second roof layer when Darren's boss showed up. Shadley Grem parked his truck on the street in front and got out. He stood at the curb breathing hard, watching.

"Hey!" Darren called down when he caught sight of the round shape of the man below.

"You got someone with you?" Shadley yelled. He held a flat hand on his brow to shade his eyes.

"Isn't he great?" Darren said. He watched Bugs push a shower of green moss off like a waterfall. "I'll introduce you. We'll be right down."

Shadley rolled back on his heels and regarded the robot. "Back a few wars ago, we had one of those mechanical men to work here."

"How did that go?" Darren asked.

Shadley held his plump hand up high and let it drop and clap onto his other hand. "Fell off the roof!"

"Oh no! Bugs—Bugs is the name my son gave him—Bugs is a whole different kind of robot. You can see how lightweight he is. He practically floats when he wants to. And look at all the work he's already done."

"Hmmm," Shadley replied. "He does seem pretty handy with that rake. Is he dependable? Can he work in all kinds of weather?"

"Of course. That's what a robot is for."

"Well then, I guess he's hired."

Darren almost laughed. That was so easy. The night before he was so worried about it he got up out of bed at midnight to look at those papers Roland gave him. He sat at the kitchen table with the little lamp on and opened the yellow envelope. He pulled out some folded title papers. These were actually for Jeffers. They were detailed specifications on his construction and capabilities. There were other certifications and a typed diploma of ownership and documents issued by the Department of Labor. *The introduction of robots into the workforce is increasing. The reason is not only to save on the cost of labor, but to improve product quality. This is achieved in part by...*Darren stopped reading. There were stamped documents, tax codes and authenticated permits. Would it be enough though? He folded everything and pushed it back in the envelope and sat at the table. He listened to the steady tick of the kitchen wall clock. Was it enough to replace himself with a robot?

Darren waved to Bugs and said, "Okay. I'll be back at 5 o'clock to pick you up. Or you can just head home." That was it. He took one last look at Bugs up on the roof and then he left. Darren was a free man!

Suddenly the whole world was different. He could feel the sunshine on him. He loved the breeze in the air, he felt he could follow it anywhere.

He turned the corner on Cedar Street. The road went steeply towards the sky blue water. A laugh formed in him like a balloon.

Darren followed the waterfront. He passed a pile of nylon fishing nets. A seagull stood next to them, wishing they were full. There were boats up on wooden racks, all done with the sea. One of them was half covered with blackberry vines that had crept down from the hill.

A pelican was carved on top of a gate post. It wore a captain's hat and smoked a corncob pipe. Its blue eye was painted with a twinkle; it seemed ready to lift a wooden wing to clap your shoulder and welcome you through. There was also a sign nailed to the post: Seawater Estates. The ends of the board were wrapped with taut gray nautical rope.

Darren tried the rusted metal gate. It was locked. That was alright. Mike had told him the combination: 4-14-12. That was the night the Titanic sunk.

It was a little funny he supposed, that the gate even needed a lock. Seawater Estates resembled a scrapyard. Darren followed a rickety stairway to the docks on the water's edge. The estates began at sea level. Tied to the docks that warped and bent from the shore were dozens of houseboats. Some of them were little more than rafts with a shack propped on top. But what they lacked in expense, they made up for in far more wondrous ways. Everything had been handmade by the artists living there…all the way to the end of the last dock, where a Ferris Wheel creaked in the wind.

Darren stopped at Mike's houseboat and stared. It was impressive. An ancient looking airplane was tacked to the slanted roof, like some flying dinosaur resting before catching the sea breeze. Mike had built smaller airplanes before, out of wire and wood and cloth, but this one looked like the real thing. It looked ready to fly.

A narrow gangplank stretched from the dock to Mike's houseboat. It sagged as Darren stepped onto it. Below him was deep green water. A pack of tiny silvery fish moved in its shadow and hurried to hide under the legs of the dock as Darren walked. His weight in the middle made the plank dip to the surface, but a few steps more and he was safely aboard.

He was on a deck crowded with tomato plants and all kinds of flowers growing from paint cans and wooden boxes. The only sound was the nuzzling bees and the steady lap of water. But Mike wasn't at home.

Darren wanted to leave him a note, until he patted his pockets and realized he didn't have a pen or paper. Some writer I am, he sighed. Then he remembered, that's what no work was supposed to let him go do.

Now he was given the chance for his dream to come true. He left the shade of Mike's airplane wing, made it luckily over the gangplank again, to bid Seawater Estates a fond farewell.

It was such a sunny day he felt like a prisoner set free. By some stroke of luck the iron door had been opened and he could choose wherever he wanted to go. That would be Fuji's Five and Dime Store. It waited for him on 45th Street, behind some red leafed cherry trees planted in the pavement. Black painted trim around windows stock full of bright fruit colors.

Old Man Fuji was sitting at the counter, listening to a radio baseball game. His concentration broke only for a moment to wave as Darren passed him. It was a San Francisco swing and a miss.

Darren found the stationary and paused to hover over the rows of notebooks. He wondered which one was waiting for him.

He had to go back to Fuji's again to buy a pen. Then that was all he needed to begin his new life. He sat at a bench in the park and started to write. It must have been something waiting a long time in him—the words just flowed right out of the pen onto the crisp turning pages.

The world was around him—he would look up now and then and notice the park, the chatter of kids singing and playing, coming and going—otherwise he was in his own dimension.

Later, when Darren brought the kids home from school, he felt good. He had the notebook in his pocket. It was starting to fill with words; he felt like he had accomplished something great.

He was even cheerful making supper. It didn't seem so terrible that Zombo still hadn't reappeared. He played music while the food cooked on the stove.

It wasn't until after he fed them, when he went out to the mailbox, that his good mood began to change.

Amongst the bills and a cabbage-like handful of junk mail adverts, was a brown paper box, taped up with shiny cellophane. Darren read the return address. It was written in precise black pen. It was from Roland Traffic.

That made him remember Bugs.

The robot should have been home by now. Darren looked down the street the way they had gone to work in the morning, but there was no weary sight of Bugs trudging along. Darren supposed he better get out a bicycle and go looking.

He opened the front door and carried the mail to the table. First he wanted to see what Roland sent him.

Opening the package was difficult. It reminded him of Pandora's Box. Old Roland had covered it so carefully in tape that it had been mummified. Finally, with a knife Darren managed to get a side of the card-board open.

What was held inside, trapped by newspaper and wrapped in a yellow paged letter, was a black unla-beled video cassette. Darren unfolded the letter and read it.

Darren. Play the tape. I wonder if you've seen anything similar to this since bringing home that robot?
Roland.

The kids were in their own worlds. Darren brought the video to the television set to see what Roland sent.

The video began shakily, careening through Ro-land's kitchen, dipping over the silver sink, while the old man narrated. "I wanted you to see this," as the camera stopped, pointed at the window, taking in the view of his backyard on Lemon Island. There was grass and a swing-set that had been turned into some sort of musical instrument. They were the things you would expect to see in Roland Traffic's backyard.

The old man's breath sort of wheezed as he spoke again. "What I want you to see is a little off in the trees over there…" The camera bobbed to a location of thick fir trees and a blue sky. Roland zoomed the lens and focused on one of the trees…something red in one of the trees.

Darren couldn't tell if it was the remains of a red

kite or a balloon, maybe a big bird.

"I just noticed him there last week. I'm not sure how long he's been showing up. He stays for a little while then he goes…Sorry, I lost the focus button…" Roland lowered the camera back to a view of the sink.

"Okay," his voice continued, "I got it now." The camera went back to the window view, looking across the pleasant artistic yard, finding the not so distant fir trees, and zoomed in on the red smudge. Suddenly Darren could see what it was.

A man. He looked painted red. He was holding to the rough trunk effortlessly and then his head turned. He faced the camera. He had horns and a pointed beard, and as his eyes seemed to bore right into the camera lens, as his lips curled up into a sharp smile.

Darren quickly turned off the television. He glanced over his shoulder to make sure his kids hadn't seen. That was good—they were busy. His hand was actually shaking as he ejected the video and returned it to the envelope. "What the hell, Roland?" What was that crazy old man up to? Of course it looked like The Devil in that tree—it couldn't have been more jarring and blatant. But how could that be? Darren took a deep breath. The old man was an artist, right? This was probably just a part of a movie he was making, something to give a scare. Darren felt like a child who had fallen for some frightening story. It was easy to believe when it was late at night and the lights were out.

Darren tried to put it out of his mind. Besides, there were other things to worry about—Zombo was still missing, and Bugs had not returned home either. Darren got the kids started on a project and it was nice to listen to their chatter.

They were busy making Lost Monkey posters when Lila got home. Darren gave her a kiss and told her he had to go out and search for the robot. He put on a sweater and left through the kitchen, grabbing a banana on the way. Maybe he'd spot Zombo too.

The neighborhood street was quiet, lit by house windows along the sidewalk. He was looking for the forlorn shape of his robot returning. Also, every once in a while he would call out, "Zombo!"

There were plenty of places for a monkey to hide. There was even the chance that Zombo had been taken in by some new family. So Darren gave every passing window a look, hoping to see Zombo swinging from a chandelier.

A block away from the Moss Temple, Darren discovered Bugs. The robot stood beside a streetlamp, stock still, head tilted back, looking up into that pale blue glow. Something about him reminded Darren of a moth, as if any moment the robot would drift into the light and buzz out of existence. When he was close, Darren called out, "Bugs!" and the robot gave a jump.

Its spell was broken. Bugs looked at him with moony blank eyes and waited for a command.

Who knew what the robot was doing out there in the night, staring at a streetlight?

It couldn't explain itself to Darren. It just walked along beside him as they returned home. Darren tried out some questions, "How did it go today?" and, "Was the work okay?" but Bugs would only stare back at him. "So I guess you'll be working tomorrow too?"

To that the robot seemed to nod affirmatively. Darren guessed it couldn't have all been bad. He wasn't sure why Roland Traffic had designed a mute robot though. You needed some sort of communication. He would ask Roland about that when he got home. He'd give him a call. Of course he also had to ask about that devil in the tree. What in the world was that about?

Darren, deep in thought, wasn't watching the sidewalk where his right foot suddenly stepped on the banana peel he had dropped ten minutes ago. He gave a hoot as he slipped and in the next moment he hit the ground.

Getting himself back to his feet, he was further surprised.

He heard something he never heard before.

A dry, chuffing laughter came from the robot, watching Darren stand up again.

"I get it now!" Darren said. "You've got a sense of humor." He was limping. They were still a couple blocks from the house.

Bugs slowly walked with him. Even on the dark street, Darren could still see the robot smiling at the memory.

Darren said, "You know slipping on a banana peel is considered the lowest form of humor." It was something else to tell Roland about. Then he remembered the devil in Roland's movie. He cleared his throat and called, "Zombo!" The name got lost among the neighborhood silhouettes. "Zombo!"

"I got him!" Darren announced as he opened the door.

He could hear Lila say, "Dad's got him!" and the kids came running.

"Zombo!" they both cried down the hallway, before they saw Darren was standing by the door with Bugs.

"Oh, Dad…" Edith said.

Leo held up his hand in a flat greeting, "Bugs."

As they turned and left back to the kitchen, Darren said, "That's okay, Bugs. I know they're glad to see you again. We were all worried about where you were." He was afraid to look at Bugs though. He didn't want to see if the robot was sad. Wasn't it enough that he could laugh? Robots weren't supposed to have feelings.

Once Darren got the robot settled in its favorite corner, he took the telephone to the chair by the window. He dialed and looked out at the nighttime. Across the street, down the cul-de-sac along the horizon above the trees, Darren could see Lemon Island. It was a darker shape than the sky, like a whale surfacing. At the peak of the island was a radio transmitter tower with a steady red light at the top.

It took Roland a few rings to answer. "Yes?"

"Roland, this is Darren Birch."

"You watched the video," the old man interrupted.

"Yeah, I saw it."

Roland said, "I have a theory." He took a deep breath. "I'd like to tell you in person, but I'd rather not see that…*robot* in my house again."

"Just tell me, Roland. It's been a long day."

"I first noticed that creature I call The Devil soon after your robot appeared." The old man sighed, "I guess I should come clean on that too. It's not a robot. I'm sure you've had your doubts. Actually, I think it may be the physical manifestation of someone long deceased."

"A ghost," Darren said. "I figured…"

"A ghost. Yes, that's correct. I unearthed it accidentally when I was digging a hole in my field. Who would have thought there were bodies buried there? Anyway, it followed me around. I think he was lonely. I taught him simple repetitive tasks, which he accomplished satisfactorily. I guess to ease my sense of culpability, I began to think of him as a robot. He helped me out about the shop. But then," he sighed, "The Devil showed up in my tree. I wondered if maybe he wanted that ghost back."

"So you stuck me with the ghost?"

"No," Roland said. "Perhaps it would seem that way, but being a scientific observer I needed to see if the appearance of The Devil was in fact connected to—"

"Couldn't you have given Jeffers the ghost to take for a nice long walk somewhere?"

"Oh no. Jeffers won't go near the ghost. Don't you remember the way he hightailed it that day you were here?"

"So, are you telling me I should be on the lookout for The Devil?"

"In a manner of speaking, yes."

Darren stared at the little red light far out on the island and wondered if something else that red was out there too. "Listen, Roland. If that devil thing does make an appearance, I'm not making any deals! I'm handing the ghost right over."

"Ohh," the old man sighed. "I just hope it's that easy."

Darren couldn't sleep. He tossed and turned. His first day free of the grind of a fulltime job and instead he was faced with a missing monkey, a robot that was actually a ghost, and worst of all: The Devil. At this very moment The Devil could be sitting in the alder beside their window, looking in. The window was open. Darren could hear the leaves crackle while he tried to find sleep.

The alarm clock went off like a marching band at 6 AM. Even though he wasn't going to a job, there were still plenty of things to do. Darren stopped the alarm and lay still for a moment, gathering himself. It hadn't been a good sleep and he remembered why.

He looked at the window, half expecting to see a red devil clinging to the sill.

The curtains breathed.

Darren got up and with his face to the soft green skirt of cloth, looked past the curtains into the yard. He checked the trees first. He checked the lawn and the plastic slide and the garden planted with ripening vegetables and flowers. He was happy they were safe, almost ready to turn from the sight, when he stopped, caught in a cold freeze. A wooden fence separated their yard from the neighbor. It was made of tall old boards. Some of them had been in need of replacement for a while. Some of them hung like sharpened teeth. One of them had a hole just large enough for a bright red face to stand behind and look in.

That's all it took for Darren to decide he was done

with the ghost. Just when he found a way out of working a job too! But unlike Roland Traffic, he didn't want to pass the poor spirit off on someone else. First thing though was to get it out of his house, away from his family as fast as possible. Knowing that devil was right outside their door was too horrifying.

Darren dressed quickly and hurried to the other room where he reached to the ceiling, grabbed the floating ghost by the leg like a balloon string and rushed him out the door.

Darren took the ghost across the street and they turned down an alley at a run. They hurried past a fence with a barking dog, an old Volkswagen up on blocks, a garbage can stuffed with growing bamboo. Out the alley, Darren led the way in a zigzag jog, looking back behind as they plowed over streets, more alleys, and stopped to rest in a parking lot.

Darren was out of breath. Unfazed, the ghost sat quietly on the hood of a Pontiac while his human companion rested and regained his strength.

At last Darren was able to hold his hand up and say, "I found out you're a ghost."

Those weird aquarium eyes stared at him.

"Roland finally told me about you." Darren kept an eye on the wake they had left as he continued, "He also told me there's someone looking for you."

The ghost jolted itself off the hood. It gave Darren a worried look and seemed ready to bolt.

"So you know about The Devil?"

The ghost's head periscoped in a circle, searching the parking lot.

"I'm sorry. I don't mean any offence, but I don't think we can be around each other anymore. I've got a family and—"

But the ghost had spotted where it wanted to go. Planted above the car roofs and across the street on the corner was the tall tower of the Mt. Baker Theatre. The ghost pointed to itself, then at the theatre. It pressed a finger to its lips.

"Yeah," said Darren, "I won't tell."

The ghost nodded. There was no other goodbye. It vanished into the wind. It left a cold spot where it had been.

Darren started to walk. He left the parking lot. He knew there was a place he should be at this time every day: The Moss Temple…He kicked a stone out of his way. It bounced and clattered across the cracked pavement. Back to work…I was so close, he thought, I should have known.

He turned to look over his shoulder. He was still wary of that devil.

There was no sign of a blood-red man walking among the street commuters. Even the Mt. Baker Theatre tower was hiding itself behind a tree.

When Darren returned to the Moss Temple, Shadley Grem was waiting for him. Nobody wants to show up late for work with their boss already there. Shadley sat in his truck with the window rolled down, watching the sidewalk.

Darren felt those eyes lock on him.

"Where's your robot?"

Darren cleared his throat. "Uh, he didn't work out."

Shadley took a sip of coffee. "Didn't I tell you about that other robot I hired on?"

Darren nodded.

"Something always goes wrong with them."

Darren nodded again. "I guess so."

"No such thing as a free lunch," Shadley explained. He had some more coffee and sighed. "Well, I better let you get to work. Time's wasting. That moss won't fall off by itself."

A few hours passed. Darren was getting tired. His back, shoulders and arms hurt from the shoveling. Maybe mostly because he thought he was done with it. He thought of Shadley with his elbow out the window of his truck, telling him, "No such thing as a free lunch." No, but it had been nice for a day.

As he tossed another scraped up shovel load of bright green moss at the dumpster below, Darren glanced across the street. He lost his balance and almost fell. Only clocking the shovel like a ski pole against the tiles kept him on the slanted roof.

The Devil watched Darren's recovery and snapped his fingers, rueful that death had been so close. That blood-red man stood beside the same lamppost where only last night Bugs had been planted. With a chuckle that Darren could hear all the way in the air, The Devil removed his bowler hat in a bow that clearly showed the two sharp horns sprouted from his head.

There was really no other choice but to leave the Moss Temple roof and talk with The Devil.
Darren carried the shovel with him, the weight of it held like a sword, as he left the temple and walked onto the sidewalk.
The street had gone silent. It felt like the two of them had been dropped into a glass jar. The world was around them, apart from them and shimmering. Darren cleared his throat just to see if he could make a sound.
The Devil had approached the curb on the other side of the street and stopped. He had his hands in the deep pockets of his long black coat. He was still smiling at Darren.
Darren did think it strange there were no cars breaking the stream between them. The city seemed to be frozen.
When The Devil spoke, his voice sounded as close as a whisper in Darren's ear. "Where is he?" The Devil added, "You know who I mean."

The shovel grew heavy in Darren's hand. As The Devil stepped across the street towards him, he could no longer hold onto its weight. It fell with a clang onto the cement.

Darren tried to say something but found he couldn't. All he could do was stand there watching as the red man approached, bringing with him a cloudy acrid smell of fire. The Devil's long coat and black clothes roiled, as if the movement of crossing the road took him through a stormy cloud.

Darren's eyes teared up from the sulfurous hot closeness, yet he couldn't move his arm to brush his sight clear. The blood-red man stood smeared as a crimson streak of paint in front of him. The words chuffed again, like a steam locomotive, "Where…is… he?"

Darren took a step backwards. His heavy shoe scraped the cement. That effort had been all he could do, but he found that just that little bit of distance from The Devil gave him more strength. He dragged his other foot back too and kept moving, leaving The Devil scowling at him from the curbside, unwilling to take that last step up onto the sidewalk to follow, as Darren escaped in reverse, into the green shadows of the temple.

Darren turned as he went between the pillars and when he looked back at the street again, The Devil was gone. Like a faucet, the sound of traffic had been turned on and a big green truck passed by. There were cars and a bicycle.

Darren leaned against a pillar.

He was soaked with sweat. He felt sickly hot and then like a switch had been thrown, his skin was icy cold. He followed the smooth pillar down to the ground. All the air seemed to have rushed out of him. His hands opened flat and clutched at the crumbles of moss scattered on the unswept floor.

"Is this what I pay you for?" said Shadley. "Sleeping on the job?"

Darren woke up and stood. "I'm sorry!"

"Well, never mind. I'm done with you here." Shadley pointed at the sidewalk, "There's your replacement."

Darren saw a silver riveted metal robot standing at the curb. It held the shovel that Darren had dropped there earlier.

"Yeah," Shadley told him, "I'm giving your job to another robot." He slapped Darren on the shoulder and laughed.

There was blue sky over the town and all the buildings were washed with sunlight and shadows. Darren walked down Indian Street, with a view through the trees of the bay and Lemon Island.

He was just walking and thinking, letting himself be a part of the invisible breeze that pushed at his back. The little ferry plied its way across the fluttered water towards land. It was too far away for Darren to see Roland Traffic's old red truck, with its coppery passenger Jeffers standing in back. Darren's view of the sea was blocked by an apartment building and then, as he kept walking, by a billboard and a tree full of chirping birds.

Fifteen minutes later, Darren followed the shoreline on Harbor Street. Here he was again, taking the same route as yesterday, without a job, walking to Mike's houseboat.

Seagulls rested on the remaining pilings where the old pier used to be. He could see the ferry boat returning to Lemon Island, a little ribbon of smoke on the water.

The road ended at Boulevard Park. Across all that grass were the docks and Seawater Estates. People used to fly kites on happier days.

On this day, a long way from kites, as Darren left the street and stepped over the curb below the chestnut tree leaves, he stopped and stared at the park before him. It had been snowed over. He walked out into white paper that piled around his ankles. He stopped in the rustling and bent down to pick up one of the leaflets. There were tiny words pecked onto the strip of paper:

Read this carefully as it may save your life and the lives of those close to you:
Very soon your city will be destroyed by bombs. This city contains military installations, workshops and factories which produce military goods. We are determined to end

It hadn't taken Darren that long to read, but already on the other side of the park, there were firefighters edging along and setting fire to the white blanket of leaflets. A gray smoke was rising from their work and the flames were catching and spreading, burning away all mention of the warning.

Darren stuffed the leaflet into a pocket and retreated to the trees and the road he had taken. A firetruck was approaching. He tried to look like he was just out for a walk. He was innocent, he hadn't even noticed the park, or the air that was filling with smoke.

The big red truck growled past him as he left Harbor Street to follow an alley between two warehouses.

One rusted wall was covered in morning glory. The white flowers pointed towards him like trumpets. He would keep to the alleys, follow their winding paths back into town. Overhead, the sky was charred.

Every once in a while, a bomb would go off in the city—there had been times when a lot of them did. People got used to it. It was war. Darren could almost understand why the firetrucks would burn all the warnings. There was no need to scare everyone.

Anyway, looking around himself, it looked like every other day. Traffic filled the streets of downtown, people passed each other on the sidewalks going to stores and markets, cafés or work. You tried not to think of the war.

The Mount Baker Theatre was old, built in a long ago time when entertainment meant golden walls, chandeliers, red curtains that opened on magicians, dancers, singers, sideshow acts and films that sparkled on the big screen. Just off the sidewalk, before the carved doors, was a ticket booth. It looked like something suspended from a whirring zeppelin. It was a streamlined silver carriage with windows engraved around its sides. There used to be someone in there for every matinee or evening show.

Darren thought Bugs would be in there. It would have been a perfect spot for him to hide. He peered in a window at the dust, the chair, the left open register.

It was a museum of dust.

"Darren!"

He turned at the familiar voice. Roland Traffic and Jeffers stood on the sidewalk behind Darren.

"My conscience got the better of me. We decided to come give you a hand."

"That's good." Darren motioned them closer into the alcove next to the ticket booth. "You're not being followed, are you? No sign of that devil?"

"I haven't seen him," the old man replied. "Jeffers is keeping track." He pointed at the contraption the robot held. It was a shoebox-sized block of metal with a spinning silver aerial hoop on top. Jeffers was watching a green circular screen that pinged like something in a submarine. Roland whispered, "What happened to your robot?"

Darren nodded slightly at the chained, locked front doors of the theater. It looked like only a ghost could get through. "I think he's somewhere in there."

"Jeffers," Roland said. "If you will do the honors."

With a steamy wheeze of gears, the robot clanked forward. It paused at the shackled door and held out its hand toward the padlock. The tip of a finger opened like a flower blossom to reveal a skeleton key underneath.

Roland chuckled at Darren's expression. "Jeffers comes equipped for all eventualities."

Jeffers had the lock open in one turn and as the old man and Darren removed the coil of chain, that metal hand pressed the door inwards.

A lantern shone from Jeffers as the three of them crossed the gloomy interior of the theater. It reminded Darren of those sunken photos of the Titanic, all that broken splendor from in a dream. A grand stairway led up to the balcony. The red carpet unrolled from the shadows down like a tongue.

Roland tapped Darren, "You go up there. We'll look for him down here."

Darren stopped. "What? What am I supposed to do if I find him?"

"We've got to convince him to go back," said the old man, matter-of-factly. "Better us finding him than The Devil, don't you think?"

"I don't know…"

"Believe me, Darren. You go upstairs and call out if you find him. I'm following Jeffers." The robot's heavy feet made a slow thudding heartbeat. The devil detector whirling in Jeffers' hands pinged them away, leaving Darren in the dark.

He did make it up the stairway, though it wasn't easy. He went slowly and ran his hand along the wall-paper, once through a spider web and once into a hole big enough to nest a bat. When the stairs stopped on the top floor, there was more stained glass that allowed some bit of rainbow light to fall on the switch on the wall.

As Darren pressed it, little orange airport lights blinked to life. Around him, spaced every twenty feet or so, there was an electric candle flickering on the wall. They showed the way to a narrow hall leading to the balcony.

Below Darren, Jeffers trolled down the aisle with his pinging sound and meshing gears. The robot spread out a wide beam of yellow lantern light. All the seats barked out shadows like teeth.

"Hellooo!" Darren called.

The silhouette of Roland turned jaggedly. "Can you see anything up there?"

Darren laughed. What was there to see? The tiny lights ran only on the aisles, leaving the wide balcony level of seating a black area. Way at the top was a faint reflection on the window of the projection room. A smoky white blur waved on the glass.

Darren said, "Maybe…" and headed for the last row of seats, where the projection booth was perched in the center. He felt the seams of a door in the wallpaper, found a latch and opened the hatch. The narrow room glowed with the pearly haze of his ghost. Darren said, "Hello Bugs."

There were reels of film on the floor, big round metal canisters with the shiny celluloid unspooled. The ghost was holding up one of those long streamers as Darren let himself in.

After a little time and pantomime, Darren understood what the ghost had in mind. Bugs wanted to see a movie. There was no denying the spirit's absolute sense of joy, the cramped projection booth radiated with the firefly light buzzing off the ghost.

Darren helped him thread the film into the projector. He remembered how. Long ago, he used to have a machine like this, with a cardboard box full of short movies he would play on the wall in his house. And in those distant summers, he would tie the projector to an extension cord and set it up in the backyard at night. It was his own drive-in movie theater, playing movies on the back of the neighbor's garage.

Bugs' eyes shined like polished stones and he smiled eagerly when they were done and the projector waited, pointed like the cannon of a galleon out at the black night of the theater.

Bugs gestured for Darren to start the projector. Before he did, the ghost tipped his flat hat and slipped out the hatch.

Darren put his fingers on the switch and turned it.

All of a sudden there was a loud clacking noise and the steady drone as the projector turned its reels and pulled the film through. A beam of light shot from the lens. Darren took a couple steps over to look out the little glass window.

The theater was laid out like a landscape in front of

him, all the rows of chairs and the balcony drop-off to more chairs growing below. Everything flickered with the silver projected light. It looked like miles away, where a strange and magic window appeared on the screen.

Darren watched a movie steam locomotive pouring out black smoke, hurrying through a forest. Then the screen became the cab of the train and Darren stared as a hand entered the frame.

The ghost reached into the light of the movie river. He was on the other side of the projection booth, leaning out into the air. With a quick pull, the ghost climbed into the film and stood at the controls of the movie train.

"Bugs!" Darren shouted.

His robot ghost tipped his flat hat again. The train roared on silently until the torn roll of film was gone. The empty projector clacked. The screen was white as snow.

Darren made his way back to the lobby. Mostly in the dark, he couldn't see much until he opened the door to the mezzanine and there was Jeffers' lantern. The robot and Roland climbed the aisle.

"Did you see that?" Roland called. "The movie started and the ghost disappeared into it!"

"I saw it," Darren said, "I helped him get away."

The old man hooted with laughter.

Darren shielded his eyes from the bright robot lantern.

"I guess our work is done," Roland said.

Behind him, Jeffers made a coughing sound and said, "Not quite…" He turned up the sound of the contraption he carried. The beeping came in a trembling hurry.

"Oh no," Darren said.

It wasn't hard to find The Devil.

Jeffers pointed the detector and they walked.

The trilling beeping of it became a steady high pitched whine as they stopped at a door.

Gray colored daylight showed in the open gap they had left. A red hand pushed the door more and there was The Devil standing before them. He was laughing.

Darren said, "You can't get him. He's gone."

"I don't care about him anymore." The Devil took a step backwards to allow them leave of the theater. "Who cares about one ghost? Soon this city will be full of dead." He laughed again and added, "Come on out, join the parade," and he swept his arm to let them through.

They stood in the doorway and watched The Devil. He walked past the ticket booth, crossed the street between cars and continued on the sidewalk, red as blood, unseen by everyone else in town.

Roland finally asked, "What was he talking about, the city being full of dead?"

"I think he means this," said Darren. He reached in his pocket and got hold of the leaflet. "The park was full of these today."

"Can I see it?"

Darren passed it to him. "These fall on the city all the time. You think it's true this time?"

The old man shuddered. "Jeffers and I better hurry back to our island." He was already in motion.

Darren ran from the movie theater. He thought of his family, he thought of all the families, everyone and everything that made a town. Would it all be gone? The streets were only a blur, the people he just flew around, crossing roads, dodging cars and a bus and bicycles. The city was a melting candle; there wasn't much time left before it would be gone.

In his hand he held the crumpled warning. If The Devil was right, if the warnings were true, Darren would end up like everyone else in town, like every leaflet in that park, burned up and turned to smoke and cinders. There must have been thousands of warnings—one for every person in the town. Each one could have saved a life.

He was almost home. His street was around the next corner, a row of familiar houses, yards, parked cars. But he had to stop for a moment, just a second. He had to rest against a tree. His heart felt like the hot iron engine of a train, his legs could barely hold him. As his breath caught up with him, the leaves shook above. A smudge in a red cap and uniform ran along a branch. "Zombo!" Darren smiled, "What are doing up there?"

The author at time of writing *The Schubert Story*, on WWU campus, underneath an empress tree.

Laura Vasyutynska is an accomplished visual artist who has been pursuing a career as a professional artist since her youth, beginning formal training in her hometown of Zhytomyr, Ukraine. Laura moved to the United States in early 2001 and continued her career in Seattle. A former student at Western Washington University. She works primarily with oils on canvas, but also uses other media such as watercolors and graphite.

DIFFERENT PLANET
written by Allen Frost

The Next President (2004-2005)
The Schubert Story (2010)
Convenience (2011)
Moss Temple (2013)

Books by Allen Frost

Ohio Trio (Bottom Dog Press 2001)

Bowl of Water (Bottom Dog Press 2003)

Another Life (Bird Dog Publishing 2007)

Home Recordings (Bird Dog Publishing 2009)

The Mermaid Translation (Bird Dog 2010)

The Selected Correspondence of Kenneth Patchen
    edited by Allen Frost (Bottom Dog 2012)

The Wonderful Stupid Man (Bird Dog 2012)

Saint Lemonade (Good Deed Rain 2014)

Playground (Good Deed Rain 2014)

Roosevelt (Good Deed Rain 2015)

5 Novels (Good Deed Rain 2015)

The Sylvan Moore Show (Good Deed Rain 2015)

Town in a Cloud (Good Deed Rain 2015)

At the Edge of America (Good Deed Rain 2016)

Lake Erie Submarine (Good Deed Rain 2016)

The Book of Ticks (Good Deed Rain 2017)

I Can Only Imagine (Good Deed Rain 2017)

The Orphange of Abandoned Teenagers
    (Good Deed Rain 2017)

Different Planet (Good Deed Rain 2017)

Also published by Good Deed Rain

A Flutter of Birds Passing Through Heaven:
A Tribute To Robert Sund edited by Allen Frost
    and Paul Piper (2016)
and Light poetry by Paul Piper (2016)
In the Valley of Mystic Light: An Oral History
of the Skagit Valley Arts Scene edited by Claire
    Swedberg & Rita Hupy (2017)

Coming Soon

Go with the Flow: A Tribute to Clyde Sanborn
    edited by Allen Frost (2018)

I hope you have enjoyed these books. There are more
on the way.

www.ingramcontent.com/pod-product-compliance
Lightning Source LLC
Chambersburg PA
CBHW030519120726
47904CB00005B/1537